PLAY

with the

PHANTOM

USA TODAY BESTSELLING AUTHOR
AMANDA RICHARDSON

Play with the Phantom
Amanda Richardson
© Copyright 2025 Richardson House Press LTD
www.authoramandarichardson.com

Copy/line editing: Rumi Khan
Cover Design: The Pretty Little Design Co.
Cover Photography: Ren Saliba

BLURB

She has no idea she's being hunted... or that the Phantom has already *claimed* her.

Ari

I thought I wanted stability—security—someone safe. For two years, I convinced myself Asher—my polished, predictable, perfect boyfriend—was enough.

Until the letters started. Cryptic. *Obsessive*. Meant only for me.

Then, I meet Asher's twin. Maddox Cross. A name no one speaks. A convicted felon.

Asher warns me to stay away, but Maddox peels me open, piece by piece, like he already knows my secrets.

And when the truth comes out, I won't have to choose between two brothers.

Because one of them will never let me go.

Maddox

Twenty years in a cage does things to a man. Gives him time. Time to think. Time to remember. Time to obsess.

Asher never deserved Ari. I knew it the second I found out about her.

She doesn't belong in his perfect world. She belongs in *mine*—where good girls get ruined, and bad men don't let go.

Now, I'm here. In her dreams. In her room. In the dark—touching, tasting, waiting.

She was never running. Just waiting for me to catch her. And now that I have?

She'll say my name in the dark, shattered and breathless—until she knows she was never meant to belong to anyone else.

Play with the Phantom is a full-length, dark standalone romance with an age gap and stalker themes. It has a HEA. Please check the triggers.

TRIGGER WARNING

This book contains themes that may be problematic for some people.

For a complete list, please visit my website here:
www.authoramandarichardson.com/triggers

Happy reading!

Author's Note

Welcome to *Play with the Phantom.* A few quick things before you dive in...

This book contains **dubious/coerced consent**, particularly during a pivotal scene in which the heroine believes she's with her boyfriend—only to later learn it was his identical twin. If that's not your thing, it's okay to walk away now.

Still here? Good.

This book walks a deliciously fine line—sometimes dark, sometimes funny, sometimes a little too honest. It's spicy. It's chaotic. It doesn't pretend to be morally clean. If you're into **antiheroes who would burn the world down for the one they love**, Maddox Cross is here to ruin you.

If you like stalkers, obsessed men, a little dubcon, and a lot of tension that makes you want to scream into a pillow—you're in the right place.

Maddox is completely unhinged in the best way. He's not the kind of man who asks permission twice. Once he's chosen Ari, there's no going back. He is single-minded in his devotion, dangerously protective, and he *will* wait outside your house with a bouquet of forget-me-nots and an arrogant smirk.

This is not real life. This is fantasy. You'll get your happily ever after in the end, I promise.

And yes—Maddox does unspeakable things to her perfume bottle.

Buckle up and enjoy the ride…

Xo,
Amanda

For all the book lovers who break free from their stifling beginnings.

May your middle and end have lots of hot, dirty sex.

THE PHANTOM LETTER
ARI

I LICK MY HAND AND REACH DOWN BETWEEN MY legs, finding my clit and circling my fingers around it furiously. Across from me, Asher watches. His expression is neutral. Almost *polite*. Like fucking always. Even when I lift my hand and slap it down against my pussy, he doesn't react. The sharp sting sends an electric shock through me, and my whole body shudders.

"Yes," I whimper, rubbing myself harder. "Just... like... that..."

Asher's brows shoot up.

When I glance down, his cock is still soft.

That's a problem.

Pausing, I sit up slightly. "Is something wrong?"

He exhales, rolling his shoulders like he's forcing himself to stay engaged. "Ari, you don't have to hurt yourself."

I groan as I flop back onto the bed, exhaling with frustration. "That's the point, Ash. I like it."

His mouth forms a tight line, and I resist the urge to roll my eyes. Reaching between my legs, I press two fingers inside myself this time. It's not enough. It never is when I do it myself.

Asher leans forward, reaching out toward me like he wants to contribute, but I swat his hand away.

"Pay attention," I growl. "I like it fast and furious. And *hard*. Don't be afraid to hurt me."

"I'm not going to hurt you," he says, rolling his eyes.

My frustration spikes.

I remove my hand and gesture for him to try. "Go on. Try again."

His gray-blue eyes bore into mine, and I swear I can feel the impatience broiling underneath his good-natured, golden retriever persona.

He slips his large hand between my legs, circling my wet clit.

"Spit on it," I tell him.

He stares at me like I've suggested something illegal. Instead, he inserts one finger into my cunt and uses my arousal as lube instead.

Fine.

"My clit," I direct, placing my hand on top of his and pressing down. "Focus on the clit, and you'll be golden."

Why is it that I'm the one who's always carrying the burden of making sure things go smoothly? Work, life... and now, apparently, sex. Even in bed, I can't catch a break.

Asher's finger moves in slow, careful circles, and I suppress a groan.

"Harder. Slap me. Pinch it, if you need to."

"Ari—"

I groan and shove his hand away. "You always say you're willing to learn what I like, and yet you always get frustrated by what I try to teach you."

He drags a hand down his face as he sighs. "Can't we just... do it normally?"

I press my lips together. What's the point of a man having a massive cock if he doesn't know how to use it? Because, sure, his dick is big. But I've never gotten off from it. Not once. I'm a clitoral orgasm girlie, and Asher isn't too pleased about having to learn my hot buttons.

And honestly, I'm tired of teaching someone who clearly has no desire to learn.

I sigh and tilt my head. "Yeah, sure. Just fuck me, then."

He kisses me, but it feels forced, his hand jerking at his cock in frustration. It takes a few minutes—too long—before he finally positions himself between my spread legs.

I press a hand on his chest before he can push in. "Let me go on top."

He nods immediately, and something in me deflates. He always acquiesces.

I slide off him, walking toward my bedside table, yanking the drawer open. I grab my clit sucker, because if he can't bother to learn how to do it, at least I have this magical invention. Climbing back on top of him, I straddle his waist but I don't let him inside me yet. Instead, I turn the vibrator on and press it against my clit.

The sensation hits me instantly. I jerk, my body tensing with pleasure.

Asher groans beneath me, his hands coming to my hips, dragging me against his cock.

At least he's pretty.

At almost six-foot-five, he's massive compared to my petite five-two. And sure, he makes me feel safe. Sure, the sex is okay.

But we've been dating for two years without progressing forward, and I keep wondering why I'm still here.

"Ari," Asher mutters, squeezing my hips as I slide against his shaft. "I want to be inside of you."

"Then you know what to do."

His brow furrows slightly. But then he lifts me up, and I

angle his cock against my entrance. I don't give him time to gently set me down on his cock.

Instead, I slam down on him.

"Fuck," he growls. "Are you okay?"

I huff a laugh as I grind down on his cock. "I'm a big girl, Ash."

Then, I lean forward, whispering in his ear.

"And I like it when you hit my cervix."

Asher exhales through his nose, shaking his head. "You're a fucking psycho."

Turning my vibrator up, I slide up and down his cock, rolling my hips as I lift myself and slam back down. The rough friction brings me close and I throw my head back, lost in the sensation.

"Pinch my nipples," I beg. He reaches up and gently twists my right nipple. "Harder."

He twists it a bit rougher, but not how I like it. I push his hand away and grab my own breast, rolling my nipple between my fingers, tweaking it the way I actually like.

Pain and pleasure, sharp and perfect.

I'm close, and I close my eyes as I ride him. His hands squeeze my thighs, and I can tell by the way his breathing changes that he's close too. I wish he'd talk dirty, or moan, or something. It's like he holds it all inside.

Silent. Detached. Always holding back. Like he's doing this for the sake of doing it, not because he actually craves it.

I crave it. I always crave it. But no one ever seems to crave me back the same way.

"Talk to me," I beg, my voice tight as I open my eyes. "Say something dirty."

"You're so hot," he says, sounding unaffected. "So perfect, so sexy."

"Call me your little cockslut," I whisper. Adjusting the clit sucker *just so,* my mouth drops open as the different angle makes my climax creep up quickly.

"Jesus, Ari."

"C'mon, humor me. Just once. For science."

He groans instead of answering, so like every time I have sex, I close my eyes and imagine a different scenario. I imagine someone *claiming* me. I imagine the noises, and maybe even them pushing me onto my back and taking charge from above me.

I imagine how it would feel to have strong hands holding mine above my head as I'm fucked relentlessly.

Sometimes I even imagine it's not consensual. That the person I'm fucking is *taking* me—overwhelming me. Leaving me powerless beneath their touch, lost in the intoxicating mix of fear and desire.

Strong hands grabbing my hips, forcing me down harder.

A rough, desperate pace that leaves me gasping, completely at his mercy even when I'm the one on top—

"I'm coming. Oh, fuck—"

My orgasm slams into me like a goddamn wrecking ball.

I writhe against him as I ride out the wave of ecstasy. The clit sucker pulls everything out of me, and I moan, shaking and twitching as I contract around him. I open my eyes and don't look away from him as it rolls through me. I drop the clit sucker off to the side, completely spent.

I blink down at him, still perched on his cock. "You didn't come?" I ask, moving gently on top of his cock.

He shifts beneath me, his expression tightening. "I've had a busy day at work."

Then, he lifts me off him and sits up, his dark blond hair slicked back as he reaches for his clothes. I watch him for a beat, admiring the way his muscles contract along his back, that perfectly round ass I could bounce a quarter off of, and those thick, long legs.

He pulls his pants on, and something deflates inside me.

"Do you want a blow job?"

He pauses. "I have a meeting soon. I should get back to the office." He continues putting on his button-up, not even meeting my gaze.

I swallow something bitter, forcing a small smile. "Maybe you could come over after work and we could watch a movie?"

He smiles at me, but it doesn't reach his eyes. "I'd like that. I'll call you, okay?"

With that, he leans down, presses a light kiss to my forehead, and leaves.

A minute later, the front door clicks shut. I stare at the ceiling.

Yeah. He's not coming over.

I roll onto my side, frowning at my dresser. Something like disappointment coils in my stomach.

Two years of this. Two years of careful space, of lingering just outside of something real. And now, I don't even know how to close the gap—if it's even possible anymore.

I shove the uncomfortable feeling down.

Then, I push myself off the bed and head for the bathroom.

I clean myself up, change into pajamas, and wander into the kitchen for a glass of water.

The mail from earlier is still sitting on the counter. I sort through it mindlessly—bills, junk ads, and an envelope with handwriting I don't recognize. I pause, my brows drawing together. It's not a bill, or spam, or one of the many postcards my grandma sends me from wherever the fuck she is in the world right now.

It's a white envelope.

I flip it over, scanning for a return address—*nothing*.

Huh.

My stomach squeezes. I peel the envelope open, letting a piece of lined notebook paper flutter onto the counter.

The handwriting is rushed—sharp—like it was written in a hurry.

I pick it up, scanning the words, my pulse thrumming unevenly.

> A,
>
> You don't know me. Not yet. But I know you.
>
> I know how light must fall on your skin, how the world must hush when you walk through it.
>
> I know you the way a man knows the thing he was never meant to have—too well, too deep, too much.
>
> They say time changes a man. That's a lie.
>
> Time only sharpens what's already there.
>
> And me? I've had nothing but time.
>
> I'll see you soon, angel.
>
> M

I let out a breathy laugh, though it doesn't quite reach my chest.

Ever since moving into my grandmother's 1920s bungalow, I've received my fair share of strange mail. This isn't the first strange letter I've gotten since moving into this house. I mean, my grandmother never married, had my father out of wedlock, lived on a commune for twenty years, and has recently decided to spend her retirement years hopping from one country to another.

And honestly? I admire the hell out of her for it.

Plus, now I can live in her house for half the price of other houses in the area.

I snap a quick picture of the letter for Frankie, my best friend. Then, I fold it up and set it on the counter.

> I either have a stalker or this is another one for Anastasia's collection.

FRANKIE

> Oh my god. That is so ominous. You should frame it.

> Why doesn't Granny get normal mail?

FRANKIE

> Lol. She's lived a life. I'm a little jealous, to be honest.

> Me too. Here I am, fapping myself raw in front of Asher so he can see firsthand where my clit is. My life is soooo glamorous.

FRANKIE

> 💀

FRANKIE

> I should send him a book on female anatomy.

> Please do. Highlight the clitoris in yellow and write "X marks the spot" in the margins.

Smiling, I walk back to my home office and open up my

email. I recently opened up my own virtual CPA practice, and the inbox is full of client inquiries.

A few hours later, I'm just wrapping up my workday when my phone chimes.

ASHER

Hey, I'm sorry but I can't come over tonight after all. Rain check?

I grimace at the screen.

No problem. See ya later.

ASHER

Ari, come on. I said I was sorry. I'm completely exhausted from earlier.

Yeah, you did work hard.

Silence.

He doesn't respond.

I smirk, tossing my phone onto the counter as I walk into the kitchen.

Maybe it's because he's older, but sometimes Asher's linguistic tendencies remind me way too much of my father. And honestly? Nothing kills attraction faster than feeling like you're dating a man who talks like a corporate email. He's sweet. Stable. Predictable. Exactly what I thought I wanted two years ago.

And so goddamn vanilla it makes my teeth ache.

And me? I am most definitely not.

After heating up some leftover pasta, I walk into the living room and curl up on the couch with my iPad and eat. Opening my reading app, I tap the e-book I'm currently reading. I settle under the covers, shifting to get comfortable. Five pages in, the heroine is already being chased through the woods by an eight-foot-tall demon with morally questionable intentions.

Lucky bitch.

Five and a half chapters in, my eyes begin to droop.

Quickly cleaning up my dinner dishes, I turn the lights off, set my security system, and triple-check the locks on all my doors and windows. Once in bed, my body is exhausted, but my mind refuses to shut up.

About work. About Asher. About that letter.

Something about it itches.

Not the words, or even the tone.

But the certainty of it.

I exhale, forcing the thought away. If I don't think about it, it can't bother me. I curl deeper into the blankets, pressing my face into my pillow. Except my body refuses to shut up too.

There's a persistent heat curling low in my stomach, an ache between my thighs that isn't going anywhere. I let out a slow breath, pressing my legs together. My mind slips back to earlier. Not Asher's hands or his soft kisses.

Something else.

Something darker. Firm hands grabbing me. Rougher edges, throaty male groans, sounds of desperation. Teeth scraping against my throat.

My breath catches.

I swallow hard, turning onto my stomach.

My thighs clench again, my fingers curling in the sheets.

Jesus. Why am I like this? Why is my brain wired to find danger hot? Why is the idea of someone being a little bit unhinged over me somehow deeply compelling? Probably something to unpack in therapy. Not tonight, though.

I force my breathing to slow, my body to still.

And eventually—*finally*—I fall asleep.

A Phantom at the Edge

Ari

The letter sits on my kitchen counter, exactly where I left it last night.

I tell myself I'm not avoiding it.

But I haven't thrown it away, either.

Instead, I drink my coffee with deliberate, practiced normalcy. I check my emails on my phone, skim my calendar, pretend my morning is like any other. But every few minutes, my eyes flick toward the envelope.

I'll see you soon, angel.

The words keep looping in my head, even though they shouldn't. It's just a letter. Just a misunderstanding. Maybe even a prank of some kind.

But something about it sticks.

It shouldn't.

It should unnerve me. It *does* unnerve me.

And yet…

My thighs press together as I take another slow sip of coffee. Heat licks low in my belly, sharp and unwelcome. There's something about the idea of being watched, of someone lurking just outside my awareness, tracking my every move. Wanting me. *Waiting* for me.

My pulse jumps, a slow, traitorous throb.

I could tell Asher. I should. But then I'd have to explain why it unsettles me. And why, in some dark, shameful part of me, it doesn't.

So I don't.

Instead, I slide the letter into a drawer, out of sight but not out of mind. My fingers linger on the edges of the paper, as if it might reveal something more if I just hold on long enough.

I'm a couple of hours into my workday when my phone buzzes.

ASHER

> Hello. I feel really bad about last night. May I take you to dinner tonight?

Perking up instantly, I'm smiling as I respond.

> Ooh, dinner? Sounds fancy, and like something a real couple does.

ASHER

> Ha. Ha. I'll make a reservation. Italian okay?

> I guess I'll allow it. As long as you don't say 'rain check' again.

ASHER

> Noted. 7pm?

> See you then, old man.

I set my phone down, still smiling.

A *real* date.

Lately it feels like Asher and I are in some kind of half-relationship limbo, with neither of us fully in or fully out. But maybe this is him trying. Maybe this is him making an effort. It's been months since we've gone on a real date.

The rest of the day zips by, and by the time I arrive at the restaurant in the rideshare I ordered, Asher is already waiting at the table, checking his phone.

Always be a few minutes late. Make him sweat. Remind him I'm not a sure thing.

At first glance, he looks like his usual self—button-up rolled at the sleeves, hair slicked back, looking every inch the clean-cut businessman with the important job. He's a man who knows his place in the world and has never had to fight for it. My heart even does a little somersault, and I think back to when we met almost two years ago on a dating app.

I almost didn't meet him for coffee that day.

Sixteen years older. Closer in age to my parents than to me.

I remember staring at his profile, fingers hovering over the swipe left button, thinking, *Do I really want to be someone's midlife crisis?*

But he didn't feel old when we talked. He didn't *look* old, either, thanks to spectacular genes and an annoyingly good skincare routine. More than that, he was stable. Solid. The kind of man my father would call *a good investment.* No games, no chaos, no late-night fights that left me sobbing in my car. After years of men who burned hot and left scars, Asher felt like safety.

And for a while, that was enough.

Until it wasn't.

Lately, I catch myself staring at him, watching the way he smiles at all the right moments. I know exactly what he'll say before he says it. At one time, I enjoyed the gentle predictability of it.

I'm just not sure when the stability started to feel like stagnation.

And of course there's *the letter.*

I know how light must fall on your skin, how the world must hush when you walk through it. I know you the way a man knows the thing he was never meant to have—too well, too deep, too much.

The words branded into my skin long after I shoved it into the back of a drawer, the raw, hungry want tangled in every line. It's terrifying, that level of obsession. And yet, beneath the fear, there's something else. A spark. A reminder of what it felt like to be wanted—not just chosen, not just loved, but *craved*.

But Asher isn't that. And maybe that's a good thing. After all, I am a goddamn adult.

I slide into the seat across from him, watching his reaction carefully. The way he puts his phone down, like he wasn't just checking it for the third time in a row.

"Miss me?" I tease, arching a brow.

His lips twitch in what should be amusement. But there's a fraction of a second, so quick I almost miss it, where something flickers in his expression.

There. Right there.

A tightness around his mouth. A hesitation in his eyes. It's nothing. But it's also everything. My stomach clenches, my brain already spinning into worst-case scenarios like a machine that never shuts off. He's pulling away. He's bored. He's going to break up with me over appetizers.

Or worse, he's staying out of obligation.

The logical part of my brain, the CPA who crunches numbers for a living, tells me I'm being ridiculous. That I can't possibly analyze every facial expression, every half-second shift in body language, and assume it means something.

And yet, he's distracted, shoulders tense in a way that isn't work-related.

"Hey," I say, nudging his foot under the table. "You look

like you're debating running for office or confessing to murder."

That earns a huff of laughter, but it's delayed, like he had to think about it first.

"Long day," he says.

I raise an eyebrow. "Bad or just boring?"

"Neither. Just... family stuff. I'm a little distracted."

I pause, twirling my straw in my drink. I've met his parents, Otto and Hannah, a couple of times. They're nice, retired, and live just outside of San Diego in a massive house.

Certainly not a reason to be as anxious as Asher looks.

I should pry. I want to pry. But the way his fingers tighten around his glass makes me hesitate.

Instead, I take a sip, and say lightly, "So, dinner means I forgive you for last night, but only if you make an actual effort in the conversation."

The outer corners of his blue eyes crinkle, and there's a touch of amusement twinkling in his irises. But then it disappears. He's present physically, but he's somewhere else, too.

A second later, he tells me about work—his morning meeting, as well as a new, difficult client. However, his words feel measured.

Like he's talking just to talk, because I asked him to, instead of actually engaging with me.

The server takes our orders, and I continue listening to Asher explain the difference between two accounting regulations I stopped caring about thirty seconds ago.

I nod along, absently swirling my wine, but my mind drifts. Normally, I like listening to him talk—there's something reassuring about how steady he is. Predictable. Reliable.

But tonight?

He's saying all the right things, but it doesn't feel right. Whatever family drama has him preoccupied is really messing with him it seems.

I take another sip of wine and decide to test the waters. "You know, I read somewhere that murderers are more likely to work in finance than any other field."

That gets his attention. His glass stills halfway to his mouth. His eyes flick to mine, lips quirking, but there's a fraction of a second—so quick I almost miss it—where his expression tenses.

"That's a weird fact to bring up during dinner," he says, his voice a little too even.

I shrug. "Just saying. You fit the profile."

He exhales sharply through his nose. "Do I?" he asks, but there's no real challenge in his voice.

He picks up his glass and takes a longer sip than necessary, like he needs the extra second before looking at me again.

My fingers tighten around my stemware.

I was joking. He knows I was joking.

So why does he look like I just hit a nerve?

Smooth it over, Ari.

"Buttoned-up businessman with a secret dark side?" I tap my fingers against my glass. "Definitely."

He ignores my teasing. A second later, the server brings our food over, and for the next few minutes, we eat in comfortable silence. The risotto I ordered is incredible, and I can't help but moan out loud as I clean my bowl. Asher grins, his foot tapping mine playfully under the table.

He finishes his chicken, and when he pushes his plate away, I expect him to make eye contact with our server to get the bill.

Instead, he does something unexpected.

"So," he says, setting his napkin on his plate. "Tell me something I don't know about you."

I pause, caught off guard.

A small, startled laugh escapes me. "What?"

His lips curve slightly, but I don't miss the way he shifts in his seat. "I mean it. We've been together for a while now, but I feel like... I don't know. Maybe I should ask more questions. Make more of an effort."

I blink, tilting my head. Asher has never been bad at conversation, but he's never been one for deep dives into my personal history, either.

"You already know the basics," I say, playing with my napkin. "I'm a CPA, I have questionable taste in reality TV, I collect vintage Polly Pockets, and I have unresolved daddy issues."

He lightly chuckles. "Right. But I mean something I wouldn't already know. And please God don't tell me you collect something even more weird than the Polly Pockets."

"Hey. They're not weird," I say, my chest lancing briefly with hurt. But I don't elaborate. For some reason, I've never told Asher why I collect them.

I study him for a second, wondering where this line of questioning is coming from. But he's waiting for my answer. *And* he's actually trying. I have to give him some credit for that.

I lean back and tap my fingers against the stem of my glass.

"All right. Let's see." I purse my lips, thinking. I could tell him about the fact that every Sunday night since I was in high school, I spend a couple of hours writing and uploading monster erotica to a fan fiction site. Or I could tell him about the way I fall down conspiracy theory rabbit holes until I could probably write a dissertation on the Denver International Airport or the missing Roanoke colony.

But those feel too personal, somehow.

"Oh. I had a goldfish named Titan when I was eight. He committed suicide."

That earns me a full-blown laugh. "Jesus, Ari."

"What?" I say innocently. "He jumped out of his tank in the middle of the night. It was a tragedy."

He shakes his head, still chuckling. "And here I thought you were going to tell me something sweet."

"Well, you asked." I take a sip of wine, but my amusement doesn't fully settle. There's still a weird energy between us, like he's here but his mind is somewhere else.

Still, this is better than before. At least he's trying right now.

He leans back in his chair, watching me for a beat, his expression softer now. "You know... I think I get it."

I arch a brow. "Get what?"

"You," he says simply. He swirls the last of his wine in his glass. "You like to be understood without having to explain."

Something in my chest aches, just a little. "Well, yeah. Most people do."

He nods, conceding the point. "Yeah. But with you, it's different. You don't just want it—you expect it." He sets the glass down, fingers still resting against the rim. "And maybe I haven't been great at that."

I blink, surprised by the admission. "That's very... introspective of you."

He gives a small smile, but there's something searching in his gaze. "I guess I'm saying I'll try to read you better." His voice dips just slightly.

The air between us shifts, just for a moment.

Huh. I'm pleasantly surprised.

But also... thrown off. For two years, Asher has been consistent. Not in the way that meant stability, but in the way that meant routine. Predictable. Safe. So why now?

Why, after months of ignoring the way I practically had to map out my pleasure for him, is he suddenly saying this?

I could make a joke, turn it into something teasing and light, like I always do when things get too serious.

But I don't.

Instead, I just nod and say, "That would be nice."

"And while we're on the topic of getting to know each other... I wanted to ask you something. Feel free to say no. My mom would kill me if I didn't ask."

I go still. "What is it?"

Running a hand through his hair, he looks at me with dark contemplation. "They invited you to go away with us next week. Every year, they rent a house on the coast up in Malibu..."

I blink. He's asking me to go this year? He'd gone last year and hadn't invited me. Not that I ever asked why, but still.

"You want me to go this time?" I say carefully.

He gives a small, almost sheepish smile. "Yeah. I mean, my parents will be there, too, but..."

A slow, cautious excitement stirs in my chest, but I force myself to keep my expression neutral. "And if I asked *you* if you actually want me to go... what would you say?"

He clenches his glass harder, his knuckles flexing just once before he exhales, his voice careful. "I'd say... it would be really nice to have you there."

"Okay," I say. "I'll go."

His shoulders relax slightly, and that same small smile tugs at his lips. "Good."

He doesn't push the moment further, just gestures for the check.

A few minutes later, he offers to drive me home in his Honda Civic. The car ride is quiet, but not uncomfortable. It's late, and the streetlights flicker past in hazy yellow streams, the hum of the engine filling the space between us.

"Thanks for dinner," I say, watching the Pacific Coast blur outside the window.

"Of course. I meant what I said, you know."

I glance at him. "About what?"

His jaw shifts, like he's choosing his words carefully. "About paying attention to what you want." He exhales, eyes still on the road. "I don't always get things right the first time, but I can learn. I think getting away for a bit will help."

"Yeah. Maybe."

Or maybe the trip will be a "make it or break it" situation, but I digress.

Asher pulls up to my house a few minutes later and shifts the car into park.

"This was nice. And thanks for the invitation," I say, quickly pecking him on the cheek before I shift over and reach for the handle.

"Sleep well, babe."

"You too."

I step out of the car, closing the door behind me before walking up the path to my grandma's Spanish-style, two-bedroom bungalow. It makes me smile every time I walk up to the door. If I listen closely, I swear I can still hear my childish squeals as my sisters and I raced from the car to her front door whenever we visited.

It's nearly the same as it was growing up, white with terra-cotta accents. I'd painted the door a light coral color a few months ago, but otherwise it's untouched and a perfectly preserved part of my childhood.

One of the only good parts, actually.

I turn around and wave goodbye to Asher.

The moment his taillights disappear down the street, the quiet presses in.

My heels click against the floor as I make my way inside, disarming the security system and tossing my purse onto the kitchen counter. I should go to bed—I have work in the morning—but something about the night feels unfinished.

I slip off my shoes and pad toward the bathroom, stretching my arms over my head. Maybe I'll take a bath, unwind a little—

My steps slow.

My front door was locked when I came in. I know it was, because I used my key to get in.

But the back door, the one leading to my small back patio, is slightly ajar.

I freeze.

For a second, my brain tries to convince me I'm wrong. That I locked it earlier—I must have locked it earlier. I *never* forget to lock the door. As a single woman living alone, I am very conscious of staying safe. But the small gap, the sliver of darkness beyond the threshold, says I did forget.

A prickle of unease crawls over my skin.

I swallow, my fingers flexing at my sides. No. Don't spiral.

It was probably me. I probably forgot.

I cross the room quickly, shoving the door closed and locking it tight, checking the handle twice, three times.

My reflection catches in the dark glass of the patio door— wide eyes, lips pressed together too tightly.

I force myself to exhale.

If someone was here, the sensors I had installed would've picked it up. I would've gotten an alert on my phone.

I turn away and flick off the kitchen light, but not before grabbing the biggest knife I own and walking around the house checking for anything that might've been stolen, just in case. I also check every closet and crevice for axe murderers before resetting the alarm system.

It's nothing. There was no alert.

Taking the knife into my bedroom, I slide the blade under the pillow on the other side of the bed just in case.

An hour later, I'm tossing and turning and attempting to sleep. It's taking me longer than usual to drift off, and my usual perusal of my favorite romance book groups used to lull me to sleep isn't working. Neither are the thirst trap live videos I frequent.

I blame the wine, the overthinking, the way my skin still tingles from the momentary fear of that unlocked door.

But eventually, exhaustion wins.

I'm drifting—half conscious, caught between wakefulness and dreams—when something pulls me back.

Not a sound. Not exactly.

More like a shift. A weight in the air.

My eyes flutter open, and the room is dark. Quiet.

Too quiet.

I strain my ears, listening. Nothing moves. Nothing creaks.

But my pulse is slow and heavy, a deep, instinctual thrum beneath my skin.

The feeling passes—or at least, I tell myself it does.

It's just my anxiety. I'm on meds now, and I've just forgotten what it feels like for that spike of adrenaline to hit.

Used to happen all the time, I tell myself.

I turn onto my side, tucking my hands under my cheek, and will my body to relax.

After a while, I fall asleep.

———

The second letter is waiting in my mailbox the next morning. Just my name, scrawled in messy, impatient handwriting. It's not anonymous to 'A' this time. Whoever they are, they know my name. My stomach knots as I tear it open, and a dried forget-me-not flower falls onto my floor. I pick it up and my breath catches as my eyes scan the words inside.

Ari,

You lock your doors at night. That's good. But doors don't keep me out, angel.

They only keep you in.

I wonder if you've figured it out yet. If you've felt it—the space beside you in the dark, the whisper of something just out of reach.

I'm patient.

I can wait.

But when you finally realize who I am, when you say my name for the first time, I want you to remember that I was already here.

I've always been here.

Sleep well, little warrior.

M

Phantom Visitor
Ari

"You're welcome to stay with us," Frankie says, breaking off pieces of her muffin and handing them to Lucia, her eighteen-month-old daughter. "You know, temporarily."

"I might buy a gun," I tell her absentmindedly, chewing on the banana bread I'm eating but not really tasting.

Frankie chuckles. "Do you even know how to use a gun?"

I roll my eyes. "Of course I do. I had Captain America as a father."

She snorts. "How is Mr. Clarke, by the way?"

This earns her another eye roll. "Oh, you know. Still waking up at 0500, still iron-pressing his jeans, still thinking emotions are a government conspiracy." She laughs, and I shake my head. "Seriously, I swear the man thinks glitter is a threat to national security."

"Classic Lieutenant Clarke."

"Classic," I agree. "It's too bad he had three daughters that he couldn't mold into the picture-perfect soldiers he always wanted."

Lucia laughs, despite not understanding, and I smirk,

reaching over to her and booping her on the nose, which makes her squeal with more laughter.

"Instead, he got you—CPA by day, misfit by night," Frankie says, gray eyes twinkling. "But seriously. Come stay with us. Dante wouldn't mind," she adds, referring to her husband.

I shrug as I push the rest of the banana bread away. For a second, I'd forgotten about why I asked Frankie to meet me for coffee.

The second letter wasn't a coincidence. The first letter could have been a fluke, just another piece of mail meant for my grandma and her adventure-filled life.

But the letter from this morning?

It means whoever sent it knows me. Knows where I live, and my name. Knows enough to make me feel... watched. And I haven't fully come to terms with that yet. Because who would send me something like that? Is it a prank? A bored stranger? Maybe an angry ex-client?

I've run through every possibility. Asher? No. Not his style. Too dramatic, too cryptic. He's blunt, direct, too logical for something like this.

Frankie? Definitely not. She'd subscribe me to a monthly "Potato of the Month" club and wait six months before telling me it was her.

A wrong address? But that doesn't explain how they knew my name. The personal tone. The way it feels too... intentional.

That leaves one option: someone I don't know.

Someone who knows *me*.

And what was up with the flower? A forget-me-not? *So cliché*.

Still, a slow chill creeps up my spine, and I tamp it down.

"I'll be fine. I'm a black belt, remember?" I add, holding

my fists up in front of my face. "But if I go missing, just know my murder was premeditated."

Frankie scoffs. "Ari, I'm being serious. The letter was fucking creepy. At least ask Asher to stay with you tonight," she adds, handing Lucia a sippy cup of water.

I wrinkle my nose. "And share my bed? No, thanks. He's a blanket hog."

"Your relationship confounds me," she says quickly, shaking her head. "You've been together for two years. That's a long time. Sometimes I wonder if you're just with him because it's convenient."

I look down, tracing my finger along the edge of the plate. "I mean, I'm also with him because of his giant co—" I clear my throat, looking at Lucia. "His giant sausage, I mean."

She giggles again.

"Have you at least told Asher about the creepy letters? If he knew, he'd probably offer to stay over in a heartbeat."

I hadn't even considered telling him.

The thought grates at something in my chest. Asking for help has never been my strong suit, but... what does it say about me that it didn't even cross my mind?

That I don't trust him to handle it?

Or that I just don't think he'd care enough to?

"I'm still considering paranormal theories," I add to break the tension.

"Do I want to know?" she asks, her voice droll.

I huff a laugh. "Well, considering it could be a demon coming to claim my soul, probably not."

"You're unhinged."

"I promise I can handle it," I say quickly, offering her a reassuring smile that doesn't quite reach my eyes. "I have my alarm system and a massive knife sitting under a pillow on my bed."

Frankie gives me a flat look. "That's not reassuring."

I grin, lifting my hands. "Why not? It's a big knife. You should see it."

Lucia babbles something in toddler gibberish, smacking her sippy cup on the table, and Frankie rolls her eyes. "You're impossible."

"I'm a survivor," I correct. "I was raised by Captain America, remember? He practically had us running combat drills in the backyard."

Frankie exhales sharply, shaking her head. "I don't get you, Ari. You say you can handle it, but you don't even know what *it* is. You got a random letter from some creep, your door was unlocked, and now you're making jokes about stabbing someone. If it were me, I'd be shitting my pants terrified and halfway moved out already."

"Well, if I actually *had* to stab someone, I'd hope my jokes would make the police report more interesting."

"Ari."

I sigh, dropping my playful expression for the first time.

The truth is, I don't want to think about it too hard. Because if I do, if I let myself fully acknowledge that someone out there is watching me, slipping notes into my mailbox, and maybe even walking into my home, my safe space—then I'll have to admit that I'm not actually in control of this situation.

And I don't know how to deal with that.

So I do what I do best. I deflect. I joke. I pretend.

"I'll be fine, Frankie." My voice is light again, easy. "I'm too stubborn to get murdered. If anyone tries, I'll annoy them into letting me go."

Frankie stares at me for a long moment, then sighs. "Just... be careful, okay?"

I lift my coffee mug in a mock toast. "Aren't I always?"

After my early coffee date with Frankie, I head back home to start my workday, albeit a little later than normal. Upon walking up to my house, I look around, checking for any clues that someone's been here. But everything is how I left it. Unlocking the door, I walk inside and immediately lock it behind me before setting the alarm. I don't usually turn it on during the day—it feels a little overkill—but every creak, every hum of the refrigerator, sends a shiver licking through me.

After a thorough check that no serial killers are hiding under my bed or in my closet, I get to work.

Or try to.

Every noise makes me jump—cars driving by, the faint sound of my neighbor, Blythe, trimming her rose bushes, the gurgle of my grandma's ancient fridge. I can't even drown it out with headphones because, apparently, fear makes me hyperaware and paranoid.

I do my best to tackle my to-do list, despite my clammy hands and racing heart.

When I get to lunchtime, I'm jittery and exhausted. I head into the kitchen, ready to slap together the least depressing sandwich I can muster, when I hear someone moving on the other side of my front door.

I freeze, bread in one hand, butcher knife in the other, as my palms grow clammy. Slowly walking to my front door with the knife in my hand, I listen for the trespasser to knock or do something, but nothing else happens, until I hear the scuffle of boots walking away. A quick peek through the peephole tells me that whoever was out there is gone, but I've seen horror movies. I know they could be hiding off to the side.

I wait.

And I wait.

My breath comes in heavy pants as my heart pounds against my ribs. Gathering the courage to open the door, I pull it open quickly as I brandish the knife, just in case.

No one is here.

Frowning, I step out onto the porch, scanning the yard for anything suspicious. Blythe, my elderly neighbor, is watering her roses, her floppy sun hat casting a shadow over her face.

She glances over and waves when she sees me.

I wave back awkwardly, knife still in hand. "Hey, Blythe! Did you see anyone come to my door a few minutes ago?" I call out.

She squints at me and motions for me to come closer.

With a sigh, I walk barefoot across the grass, knife behind my back.

"Sorry, what was that?" Blythe asks, cupping a hand around her ear.

I point back to my door with my free hand. "Did you see anyone knock on my door just now? A man? A woman? Maybe one of those kids selling overpriced chocolate bars?"

She narrows her eyes and puts a finger under her chin, tapping it thoughtfully. "You know what? I think I did. Just now, wasn't it? Tall man, blond. Gorgeous blue eyes," she adds, winking.

My breath eases out in relief. "Oh, that sounds kind of like my boyfriend."

Blythe hums, leaning on her garden wall. "Interesting," she says, eyeing me suspiciously.

I look down at myself before looking back up at her. "What?"

"Oh, nothing. It's just that he didn't seem very..." She purses her lips.

"Very what?" I ask. Arching my brows, I wait for her to continue.

"He had a bit of a rough edge to him. Looked like he was about to ask if I had a cigarette, you know?"

The description makes me pause. Asher's polished to the

point of gleaming. He wouldn't show up looking anything less than perfect, not even to stop by unannounced.

But it had to be him. Who else could it be based on Blythe's *very* detailed description?

"Huh. Maybe he was having a bad day. I'll call him. Thanks, Blythe!" I say, forcing a smile.

As I walk back toward the house, knife still in hand, I can't shake the feeling that her description doesn't quite match Asher. Once I'm inside, I text the man of the hour.

> This is a weird question, but did you stop by my house a few minutes ago?

Much to my surprise, he texts me back immediately.

ASHER

> No, I've been knee-deep in tax filings all afternoon. Why do you ask?

I stare at the message for a second too long, my fingers coiling around my phone.

A slow, creeping unease curls through me, but I force it down. There has to be an explanation. Maybe Blythe's eyesight isn't what it used to be. Maybe some random guy just happened to be passing through the neighborhood—a random guy who fits Asher's description...

Maybe.

I swallow hard, my thumb hovering over the keyboard.

> No reason. Someone came to my door and I assumed it was you.

ASHER

> Wish it were me. Would've rather been with you than drowning in spreadsheets.

His response should comfort me, but it doesn't. I set my

phone down, rubbing my arms as if I can shake off the lingering unease.

It's nothing. Just my imagination.

Still, as I move through the house, checking the locks a little more thoroughly than usual, I can't ignore the feeling humming beneath my skin.

Blythe described someone. Someone real.

And if it wasn't Asher…

Then who the hell was it?

Controversial Death of Insurance President Sparks Debate

San Diego Tribune, April 30, 2005

The unexpected passing of Daniel Whittaker, president of GoldStar Health, has certainly sent shock waves through the corporate community and ignited important conversations. At just 53, his life came to a tragic end in his downtown San Diego penthouse this past Sunday. While there are whispers of foul play, law enforcement is still gathering details.

Whittaker was a controversial figure who sparked important conversations about healthcare accessibility. The company faced scrutiny for its policies, and some employees have even gone on record saying the unofficial policy at GoldStar is "profit over people." The company is facing numerous lawsuits for denying life-saving coverage to vulnerable patients, which have been linked to the deaths of several individuals, including children.

The investigation took a dramatic turn when Maddox Cross, 25, a former Marine turned security contractor, was arrested on charges of conspiracy and obstruction of justice. Cross allegedly accessed restricted areas of Whittaker's office building on the night of the president's death.

Prosecutors claimed Cross was linked to an anonymous vigilante group targeting corrupt executives. Though there was insufficient evidence to convict Cross of murder, he was sentenced to 20 years in prison for his involvement in what authorities described as a "coordinated effort to intimidate corporate leaders."

While Whittaker's death remains unsolved, public opinion remains divided. Some view Cross as a dangerous criminal, while others have branded him a modern-day Robin Hood, pointing to his history of aiding veterans and disadvantaged families. People have even given him a nickname: the Phantom.

Cross's legal team declined to comment, but in a statement made during sentencing, Cross said, "There's more blood on Whittaker's hands than anyone wants to admit."

THE PHANTOM
AMONG US

ARI

"How do I look?" I ask Asher, twirling in my white summer dress. The fabric is a structured white linen, and it's what Frankie calls my 'good girl' dress. The neckline isn't too low, the length isn't too short, and it has adorable, puffy sleeves. I've paired it with nude, flat sandals and left my long brown hair naturally wavy.

"You look great," Asher says, looking back at his phone a second after his eyes skim down my body from his place sitting on my bed.

Grabbing my vintage pink Prada purse, I slide my phone inside, set it on top of my suitcase, and walk over to Asher.

He sighs as he pockets his phone, and his hands come to rest on my hips.

"What's wrong?" he asks, brows wrinkling.

"I'm just nervous. Dinner with your parents is one thing, but a week with them? What if they discover I reenact entire courtroom scenes from *Legally Blonde* in the shower?"

He smiles at this. "You don't really do that, do you?" I scowl down at him in answer, and he chuckles. "They love you, Ari. It's why my mom asked me to invite you."

My brown eyes flick between his blue ones. "I hope so. Because I really like you."

"I really like you, too," he murmurs, squeezing my ass and kissing my stomach.

"Do we have time for a quickie?" I ask, wiggling my brows as I look down at him.

He laughs. "Unfortunately not. I'd rather not be late, or else I'll never hear the end of it from my dad."

He stands, dropping his hands from my hips, and I miss the contact. Grabbing my things, he walks to the front door to begin loading his car. I do a once-over of the house, making sure everything is all set for me to be away for a week.

My eyes snag on the drawer where I stashed the two letters I've gotten, and I swallow.

The letters had been a quiet, creeping presence for a few days last week, but there hasn't been another since then.

Seven whole days of complete radio silence.

Maybe that should bring relief. Maybe it should make me feel safer, knowing that whoever had been watching me— writing to me—had finally lost interest.

But instead, a strange, unwelcome feeling twists low in my stomach.

Disappointment.

I shake my head, pushing the thought away as quickly as it comes. I *should* be relieved. I should be grateful that the eerie, obsessive messages have stopped. But some dark, hidden part of me—one I don't like to acknowledge—itches at the silence.

After locking up, Asher and I climb into his car. He tells me a little bit more about his family, and I give him my rapt attention. Apparently today is something called midsummer —a holiday that his father, Otto, grew up celebrating in Sweden. Asher drives with one hand on the wheel, the other resting on the center console, and every once in a while, he squeezes my thigh lightly. It feels so... domestic.

It's a three-hour drive to Malibu where his parents are renting the vacation house. And once we pull into the gated driveway, my mouth drops open. The house is bigger than I expected. More modern, too. It sits on a cliff overlooking the ocean, all glass walls and sleek wooden beams. It's the kind of place that people with money book when they want to pretend they're still connected to nature while sipping imported wine and ignoring emails.

The place is as polished as I expected, impeccably maintained and gleaming in the late afternoon sun.

"What do you think?" Asher asks, placing an arm around my shoulders as we both exit the car.

"I think it explains a lot," I tease, smiling when he huffs a quiet laugh.

"Come on. My parents are already inside."

I've met them before, of course. Hannah and Otto. They were polite the two other times we'd had dinner with them, welcoming in the way that people raised to uphold appearances always are. Asher is like that too—buttoned-up, controlled. Everything in his life fits into a neat, color-coded folder, and his parents are exactly the same.

Asher grabs our suitcases and takes my hand, leading me toward the front door. It opens before we reach it, and Otto steps onto the porch, smiling. Asher's father is a broad man and though he's white-haired, he still carries the imposing presence of someone used to being in control.

"So nice to see you again, Ari," he says, his voice warm as he pulls me into a brief but firm hug.

"You too," I reply, offering a smile. "Thank you for having me."

Hannah appears in the doorway, clasping her hands together. "We're just waiting on one more, and then we'll get seated outside."

I glance at Asher as my brows knit together. His grip tightens slightly around my fingers.

"You invited him?" Asher's voice is cold, sharp enough to make his father's brow lift slightly.

"Of course I did, son. We're a family, and we should behave as such. Besides, it's midsummer. A time for celebration, don't you think?" Otto pats Asher on the back before walking into the house, leaving us standing there.

Asher exhales, his fingers twitching at his sides.

"Are you okay?" I ask quietly, touching his arm.

He nods stiffly but doesn't say anything. Hannah gestures for us to follow, leading us through the house to the open patio doors. The backyard is breathtaking, an elegant dining table set with candles and fresh flowers, the sound of the ocean mingling with the faint trickle of the pool.

Asher is tense beside me, his body coiled tight like a spring about to snap. I squeeze his hand. "Who else did your parents invite?"

He sighs, jaw clenching. "My brother."

I pause mid-step. "You have a brother?"

Asher presses his lips together before nodding. "I never told you because I want nothing to do with him. I even changed my last name to Harrison—my mother's maiden name—so no one would make the connection."

There's something almost haunted in his voice, and I remember his words from last week.

"Family stuff. I'm a little distracted."

I frown, watching the way his throat bobs when he swallows hard. His weird mood all week must've been because of his brother.

"But why? What happened?"

"Ari," he says, voice low, "promise me you'll stay away from him, okay? He's dangerous."

My stomach knots. "Dangerous? How?"

Before he can answer, Otto's voice cuts through the air. "Ah, there he is!"

Asher rubs his temples, and I slowly turn toward the back doors.

The man standing in the threshold isn't just anyone.

My breath catches. My pulse stumbles.

Because he isn't just Asher's brother. He's his *twin*.

Identical—perfectly so.

Asher never told me he had an identical twin brother.

The revelation lingers in my mind, sticky and uncomfortable. It wasn't something casual he'd forgotten to mention. It was something he actively hid.

And now, I'm about to find out the reason why.

THE PHANTOM
WALKS FREE

San Diego Tribune, April 29, 2025

After 20 years behind bars, Maddox Cross, the former cybersecurity specialist turned convicted felon, was released from San Quentin State Prison earlier this week. Cross, now in his mid-forties, was sentenced in 2005 for conspiracy and obstruction of justice relating to the murder of Daniel Whittaker, president of Gold-Star Health, whose death sent shock waves through the corporate and legal world.

At the time, Whittaker's murder was as sensational as it was divisive. A powerful executive with a long history of corruption allegations, Whittaker was found in his luxury penthouse suite with a single gunshot wound to the head—execution style. The case gained traction when an anonymous tip led authorities to Cross, a former Marine turned cybersecurity contractor with no prior criminal record. Despite weak forensic evidence and no direct witnesses, Cross was convicted largely due to circumstantial evidence and a prosecution that painted him as a vigilante hacker who took justice into his own hands.

But in the years since his sentencing, the case has only grown murkier.

Key evidence from his case twenty years ago, such as surveillance footage, digital records, and financial transactions, has disappeared from police and court archives. Authorities are baffled, and the missing evidence only undermines the strength of the case against Cross. When pressed for comment, law enforcement officials have repeatedly cited "technical malfunctions" and "archival discrepancies", an explanation that legal experts and investigative journalists find convenient at best.

"It's like the evidence against him was scrubbed from existence," said one former prosecutor who worked on the case but wished to remain anonymous. "You don't just lose an entire digital and forensic trail. Not unless someone made it disappear."

Over the years, Cross has maintained a near-silent stance on his conviction. Unlike many inmates who fight for their exoneration, he never appealed, never sought parole, never spoke to the press—as if waiting for his time to run out.

That time has finally come.

His release, though expected, has reignited public curiosity and quiet unease. Cross was known for his deep web connections, encryption expertise, and rumored ability to make people—and evidence—disappear. With no official employment prospects and a fortune that authorities were never able to trace, speculation runs high about where he will go—and what he will do next.

When reporters reached out to Cross upon his release, he gave only one response before disappearing into the crowd:

"Freedom isn't something you win. It's something you take."

And now, after two decades, Maddox Cross, also known as the Phantom, has finally taken his.

The Phantom at the Table

Ari

"Ari, this is Maddox."

The air shifts the moment he steps fully onto the back patio.

I don't know what I expected when Otto announced his arrival, but it wasn't this.

For a moment, my brain refuses to process what's happening. Why hadn't Asher ever mentioned it? Why hadn't I ever met him the other times we had dinner with his parents? The similarities are undeniable—the same sharp jawline, the same height, the same storm-colored, bluish-gray eyes. But where Asher is put together, Maddox is unraveled in a way that feels deliberate. His tattoos peek out from the pushed-up sleeves of his dark gray Henley, snaking down to his large hands. His stance is lazy yet controlled. The same face as Asher, but sharpened at the edges.

Different.

He looks at me, and something inside me locks up. It's not fear, exactly. It's something heavier. Recognition, maybe? But that doesn't make sense.

His eyes flick over me slowly, and I have to force myself

not to shift uncomfortably. A slow, knowing smirk tugs at his lips, and I have the distinct feeling that he knows something I don't.

My pulse kicks up.

He steps forward, extending a hand. "Ari. So nice to meet you."

I hesitate for just a fraction of a second before taking his hand. His fingers close around mine, warm and strong, his grip just firm enough to make me aware of it.

I clear my throat. "Nice to meet you, Maddox."

His smirk deepens, but before he can say anything else, Asher steps between us, his posture stiff. "You don't have to talk to him."

Maddox doesn't break our eye contact as he hums. "Come on, brother. That's not very hospitable."

The tension between them is immediate, thick. Maddox looks entirely unaffected, his amusement contained behind an arrogant smirk, while Asher's jaw is tight enough to crack. I glance between them, something curling in my stomach.

Hannah, sensing the shift, steps forward with a bright smile. "Let's get seated," she says. "I'll bring the food out."

She places a hand on my shoulder before disappearing inside, and Otto gestures to the large dining table set on the patio. Asher pulls out my chair, and just as I sit, Maddox takes the seat beside me, completely ignoring his brother's glare.

"So, Ari," Maddox says, stretching an arm over the back of his chair. "What do you do?"

I blink at the directness of his attention, but before I can answer, Asher speaks up. "She's a CPA."

Maddox keeps his eyes on me, nodding like he already knew. "Numbers girl. Smart."

I open my mouth to respond, but Asher cuts in, voice clipped. "Stop interrogating her."

Maddox doesn't even look at him. His eyes stay on me, waiting.

Before I can answer, Hannah returns, setting dishes down with a practiced ease. The table fills with food: dill potatoes, Swedish meatballs, smoked salmon. The scent is warm, rich with butter and herbs.

"It's been too long since we had a meal like this together," Otto says, exhaling contentedly.

Asher stays quiet, his fingers drumming once against the table before stilling. I glance at him, sensing the echo of something unsaid, but before I can ask, Otto turns to me.

"Have you ever had Swedish food before, Ari?"

I shake my head, offering a small smile. "I can't say that I have, but it looks amazing."

Hannah beams. "I'm so glad you think so, sweetheart."

I take a bite of the dill potatoes, and my eyes widen involuntarily. "Oh my god," I murmur as the flavors hit my tongue. Garlic, fresh rosemary, olive oil. "This is incredible."

Maddox chuckles, and the sound sends a ripple of awareness dancing along my nerves.

"It's Maddox's favorite too," Otto adds, taking a sip of his drink.

The words land with weight.

A hesitation lingers between us, a fraction of a second where something shifts. My grip tightens around my fork as I glance at Maddox. He's already watching me, his expression unreadable.

Something is wrong.

I don't know what, but I feel it in my bones.

I force myself to look away, focusing on my plate, on the way Asher's shoulders have gone rigid.

"You guys don't see each other often?" I ask, keeping my voice casual.

More silence, and then Asher sighs before answering.

"No," Asher says, his tone final.

I glance at Maddox, expecting a matching response, but instead, he smiles slowly. "I was... away for a while."

The way he says it makes the hair on my arms rise.

Something about it isn't right.

My brain is already working through the possibilities, trying to make sense of the feeling in my gut. The way everyone is suddenly avoiding looking at one another. The way Maddox is watching me, waiting for a reaction.

"What, were you in jail or something?" I joke lightly, taking a sip of my wine.

Otto clears his throat. Hannah drinks deeply from her glass. Asher flinches.

And Maddox smiles.

It's slow. Amused. Something dark glints in his eyes.

"Something like that."

The air shifts again, thick and cloying. I clench my fingers around my wineglass as my thoughts swirl around my mind.

It was a joke, but everyone is acting like I stepped on a live wire. "Really?" I ask, almost incredulously.

Maddox holds my gaze a second too long, like he's letting the gravity of this conversation settle in. Then, as if the tension wasn't suffocating the table, he reaches for the plate of smoked salmon and casually piles some onto his plate, completely at ease.

Asher exhales sharply, his hand tightening into a fist on the table. "We don't need to do this right now," he mutters.

Maddox doesn't even acknowledge him. "You should try the meatballs, Ari," he says smoothly, sliding the dish in front of me. "They're a family recipe."

The way he says family makes something twist in my stomach.

I glance at the dish, then back at him. My hands feel clammy, but I force myself to appear unbothered, to match the casual tone he so effortlessly holds. "You're very invested in my meal choices," I remark lightly, spearing one with my fork.

He smirks. "You strike me as someone who likes to be taken care of."

A flicker of heat ignites in my chest, unexpected and frustrating. I shove the bite of food into my mouth, chewing slower than necessary as I try to push away whatever strange pull Maddox has. The meatball is rich, savory, and frustratingly delicious.

He watches, clearly waiting for my reaction.

I swallow and pick up my wine. "It's good."

Maddox hums, pleased. "Told you."

Across the table, Asher clears his throat. "I don't remember you being this talkative, Maddox."

Maddox finally, lazily, drags his gaze to his twin. "Maybe you just never listened."

The words are deceptively light, but I catch the razor edge beneath them. The tension between them is thick as years of resentment press in. Hannah shifts uncomfortably. Otto sighs.

"Now's not the time for arguing," their father interjects, but his voice lacks real force. It makes me wonder if perhaps this is an old battle, one he's tired of refereeing and one he's used to.

Maddox picks up his drink and takes a slow sip. "You're right." His tone relaxed—*too* relaxed—and something about it feels mocking. "It's a time for celebration." His eyes flick back to me and amusement curls at the edges of his lips. "Tell me, Ari, what exactly do you see in my brother?"

Asher stiffens beside me. "What the hell is your problem, Maddox?"

But Maddox just waits, eyes locked on to mine, expectant.

I should brush it off. I should shut him down. But there's something in his gaze that makes me hesitate—something dark, something knowing. Like he's already decided he won't like my answer.

I wet my lips, placing my fork down carefully. "Asher is a good man," I say evenly.

Maddox tilts his head, studying me. "Good," he echoes, as if tasting the word. "Safe."

I hesitate. "Yes."

His smirk is slow, like I just confirmed something for him. "You like safe, then?"

Asher bristles. "Enough."

His tone lacks force, though, and I ignore the way my stomach twists—not just with unease, but with something closer to disappointment. Like a part of me was waiting for Asher to shut this down, to put Maddox in his place, to *win* this fight before it even started. But he doesn't.

And maybe, deep down, I already knew he wouldn't.

I keep my eyes in my lap, avoiding eye contact with Asher.

Maddox ignores him, leaning in just slightly so that Hannah, Otto, and Asher can't hear his next words. "You don't strike me as someone who wants *safe*." He's so close that his breath brushes against my ear.

My breath catches. There's something about the way Maddox says it, the way his voice dips low like he's exposing something I didn't even know about myself. My fingers curl into my lap.

"I don't know what you mean," I whisper, looking directly at him to show that I'm not afraid.

Maddox holds my gaze for another beat, then leans back in his chair, stretching lazily. "Sure you don't."

Asher watches us closely, and I squirm in my seat.

The conversation shifts to something different after that. Hannah's light chatter about some distant relative's recent wedding is distracting enough, and Otto asks Asher about work. But the whole time they talk amongst themselves, I can feel Maddox's unwavering presence beside me.

He doesn't speak to me.

He just waits—like a patient predator watching its prey.

Like he knows the chase is inevitable.

And for the first time in a long time, I wonder if I'm the one being hunted.

Phantom Promises

Ari

I stare at the small bedroom where Otto had deposited my suitcase earlier. It's cute, in a beach cottage kind of way. Lots of white and seashell accents with a bathroom off the opposite wall of the bed. But it's not the decor that gives me pause.

It's the bed. A very small... *single* bed.

Turning toward Asher, he rubs the back of his neck and gives me an apologetic look.

"My parents are quite traditional," he explains, shuffling his feet. "My room is just down the hall—"

"Separate bedrooms?" I ask, arching a brow. "They do realize you're pushing fifty—"

"I'm forty-five, Ari," he deadpans, glowering at me. "And I know. It's not ideal, but we have to respect their rules."

I bite my tongue and nod once. "Fine. But are there rules against sneaking around?" I ask, giving him a conspiratorial smirk.

He shakes his head and averts his gaze, but doesn't answer right away. Then, after a pause, he sighs.

"Ari, I think it's best if we don't... you know, on this trip."

My smirk fades. "Wait. *At all?*"

He shrugs like it's no big deal. "I just don't want to make things awkward. It's only a week."

I stare at him for a second, something pulling taut in my chest. *Only a week?*

How romantic.

I force a small nod, shoving the frustration down. "Sure. Whatever."

Should've packed my vibrator.

He bends down and gives me a chaste peck on the lips. "I'm sorry about my brother," he adds, rolling his eyes. "It appears that twenty years behind bars did nothing to assuage his arrogant attitude. If you feel uncomfortable—"

"Asher," I say quietly, placing a hand on his chest. "I can handle myself. I promise. But thank you." Still, his words from earlier snag in my mind.

"Promise me you'll stay away from him, okay?"

"He's dangerous."

I want to ask what he went to prison for, but I also don't want to know.

"Okay. Well, I have a few meetings in the morning, so just help yourself to the house," he says, already halfway to the door. "My parents will be around."

I nod slowly, but something about that feels... odd. I don't *know* his parents well. I was hoping to rely on him to navigate this whole week, but now it seems like I'm supposed to figure it out on my own.

"Right," I murmur. "I'll just... make myself at home."

He gives me a knowing smile before running a hand over his mouth. "We're doing a gift exchange tomorrow, by the way. Sort of like a white elephant, but for midsummer."

My stomach drops. "What? Shit, I didn't get anyone a gift."

"It's fine, we can figure something out tomorrow, okay?"

Guilt, heavy and suffocating, clogs my throat. So much for making a good impression...

He quickly kisses me once on the head and turns to leave. Once the door closes behind him, I sigh and walk over to my suitcase. I'd probably packed too many clothes, but I had no idea what to expect this week.

Flipping open the lid, my stomach sinks for the second time.

A sticky, oily mess coats the inside of my bag. I groan, lifting my favorite and now ruined silk camisole to find that my face oil and shampoo have exploded, soaking through half my clothes. I manage to salvage a few things, but I already know I'm going to need replacements since we're here for a week.

I sigh, resigned. "This is *definitely* not how I imagined this trip going," I mutter under my breath.

Grabbing my toiletry bag, I clean up as much as I can before tossing the ruined clothes in the corner of the room. Looks like I'll have to go shopping tomorrow.

Maybe I'll go alone.

Or maybe I won't have a choice.

At least I'll be able to get a midsummer present while I'm out.

A soft creak sounds outside my door, and I freeze. My eyes flick to the handle, but it stays still, unmoving. Maybe it's just the house settling. Or maybe it's someone walking by in the hallway.

Shaking it off, I grab a fresh oversized t-shirt from the undamaged side of my suitcase and change quickly before getting ready for bed. A few minutes later, I flick off the light and climb into bed, curling up under the blankets.

The house is quiet. Too quiet.

As I close my eyes, something lingers at the edges of my

thoughts, like an itch I can't quite reach. My body is restless, and I can't shake the ominous feeling off.

I toss. Turn. Glance at the clock.

Ten p.m.

Pulling my Kindle from under the covers where I stashed it, I attempt to read, but my eyes skim the same page over and over again. Groaning, I throw my covers off and check the time.

11:42 p.m.

This is futile. If I'm awake, I might as well be *doing* something. Catching up on work emails, or learning French. *Something.*

I toss back an Ambien, something I take whenever I have trouble sleeping, and then I pull my laptop onto the bed. I have about thirty minutes before it kicks in, so I might as well be productive.

Clicking into my fan fiction account, I use the Wi-Fi password Asher had texted me as I check the recent comments for the story I'm writing. It's a mash-up of *Eragon* and *Game of Thrones*. My main character is currently on her knees for a seven-foot dragon hybrid, begging him to wreck her life.

In iambic pentameter.

Because I have range.

The comments have me cackling as I roll over in bed.

Mommy? Sorry. Mommy? Sorry.

Absolutely feral for this unhinged insanity. Pls write faster.

Genuinely concerned for your mental health but in a good way.

The last one makes me laugh harder. *You and me both, bestie.* This is what I get for writing erotica in the style of Shakespeare.

Half a chapter in and six rhyming scenes later, my phone buzzes, and Asher's name flashes on the screen.

ASHER

Hey. I feel like I kind of brushed you off earlier, and I'm sorry. Maybe I'll sneak in later for some PG-13 fun?

I blink at the message, my eyes already feeling heavy. The Ambien's starting to kick in.

That's fine. I took an Ambien, though, so you can't hold me accountable for anything I say or do.

His reply is almost immediate.

ASHER

Lol. Okay. Maybe tomorrow?

My lips twitch into a faint smile. I want to text something back, but the effort feels like too much.

Yeah. I just need to sleep right now.

The words blur slightly on the screen, and I lie back and close my eyes for what feels like just a second.

"Then sleep. I'll take care of everything."

The voice is soft, familiar, just enough like Asher's to make sense in the haze of the Ambien.

My lips part to respond, but my body feels heavy, sinking deeper into the mattress. Sleep pulls at me, warm and slow, until I'm not sure if my eyes are closed or if the room is just dark.

Maybe both.

Maybe neither.

———

I don't know how much time passes before I feel it—the mattress dipping beside me.

I open my eyes, but my vision swims, shapes blurring into shadows.

"Asher?" I mumble, the word thick on my tongue.

The figure leans closer, a hand brushing my cheek. The warmth of the touch grounds me, but something about it feels... different.

"Shh," the voice murmurs, low and soothing. "Go back to sleep."

I blink, trying to focus on his face, but it's hard to make out anything beyond the dark outline.

I swear I see a dark, whirling pattern on his neck, but I can't focus enough to truly determine if I'm seeing things again or not.

"You came to my room," I whisper, more a statement than a question. My limbs feel heavy, my head too foggy to question why.

"I needed to see you," he says softly.

I smile faintly, my eyes drifting shut again. I'm not sure if I'm awake or dreaming when I feel his hands on my arms, pulling the blanket higher around me. His touch lingers, trailing down my shoulder, then back up to cup my cheek.

"You smell different," I whisper, my voice barely audible.

"Do I?" he asks.

The words echo strangely, like they're both too close and too far away.

I try to laugh, but it comes out weak. "Yes." He chuckles softly, and the sound ripples through the room. "What's so funny?"

"Nothing, angel. Go back to sleep, okay?"

"You've never called me that before," I tell him, feeling sleep tugging at my consciousness.

I feel the bed shift as he leans closer, his lips brushing my temple. It feels... unfamiliar.

But it's Asher. I can see him with my own two eyes. Barely—but it's him.

"Sleep," he whispers.

I nod, the motion sluggish, and let the darkness take over.

———

When I wake up, the first thing I notice is the heaviness in my limbs. The Ambien always does that—leaves me groggy and unsure of where dreams end and reality begins.

I sit up slowly, blinking against the sunlight streaming through the curtains. It takes me a second to orient myself.

Asher. Beach house. Malibu.

I smile when I remember how he tucked me in last night, how his rich laugh made me feel safe.

But as I rub the sleep from my eyes, something itches at the edges of my memory, like a half-forgotten melody. The way he touched me, his lips on my temple, the quiet rasp of his voice. Something about it feels... off. I was alone when I fell asleep.

Wasn't I?

"Nothing, angel. Go back to sleep, okay?"

A flicker of unease skates down my spine as I grab my phone, texting Asher before I even have a chance to second-guess myself.

> I enjoyed last night. ;)

It takes a few minutes for him to respond, and when he does, it's not what I expect.

ASHER

What are you talking about?

My stomach twists. *Did I dream it?* I suppose it wouldn't be the first time Ambien made me dream about something silly.

Um. I think it must've been the Ambien
making me hallucinate again.

Three dots appear, then disappear. Then, finally—

ASHER

How much Ambien did you take?

I bite the inside of my cheek at his condescending tone.

The normal amount.

ASHER

You've told me before it makes you do
weird things. Remember that time you
ordered an entire pizza and forgot about it
until the delivery guy showed up? Or what
about the goat?

I sigh.

I'll never live the goat down, will I?

ASHER

You tried to adopt a goat off Craigslist. A
real, live goat, Ari. What do you think?
You're not yourself when you're on that
stuff. You shouldn't be taking it.

Yeah. Tell that to my insomnia.

I exhale, running a hand through my hair. I stare down at his texts again, and that unease doesn't fade.

Because no matter how much I try to logic my way through it, I know one thing for certain.

Asher has never called me *angel,* so where the hell did that hallucination even come from?

Phantom Menace

Ari

THE MORNING AIR IS CRISP, BUT THE SUN HAS THAT low heat that tells me it's going to be hot later, once the marine layer burns off. Sunlight filters through the tall windows in the house in thick beams as I step into the kitchen, freshly showered and wearing the same outfit as yesterday. Hannah and Otto are already seated at the dining table, sipping coffee and reading the paper. Asher is nowhere to be found, but that's not surprising. He mentioned having a meeting this morning, though I thought he'd at least have breakfast with me before disappearing into work mode.

I grab a cup of coffee and make my way toward the study, where I find him exactly as expected—seated at a large wooden desk, laptop open, phone pressed to his ear.

"Asher," I say softly, stepping inside.

He doesn't look up. Instead, he holds up a single finger, signaling me to wait. My stomach twists, the gesture making something small and bitter rise in my throat. It's not the first time he's done this when he's on an important call, but somehow, here, where I don't know anyone but him, it stings more.

I stand there awkwardly, shifting from foot to foot as he

continues speaking, completely immersed in whatever conversation he's having. Minutes pass, and the longer I stand there, the more I feel like an interruption rather than his girlfriend. Finally, he types something into his computer, glances at me, and presses his hand over the receiver.

"What is it?" he asks, his tone clipped.

I swallow the small knot of disappointment in my throat. "I need to go shopping. My clothes—" I exhale, forcing a light chuckle. "Let's just say they didn't survive the trip."

His brow furrows, but his attention is already slipping back to his laptop. "Can you take a rideshare?"

I blink. "I... I don't really know my way around here."

"I'll send you the address of a good shopping center," he says, already refocusing on his screen. "I'll check in later, okay?"

I hesitate, waiting—just for a second—to see if he'll change his mind. If he'll look at me properly, see the way I'm standing here feeling wholly uncomfortable. But he doesn't.

I nod, even though he's barely looking at me. "Okay."

I turn and leave, pressing my lips together as I make my way back to the kitchen. I shouldn't be upset. I know Asher is busy at work. But still, I thought—

"You need to go somewhere?"

The voice is deep, smooth, cutting through my thoughts like a blade.

Maddox.

I turn, finding him leaning against the kitchen counter, a mug in his hand, watching me with that unreadable expression. His presence is all-consuming, even when he's doing nothing but standing there. He's broad-shouldered, and though I know they're twins, he seems taller than Asher. His build is all lean muscle and coiled restraint. The tattoos along his forearms and hands shift slightly as he moves, making my pulse stutter in a way I don't want to acknowledge.

He doesn't smile. He doesn't offer anything other than quiet, weighty observation.

For a moment, I don't know how to answer. Something about his attention makes me feel exposed.

"I—uh—yes. Shampoo explosion."

"I hate when that happens," Hannah supplies, glancing up from her paper.

Maddox lifts a brow, slow and deliberate, but he doesn't say anything.

I cross my arms. "It's not a big deal."

"You should take her, Maddox," Otto interjects, setting his coffee down. "She'd probably be bored with us."

Something flickers in Maddox's gaze. Amusement. Like he knows exactly what they're doing.

I shake my head. "That's okay. I can just—"

"I'll take you," Maddox cuts in, his voice leaving no room for argument.

My lips part, but no sound comes out. He's not asking. He's *telling*.

I hesitate, glancing toward the hallway where Asher is still locked away in his meeting. I should say no. I should insist on finding my own way.

But the idea of wandering an unfamiliar city alone isn't exactly appealing.

And Maddox...

I exhale sharply. "Fine. But I'm driving."

A slow smirk tugs at his lips. "No, you're not."

Before I can argue, he's already pushing off the counter, grabbing the keys off the hook by the door.

"You coming?"

I don't know why I follow him.

But I do, grabbing my purse and sandals from where they sit by the front door.

Maddox drives a sleek black SUV, a rental I assume, since I

doubt he owned a car after twenty years inside. He doesn't speak much as we pull onto Pacific Coast Highway, and I'm painfully aware of how quiet the car is. There's no radio, no idle chatter. Just the low hum of the engine and the steady, intentional way he handles the wheel.

I glance at him from the corner of my eye. He's focused, relaxed in a way that feels unnerving, like he's completely in control of every moment.

"How are you allowed to drive?" I blurt before I can stop myself. "I mean... legally?"

His lips twitch, like he's trying not to smile. "I got my license back a week after I got out."

I nod, unsure what else to say. "Well... thanks for taking me."

He finally glances at me, his gaze sharp. "You sound like you had a choice."

I freeze for a second before forcing a small, awkward chuckle. "What's that supposed to mean?"

He doesn't answer. Just smirks, turning his attention back to the road.

Minutes pass before we pull up to an outdoor shopping plaza. He parks without asking where I want to go, cutting the engine and stepping out before I can process that we're already here.

I scramble to keep up, stepping onto the sidewalk as he heads toward one of the higher-end boutiques lining the plaza.

"I don't usually shop in places like this," I say, eyeing the designer labels on the windows. "I was thinking something more—"

"This'll do," he interrupts, holding the door open for me.

Something about the way he's looking at me makes my breath hitch. Like he already knows I'll listen.

I hesitate but step inside, the cool air-conditioned space washing over me.

And Maddox? He follows right behind me.

The store is elegant, quiet, with racks of carefully curated pieces hanging several inches apart from each other. *Oh, this place is* fancy *fancy*. I scan the shelves, already knowing I'll have to be careful not to spend too much.

Maddox walks past me, plucking a dress off the rack and holding it up. "Try this."

I blink. "What?"

His eyes meet mine, and before I can ask if he's joking, he continues. "It'll complement your eyes."

I let out a soft laugh, caught between amusement and pure disbelief. "Are you serious? You don't even know my style."

His eyes drag lazily down my body, and the way he's looking at me should be illegal. I feel the trail of electricity his gaze leaves on my skin, and I squirm uncomfortably under his gaze.

"I know what'll look good on you."

The way he says it makes my stomach flip. I should argue. I should roll my eyes and brush him off. Asher would *never* pick clothes out for me—he hardly notices what I'm wearing on a good day.

Instead, I take the dress, stomping to the dressing room as he chuckles.

Asshole.

The boutique is quiet, save for the soft hum of instrumental music and the occasional rustle of hangers sliding along racks. When I pull the dress over my head, I study it with a frown. It's a sleek, black slip dress, something far more fitted than what I usually wear. And yet...

And yet...

Fuck him. I love it. And it *does* bring out my brown eyes, dammit.

Letting out a low growl, I open the dressing room door

just enough to pop my head out and tell him to his face, but he's *right there,* holding an armful of hangers.

I snatch them out of his hand without saying a word.

One outfit turns into seven, and soon I'm standing at the register with more than I intended to buy. He knew my size... something I remind myself to ask him about later, because it's weird. And except for a *very* revealing skirt, I'm buying everything he picked out for me. It's all high quality—silks and cashmere, thin cotton that feels like butter, linen fabric that feels way too expensive, and a pair of jeans that somehow hugs my ass and hips in all the right places.

I reach into my bag for my wallet, but before I can pull it out, Maddox steps forward and hands the cashier his card.

"Wait—Maddox, no."

He doesn't even look at me. "Don't waste your breath."

I see the cashier throw some lacy underwear and matching bra sets into the bag as well, and I roll my eyes. The transaction is done before I can fight him on it, and the total makes my eyes bug out. That's a very high, four-figure number—more than I've *ever* spent on... anything. The cashier hands over the bags, and Maddox takes them without a word. My fingers twitch at my sides.

"I could've paid for my own clothes," I murmur as we step outside.

"You could've," he agrees easily, carrying the bags toward the car. "But you didn't."

I scowl. "Because you didn't give me a choice."

He pauses at the passenger door, glancing at me, his gaze steady. "You could've fought harder."

Heat prickles along my skin. I don't know what to say to that, because the worst part is—

He's right.

I shouldn't have enjoyed that as much as I did, the way he

took control, the way he decided things without hesitation. It should bother me. It *does* bother me.

I let him do it.

And I don't know why.

"Also, the underwear is totally inappropriate."

He smirks, unlocking the car. "Exactly why I picked it."

Asshole.

With a scowl, I go to reach for the handle before remembering the midsummer gift. "Oh, wait. I need to get a present," I say quickly.

He arches a brow, and damn, that shouldn't be so hot. It's unfair, really, how attractive he is. His face is so much like Asher's, yet nothing like it at all. The same sharp jawline, the same striking blue eyes. But where Asher is polished like stone, Maddox is roughly worn down by granite or lava... which makes him seem more dangerous because of it.

My stomach flips when he lets his gaze wander down to my feet briefly, and it's like my body recognizes him before my mind can catch up, like some twisted version of muscle memory. Like a trick played on me by my own instincts, lulling me into a false sense of familiarity—of safety because he's my boyfriend's twin and I recognize Asher in his features.

Because no other explanation makes sense.

Nothing else explains why my pulse jumps when he takes a slow, deliberate step closer, so close that my back presses against his car. I feel cornered, but I'm not entirely sure I want to run.

"Okay. I'll wait here," he murmurs, smirking as he gives me a knowing look.

I push past him and walk to the plant shop next to the boutique we just cleared out, and a minute later, I'm walking back to the car with a small snake plant wrapped in plain brown paper. I figure whoever I get for the present exchange will appreciate a plant that's hard to kill and easy to maintain.

I glance at him as I approach the car. His expression is unreadable, but there's something beneath it—confidence, or arrogance, maybe?

Maddox opens the passenger door for me, waiting. Not offering, not suggesting—*waiting*. Like he already knows I'll listen. I hesitate, just for a second. The sharp scent of leather and faint traces of cologne linger in the air between us, something familiar tugging in the back of my mind. I shouldn't like how expectant he looks, like he knows I'm going to obey.

I swallow and step inside.

He loads the trunk with my bags, and I shift in my seat, arms crossed loosely over my chest and the plant safely at my feet. He doesn't turn on the radio once we pull out of the parking lot—again. Doesn't fill the silence with idle conversation—again.

He doesn't have to.

The drive back to the house is quiet, almost eerie. Maddox grips the wheel with an ease that's almost lazy, but there's control in his posture, in the way his fingers flex against the leather. The quiet stretches, thick and oppressive. My skin prickles.

Finally, once we're a few blocks from the vacation house, he speaks. "You liked that."

My head snaps toward him. "What?"

His lips twitch at the corner, not quite a smile. "Don't play dumb with me, Ari." My pulse spikes, and I suddenly feel hot all over. "You liked relinquishing control."

I scoff, but I can't deny the flush spreading down to my chest. "You're insufferable."

"I'm right."

I exhale sharply, turning to stare out the window. I hate that I don't have a retort. I hate that my face feels like I got too much sun, that there's a kernel of truth in his words I don't want to acknowledge.

Maddox shifts gears effortlessly, his fingers flexing around the wheel.

I swallow, keeping my eyes fixed on the road ahead. "You don't know me."

He lets out a low hum of amusement. "No?"

I don't answer.

When we pull into the driveway, Asher is already outside. He watches as we park, his jaw hardening when he sees Maddox open my door.

"You let him take you?" Asher asks, his voice edged with something sharp.

I bristle at his choice of words. "It was your parents' idea," I say, brushing past him and heading inside.

I don't have the energy to fight about something that isn't even worth arguing over.

But just as I reach the doorway, I glance back.

Maddox lingers behind, his presence stretching the moment just long enough to make Asher uncomfortable. He already has my bags in his hands, and he winks once at Asher, whose face turns a bright, purple-ish red with rage.

Well, this should be fun.

I don't look back again, but I can feel it—the tension crackling between them, an invisible war waged in silence. I don't want to be a witness to whatever the fuck kind of family drama they're involved in.

Phantom Waters
Ari

Asher finds me in the library on the second floor a few minutes later, mumbling an apology about Maddox. I can tell he's still angry, but I'm unsure what to do about it. When I reach for his hand, he brushes me off.

"My mom wants to go to the beach. Would you like to join us?" His voice is monotone, like he's getting the words out without meaning them.

"Sure. It's gorgeous out," I offer, hoping the sunshine will put him in a better mood.

"Meet you by the front door in ten?" he asks, finally looking down at me.

"Okay." He nods once, and as he turns to walk away, I grab his hand, pulling him back. "Hey, are you okay?"

He sighs, and something in his expression deflates. "I'm fine. I just didn't... I wasn't expecting Maddox to be here, that's all. I'm still furious with my parents for suggesting he drive you... What if something happened to you?" he asks, tilting his head.

I should be flattered by his protectiveness, but instead I feel a tug of irritation. "It was fine. We went to some local boutique, I picked some clothes out, end of story. You were working. What else was I supposed to do?"

Asher opens his mouth to argue, but I squeeze his hand tightly. "Hey. Maddox is your brother, whether you like it or not. And that means I need to learn to accept him."

Asher's jaw tics. "Did he— Was he nice to you, at least?"

I hesitate. Nice isn't the word I'd use.

Overpowering, commanding, *intense*.

But I keep that to myself.

"Yeah," I say simply. "He was fine."

Asher exhales, nodding stiffly. "All right. I'll see you in ten."

I watch as he walks away, a strange tightness settling in my chest.

Shaking it off, I walk down the hallway and step into my room, shutting the door behind me. I move toward my suitcase, pulling out a swimsuit, already trying to decide if I should wear the one that still faintly smells like lavender shampoo or maybe one of my new dresses that sit neatly on my bed, still inside their shopping bags.

Maddox must've dropped my new things off when Asher and I were talking. Did he overhear anything?

My phone chimes, the sharp sound cutting through the stillness of my room. I blink, my pulse already thrumming with unease as I glance down at the screen.

Unfamiliar number.

I hesitate before opening the message, expecting spam, some automated alert, anything but—

(858) 667-9960

You liked it more than you'll admit.

A slow, crawling sensation sends a static hum through me as I stare at the words, the meaning sinking in like a stone dropping into the depths of my stomach.

I know exactly who it's from.

My fingers tighten around the phone, my grip just shy of trembling. The air in the room feels too thick, too still, like the walls are closing in.

I tell myself it's nothing. That it's just Maddox messing with me. Pushing, testing.

I exhale slowly, forcing my thoughts to steady. This is all just a game to him. A game I should ignore. I should delete it. I should block the number. I should do anything but what I actually do.

I type out a response, fingers moving before my mind can catch up.

> Go to hell.

I hit send.

The reply comes almost instantly.

(858) 667-9960

> Already there, angel. Just waiting on you.

A shiver rolls through me. *Angel.*

The word lingers, curling around my thoughts like smoke. My breath stutters, and for a split second, my mind jumps somewhere it shouldn't. Somewhere absurd. The letters at my house...

I'll see you soon, angel.

You lock your doors at night. That's good. But doors don't keep me out, angel. They only keep you in.

"Nothing, angel. Go back to sleep, okay?"

But no. That's ridiculous.

I exhale sharply, pressing the power button until my screen goes black in my palm. It's time to disconnect from reality today. I've spent too much time letting this get to me already.

It's a silly pet name. A generic one. Hell, random guys have called me angel before.

And Maddox?

I just met him.

There's no way.

I shake my head, forcing the thought away, chalking it up to coincidence and my own paranoia. Still, my skin prickles as I move through the motions of getting ready, my body running on autopilot. I pull out the lavender-scented bikini from my suitcase and change into it, the faint floral scent grounding me. Normal. Routine.

I won't let some stupid text ruin my day. He's just trying to get in my head because of whatever rivalry he has going on with Asher.

I won't let him.

I won't.

But the problem is...

He already has.

————

The scent of salt and sunscreen clings to the air as I step onto the warm sand, my damp swimsuit clinging to my skin. I managed to rinse out most of the spilled shampoo, but there's still a faint lavender scent lingering from where it soaked into the dark blue fabric.

I glance toward the shoreline, where Asher stands under the shade of a large beach umbrella, his phone already in hand. His parents are a few feet away, spreading out towels and setting up a small cooler with drinks. Maddox, of course, is watching everything in silence.

I press my lips together and drop my bag onto a nearby folding chair they must've set up for me. The sun is hot against my skin, and I adjust the straps of my bikini before sitting down.

Hannah beams at me as she settles into her chair. "So, Ari... Asher says you started your own business? You worked for a firm last time we saw you, if I recall."

I smile and nod. "Yes, I have my own CPA practice now. I started it a few months ago after working for a big firm."

Before I can elaborate, Asher shifts beside me and glances up from his phone. "She's good at it, too."

I blink, and Hannah hums in approval. "That's wonderful, sweetheart. Independent women are a force to be reckoned with."

Otto chuckles, cracking open a cold beer. "No wonder you keep Asher in line."

At the mention of his name, I glance over at my boyfriend, but once again, he's too focused on whatever's on his phone screen to pay attention to the conversation. My stomach knots slightly. This is supposed to be a vacation, yet here he is, still buried in work.

Sitting on the towel, I lean back on my elbows and let the sun beat down on my skin with my eyes closed. I'm slathered in SPF 50, so I feel no guilt whatsoever for soaking up some much-needed vitamin D. My neck tingles, and when I open them, I see Maddox watching me with a white t-shirt and black swimming trunks on. The dark whorls of ink tracing down his arms are a stark contrast to the white shirt, but I don't give myself any time to admire them.

He's only a few feet away, silent and still, his sharp blue gaze tracing over my body in a way that makes my skin prickle. Not with embarrassment—with awareness.

"You're from San Diego, right?" Otto asks.

I sit up and turn toward him, offering a warm smile. "Yes, I grew up there. Well, kind of. My dad was military, so we moved around a lot before settling there."

Asher doesn't even look up from his phone. "She has two younger sisters out of state," he adds. "One in college and one in graduate school."

I clench my teeth.

It's not a lie. It's not even offensive. But something about the way he *answers* for me—without hesitation, without even checking to see if I wanted to speak for myself—grates against my skin.

Hannah nods approvingly. "I'm just so glad Asher has met such a nice, normal girl."

Her gaze flicks to Maddox, whose lips just twitch with amusement.

As if he can see right through me.

I don't know why that makes my chest constrict, but suddenly, I feel stuck.

Trapped between a mother who's already decided who I am, a boyfriend who speaks over me, and a man whose silence feels heavier than words.

The air is suddenly too thick, too hot. The sun beats down on me, and I feel my skin break out into a cold sweat.

I push myself up, brushing sand from the backs of my thighs. "I'm going for a swim."

No one argues.

Not even Asher. He doesn't even look up from his phone.

I walk toward the water, stepping over scattered shells and warm sand until I reach the surf. The ocean rushes in, lapping at my ankles, cool and soothing.

I take another step forward, letting the waves wrap around my legs, my overheated skin drinking in the relief.

After a few minutes, I feel a presence behind me. I don't have to turn around to know who it is. He doesn't speak right away, giving me the quiet I so badly needed. Instead, he steps into the water, silent as a shadow, letting the waves roll over his feet as he stares out at the horizon from next to me.

His existence is impossible to ignore.

I can feel him there, steady, deliberate, waiting. Almost like my body is tuned into the vibrations of his, somehow.

Like the air is crackling and popping.

God, I hate this.

Finally, his voice cuts through the sound of the tide. "Does Asher always do that?"

I glance at him, surprised to see he's shirtless. *Good god. He must've spent his whole prison sentence doing pull-ups.*

"Do what?"

His eyes slide to mine, sharp, assessing. "Speak for you."

A small flash of irritation flares in my chest. Not at him. At the truth in his words.

I inhale slowly, turning my gaze back toward the water. "It's not like that."

"Isn't it?"

I don't answer. The silence between us stretches, but it isn't uncomfortable. It's something else. Something heavier. I let my eyes drift over him, taking in the ink that stretches from his collarbones, creeping over his chest, down both arms, all the way to his fingers. Black lines twist and coil into intricate designs, some pieces blending seamlessly into others, like they were added over time. The ink disappears beneath the waistband of his black swim shorts, and I wonder how far it goes.

I have to actively attempt *not* to ogle my boyfriend's twin's body, but underneath the ink is pure, carefully honed muscle.

It's hard *not* to notice.

"How long did those take?" I ask, nodding toward his tattoos.

Maddox glances down at his arms, flexing his fingers slightly before letting them relax.

"Years."

I trace the patterns with my eyes, drawn to the way the ink moves with the shift of his muscles.

"They let you get tattoos in prison?"

His expression doesn't change, but something flickers behind his gaze. "Some."

I tilt my head, waiting.

He exhales, running a hand through his damp hair. "Some of these came before. The rest... I earned."

Before.

The word lingers in the air between us, and I get the distinct impression that *before* holds more weight than just a timeline.

I press my lips together, my curiosity clawing at me. "How did you earn them?"

His jaw tics slightly, and for a moment, I think he won't answer. But then—

"Because I needed to remember the people I couldn't save." His voice is steady, but I hear the fracture underneath.

Something about the way he says it makes the air between us shift.

My fingers twitch at my sides, my curiosity gnawing at me, demanding more. But before I can ask, Maddox shifts closer. Just slightly. Just enough that his presence feels heavier.

"You know," he murmurs, voice even, unreadable, "I see through the facade you're putting on for my parents."

My breath catches.

I glance up at him, brows drawing together. "Excuse me?"

His expression doesn't change, but his gaze sharpens.

"You heard me," he says, tilting his head slightly. "You're a good actress, I'll give you that. Polite. Sweet. The perfect girlfriend." His voice dips lower, like he's letting me in on some private joke. "But that's not who you really are, is it?"

A slow, unwelcome heat creeps up my neck. Not from embarrassment—from something else.

I roll my eyes, trying to brush off the strange pull of his

words. "You've known me for all of, what? A day? Don't act like you've got me figured out."

He hums, unconvinced. "No?" His blue eyes don't waver from mine. "Tell me, then. Has Asher ever noticed how restless you are?"

I open my mouth, but nothing comes out. He waits. The waves rush in around our ankles, swirling between us, and I tell myself that's why I feel off-balance. Not because of him.

Not because he's right.

I cross my arms, resisting the urge to fidget under his stare. "I don't know what you're getting at."

Maddox smirks, like he does know. Like he knows exactly what's running through my mind, and he's just waiting for me to catch up.

"You act like you don't want more, but I see it. I know it's why you're dating my brother. Perfect boyfriend. Perfect job. What's next... a perfect wedding, perfect beige house, a few perfect kids?" His voice is low, edged with something knowing, something dangerously close to the truth.

Something in my chest tightens. That all sounds... *horrible.*

"I'm not perfect," I say automatically.

"No," he agrees. "But you sure as hell try to be."

The words strike a nerve. My stomach knots. I want to argue. I want to say something sharp, something cutting.

I don't, though. Because I can't come up with a good enough retort.

Maddox sees that too. His smirk deepens, just a fraction. He shifts his weight, exhaling as he turns his gaze back toward the water.

"Good girls crack the hardest," he says absently, almost like he's talking to himself.

I swallow hard, something tight coiling low in my stomach. "I'm not—"

"A good girl?" Maddox cuts in smoothly.

His eyes flick back to mine.

I don't like the way my pulse reacts.

I don't like the way my thighs clench with whatever the fuck is happening right now.

I don't like the way he says it like he already knows the answer.

His stare lingers, watching me, waiting for me to prove him right.

And for the first time, I'm not entirely sure I can.

"Ari!"

I jerk at the sound of my name, blinking as the spell breaks.

Asher's voice carries over the sound of the waves. When I turn, he's sitting in his chair beneath the umbrella, his phone still in his hand.

He gestures toward me lazily. "Want to go on a walk? I have thirty minutes before a call."

A call.

Not time together. Not, 'I want to spend time with you.'

I exhale, dragging a hand through my damp hair. "Sure," I yell back.

When I glance back at Maddox, he's watching me. Still, patient. A hunter letting his prey come to its own conclusions.

I turn away and head toward Asher, but with every step, Maddox's words follow me.

"You act like you don't want more, but I see it."

And the worst part? I'm not even sure I know what 'more' is.

Phantom Presents

Ari

A couple of hours later, when the sun feels too strong, too hot, too suffocating, we all head back into the house.

Asher ended up cutting our walk short because he had another call to prepare for, and I spent the next hour and a half baking in the sun, letting the heat dull the restlessness still humming in my veins.

Hannah, Otto, and Maddox partake in casual conversation, but I tune most of it out, stretching across my towel and trying to force my body to relax.

I barely succeed.

So when Asher mentions the midsummer gift exchange, my stomach knots with nerves.

I nod, swallowing, but even as I make my way upstairs to change, the unease lingers.

It's stupid. It's just a gift exchange. I'm still a little pissed that Asher didn't mention it sooner. It almost feels like he left me out on purpose. Like I'm an afterthought, or maybe just not as important as I thought I was. It shouldn't bother me as much as it does, but the nagging feeling won't go away.

My fingers still tighten around the bag where the snake plant sits, neatly wrapped in crisp brown paper, tied with twine.

It's supposed to be symbolic—resilient, easy to care for, impossible to kill. According to my quick research in the shop, it fits with the idea of midsummer, of new beginnings, of life continuing.

And yet...

A familiar, nagging voice whispers in the back of my mind. *What if it's not good enough?*

What if the person who gets it doesn't care about plants? What if they think it's lazy, or last minute, or impersonal?

I shouldn't let those insecurities get to me, but they do.

I am an eldest daughter, after all. We overthink. We measure. We try to get things right, even when no one is watching.

Even when no one else cares.

I exhale, pressing a hand to my temple. Maybe I should have gone with something else. Something more expensive, something harder to find, something that shows I put in more effort.

But then... Maddox's voice slides into my thoughts.

"You're a good actress, I'll give you that. Polite. Sweet. The perfect girlfriend. But that's not who you really are, is it?"

I swallow hard. I hate that his words won't leave me alone. I hate that he looked at me for all of one and a half days and somehow saw right through me.

I shake the thought away and run my hands over the twine bow, straightening it.

It's just a plant.

It's just a gift exchange.

Not everything is as serious as I make it out to be in my head.

Thank you, anxiety.

I take a quick shower, and the whole time I can't stop thinking about Maddox.

The way his dark blond hair was tousled and wild—so different from the short, preppy style Asher wears his.

I think about the way his muscles undulated with every movement, as if he spent his entire prison sentence honing them into perfection.

I'd have to be blind not to find him attractive. I mean, I am dating his twin brother.

Showered and changed, I scowl as I pull on the dark blue linen dress that Maddox picked out—soft as butter, loose in a way I'd never choose for myself. But the color complements my dark eyes and golden skin, and with the heat outside, makeup feels pointless. My hair, still curled from the beach, hangs down my back, untouched.

I square my shoulders, plaster on a practiced, effortless smile, and head downstairs.

And yet...

The unease still lingers.

Asher is waiting for me at the bottom of the stairs, and he smiles as he wraps a hand around my waist.

"You look so pretty," he says, kissing the top of my head. "I'm sorry about having to cut our walk short."

I open my mouth to tell him it's okay when Hannah comes around the corner. "Oh, sweetheart, is that for the gift exchange?" she asks, smiling.

I nod, handing the wrapped plant over to her.

"That's so sweet of you. Let's go to the living room," she suggests.

Hannah leads us into the living room, where Otto and Maddox are already seated. I don't let my eyes wander for too long on Maddox's dark gray, worn t-shirt and black jeans.

The coffee table is scattered with small, neatly wrapped gifts, a modest but thoughtful display of tradition.

I settle onto the couch beside Asher, tucking my legs underneath me. The nerves from earlier still linger in my stomach like butterflies that have escaped their enclosure.

Hannah claps her hands together. "All right, let's get started, shall we?"

"How does it work?" I ask.

"We pull a name and that person gets the gift we picked out," she explains.

She reaches into the bowl of names, plucking out a slip of paper. Her eyes light up.

"Oh! It's Otto." She smiles and hands him a small, carefully wrapped package.

Otto opens it to reveal a small, antique compass. His expression softens. "I love it, darling," he murmurs, pressing a kiss to Hannah's cheek.

I exhale slowly, shifting in my seat. The way they look at each other, so effortlessly in sync, makes something uncomfortable settle in my chest. I've never acted like that with anyone.

Otto reaches for the next name. "Maddox."

Maddox leans back, expression unreadable as Otto hands him a thin, square box wrapped in brown paper. He peels it open, revealing a leather journal.

He runs a thumb over the cover, but his face gives nothing away. "Thank you," he says simply, looking up at Otto.

Otto nods, a strained kind of pride flickering behind his eyes.

Maddox sets the journal down beside him, then reaches into the bowl. His lips curve slightly as he reads the name.

"Asher."

Asher stills beside me as Maddox hands him a small present wrapped in white paper. He tears the paper off, revealing a historical fiction book. Asher gives Maddox a tight smile before setting the book down, and I wince as I look at

Maddox for his reaction, but Maddox just sits there stoically. I know they're not on the best of terms, but Asher didn't even look at the back of the book—he just discarded it like it meant nothing.

"Thanks," he says, his voice curt. Reaching into the bowl, he smiles when he shows me my name written on the piece of paper.

I perk up as he hands me a small box wrapped in crisp white paper.

My fingers work at the ribbon, untying it carefully, an inexplicable sense of anticipation curling in my chest.

When I finally pull the lid off, my excitement dims.

A key chain.

It's leather, simple, with a four-leaf clover branded onto one side. It's... nice... in a practical sort of way.

"Oh, thanks, Ash."

He leans over and kisses my temple. "Figured everyone could use a nice key chain."

I nod, reaching for the last strip of paper. "Hannah," I say, setting the paper down and reaching for the gift I picked out.

She gives me a warm smile as she opens it. "A plant," she muses, tilting her head. My pulse quickens. I knew it wasn't much. I should've gotten something else, something better, something— "Oh, Ari. I absolutely love snake plants," she adds, and I physically sag with relief.

"That's good. I wasn't sure— If I'd had more time—"

Maddox glances up, eyes locking on to mine. "It suits her. She has a greenhouse and everything."

Hannah reaches for the last gift on the table. "Oh! Looks like there's one left."

She picks up the package—a slightly larger box, wrapped in deep blue paper. Maddox reaches out, his grip closing over the box first.

His voice is calm, smooth. "That's for Ari."

Silence.

The air shifts, something tense settling into the room. Hannah glances at Otto, who watches the exchange carefully.

Asher frowns. "Wait. You got Ari a gift?"

Maddox's grip clamps down slightly on the box. He doesn't hesitate, doesn't back down.

"Nobody said I couldn't."

A slow *thud, thud, thud* beats in my chest as my fingers tighten around the key chain in my lap.

I glance between them—Asher, tense beside me; Maddox, unreadable across the room.

Maddox's eyes flick to mine, just for a second.

And even though no one else knows what's inside the box, I suddenly feel like he's holding a secret between his fingers.

One meant just for me.

Maddox remains silent as I take the gift from him and tear into the wrapping, my pulse hammering. The paper gives way to a ball of bubble wrap, tightly secured, as if whatever's inside is delicate, important.

Unraveling it slowly, I barely catch the object before it tumbles from my hands.

My breath snags.

Oh my god.

I feel Asher lean in closer, peering over my shoulder. "What is it?"

But I can't answer yet—my hands are shaking too much.

I turn the package over, reading the label, checking, double-checking, because there's no way—

But it is.

It's a vintage Polly Pocket. Not just any, but one of the rarest sets ever—the Jewel Secrets collection from Bluebird Toys.

New in the package. Perfectly preserved.

My holy grail.

I don't dare look at Maddox.

How the fuck did he know?

"A toy?" Asher asks, his voice bordering on incredulous. "You got my girlfriend a toy?"

I blink, snapping out of my daze just long enough to turn my head toward him.

"It's not just a toy," I whisper, my voice unsteady, my throat aching in a way I don't expect. I press my lips together, trying to suppress the sudden, overwhelming weight of emotion pressing into my ribs.

I don't cry over things.

But for a horrifying second, I think I might.

I glance down again, running my fingers over the slightly discolored plastic, the delicate packaging that has somehow survived decades untouched.

It's perfect.

It's mine.

And Maddox knew.

Asher sighs. "So is it... worth a lot of money or something?"

Maddox shifts in his chair. Calm. Unruffled. Entirely in control of this moment.

His voice is smooth, but sharp enough to cut. "It's not about money," he says evenly.

His eyes flick to mine, just for a second. Just long enough to send something electric through my veins.

"Maybe if you paid attention, you'd know it's at the top of your girlfriend's public wish list," Maddox continues, his tone cool, edged with quiet amusement.

Asher stiffens beside me.

I inhale sharply, dragging my gaze away from Maddox, willing my heart to slow.

He's right. I've had this on all of my saved lists for as long as I can remember. I never thought I'd actually own it. But Maddox—somehow, *inexplicably*—got it for me.

Which makes no sense.

How the hell did he know?

We only just met. My wish lists aren't exactly a secret, but they aren't something people just stumble across either. Did he go looking? And if he did... why?

I swallow past the lump in my throat. "It's sentimental more than anything," I say, running my fingers along the plastic once more.

But that's not quite true, is it?

Because right now, in this moment, this means more than anything anyone has ever given me.

I'd never tell Asher this, but I used to own the same set. I was maybe three or four when my grandma took me shopping. It's one of my first memories—walking along the toy aisles, waiting to pick something out. My youngest sister had just been born, so my grandma took me back to her house—the same house I currently live in.

I spent all day playing with the Jewel Secrets set. I loved it more than anything I'd ever loved before.

And when my dad came to pick me up, he made me throw it away.

I can't even remember the reason, but as I got older, I realized it was because he prioritized discipline, practicality, and "usefulness" over anything he perceived as superficial. He viewed all feminine, princess-y things as pointless—indulgent, even. Later, as a teenager, he would emphasize obedience in everything I did.

It was never about the toy.

It was about control. About shaping me into someone who didn't question authority, who didn't make selfish choices, who didn't waste time on things that brought joy instead of function.

And I was the eldest daughter. I had to be strong. Had to be responsible. Had to be perfect. There was no space for softness. No room for mistakes. No time to be a little girl who just wanted to keep her favorite toy.

As an adult, I indulge in the frivolous things like vintage purses, nostalgic toy sets, and eight-dollar iced coffees. I make good money at my job, and I fought back against the hardened childhood I experienced whenever I could.

Because if I don't?

If I stop proving to myself that I can have beautiful, unnecessary things just because I want them, then maybe I never really escaped at all.

Hannah claps her hands together, breaking the tension. "Well, I think that was a lovely exchange, don't you?"

Asher mutters something under his breath, but Hannah either doesn't hear him or chooses to ignore it.

"Lunch should be ready in about thirty minutes," she continues, rising from her seat. "I made some open-faced sandwiches and that cucumber salad you liked last time, Ari."

I force a small smile, still reeling from the last few minutes. "That sounds great."

Otto follows his wife toward the kitchen, Maddox leaves the room without a second glance, and Asher lingers only long enough to look down at his phone before sighing.

"I have a call in a few minutes. Work stuff. You'll be okay without me?"

I blink at him, then glance around the cozy, sunlit room. "...Yeah, Ash. I think I'll survive."

He doesn't even notice my sarcasm. Instead, he nods absently, already distracted, already somewhere else. And just like that, he's gone.

I let out a slow, measured breath. The house suddenly feels too warm, too tight. I need air.

I wander aimlessly for a while, tracing my fingers along the edge of the windowsill, peeking into the tidy kitchen, the too perfect sitting room. Everything is charming, carefully curated.

Everything except me.

Why did Asher even bring me here? To watch him work? The realization stings more than I want to admit. I rub my arms, trying to shake the feeling, but it sticks.

I need air. I need to think.

Leaving the unopened Polly Pocket on the table, I slip through the patio doors, letting the ocean breeze cool the heat rising beneath my skin.

The backyard is quiet, the sound of the waves a slow, steady rhythm against the cliffs. I exhale, trying to center myself, but before I can fully settle—

I catch the faint scent of something sharp, earthy, unmistakable.

Weed.

I follow the scent, stepping around the edge of the house, where the property slopes slightly before leveling out near the cliffs.

Maddox is there, leaning against the railing, the ocean stretching wide behind him.

A joint dangles between his fingers, smoke curling lazily into the summer air.

He doesn't look at me right away, just lifts it to his lips, inhales slow and deep, holds it—then exhales, the tendrils of smoke blurring the sharpness of his features.

He looks entirely at ease.

Like he belongs here.

Like he's always belonged.

I fold my arms across my chest. "Didn't take you for the type."

Maddox hums, still not looking at me. "And what type is

that?" His voice has the echo of someone who's not surprised to find me out here with him.

"The kind to... I don't know. Get high in the middle of the day on a family vacation?"

That earns me a slow smirk over his shoulder, and the sight has my breath stuttering. "You're assuming this is just for fun."

I shift on my feet, watching the way his fingers roll the joint, the ease with which he holds it.

"You're saying it's medicinal?" I tease, lifting a brow.

Maddox turns around and leans against the railing, finally looking at me then—*really* looking at me.

I squirm under his scrutiny. There's something about him that makes me feel like he knows more about me than he's letting on—the gift he just got me notwithstanding. It's like he's already spent time inside my mind. The feeling is almost suffocating, pressing into every inch of me, searching for something I don't know how to name.

"I'm saying it makes it easier."

Something about the way he says it unsettles me.

Instead, I shift my weight, glancing toward the house. "If Asher knew you were doing this out here..."

Maddox laughs under his breath, low and unimpressed.

"If Asher knew half the shit you were really thinking, he'd lose his mind."

I freeze.

My pulse skips, then quickens, then skips again. "Excuse me?"

Maddox tilts his head slightly, considering me, his gaze unhurried. Even though his expression remains neutral, there's something in his eyes that makes my stomach knot.

He lifts the joint between two fingers, rolling it lazily, studying the ember like it holds an answer. Pushing off the railing, he walks closer to me until he's standing right in front of me. The dark blue of the ocean behind him brings out the icy blue of his eyes. *Asher's* eyes.

"You and me." His voice is slow, measured. "We're not like them."

I narrow my eyes, crossing my arms. "Them?"

He smirks, but there's no humor in it. "You know who I mean. People like Asher. People who fit into neat little boxes, who never think too much about why they do what they do. People who follow the rules."

I shift my weight, resisting the impulse to fidget under his stare. "And you think you know me well enough to put me in a different category?"

His lips twitch. "I don't think. I *know*."

I let out a short, incredulous laugh. "Oh, yeah? And what exactly do you think you know?"

Maddox holds my gaze for a beat, then exhales a slow stream of smoke, his voice dropping just enough to make my stomach flip.

"You act like you're content. Like you've got it all figured out. The steady job, the loyal boyfriend, the safe little life. But deep down?" He leans in, eyes flashing. "You're fucking starving. For more. For someone to see you. For someone to take you seriously when you stop pretending you want this kind of life."

I tense, but I don't look away.

"You've been taught to accept less," he murmurs. "To settle for whatever scraps people give you and call it love. But you don't want scraps, do you, Ari? You never did. You just never thought you could ask for more."

I frown. "I'm not—"

"You do. Maybe it was your upbringing, or maybe it's the fact that you've always had to be strong for your sisters. They're younger than you, right?" I rear my head back in surprise that he remembers that. "You pretend you're fine with it—pretend it's easier that way—but deep down?"

His voice a low rasp beneath the crash of the waves, and he sets the joint down on the metal railing. He crosses his arms, watching me with the same unreadable expression.

Was this guy doing pull-ups all day in prison? Because his biceps could probably throw boulders over this railing.

"You're restless. You're waiting for someone to give you permission to live the life you've always wanted. *Truly* wanted. Not the life you're supposed to have... but the one you want more than your next breath."

Damn.

The words land too close to home. *Way too fucking close.*

I inhale sharply, crossing my arms to hide the way my fingers twitch. "That's a big assumption."

Maddox just shrugs, casual, dismissive. "Not an assumption."

I shake my head, irritated. "Why do you act like you know me?"

His eyes flick over me once, assessing, before he lifts the joint again.

"It was my job to read people." His voice is light, but there's something dark curling at the edges of it. "Back in the Marine Corps."

I blink. That catches me off guard. I had no idea he was in the Marine Corps.

"What, like interrogations?"

He smirks, but it doesn't quite reach his eyes. "Sometimes."

A pause. I wait for him to elaborate, but he doesn't.

Maddox holds the joint out toward me, his voice low, smooth. "Go on, then."

I stare at him.

Then at the burning tip, the slow curl of smoke.

Every rational part of me tells me to walk away. To say no, to go back inside and sit with Hannah and Otto and pretend I belong in a world like this. But that's the thing, isn't it? I don't. And Maddox knows it.

So I reach forward, fingers brushing against his as I take the joint from his hand.

I don't get high. Drunk? Sure. I've been known to kill a bottle or two of wine after a long day. But drugs? I don't do things like this. My father would've disowned me if he knew I smoked weed.

But...

I think about Asher, tied to his calls, his endless meetings, his perfectly structured world.

I think about how I bend and shape myself to fit into it— how *bored* I am, yet attempting to make my dad happy by settling down.

I think about the Polly Pocket, the way it felt to be truly seen for the first time in years.

And how Maddox has never asked me to do anything other than be myself. How he just *knows* things about me, like what kind of clothing will look good on me, and what all my hidden truths are.

Even ones I'd never told Asher.

I should be perturbed by his observations and assumptions, but I'm not. It's kind of... *nice*. It feels like, around Maddox, I can almost let go of the responsibility I've clung to my entire life.

And then—

I take the joint from his fingers, lift it to my lips, and inhale.

Maddox watches the whole time.

The smoke burns, but not as much as the question rising in my throat. I exhale slowly, turning toward him. "How did you know?" My voice is quieter than I mean it to be. "About the wish list."

He studies me for a beat, then shrugs, like the answer is obvious. "They're not hard to find, for people who want to see them." His voice is even, casual, but something about the way he says it makes my chest constrict.

His gaze lingers on me, steady and unreadable. "Most people don't pay attention. Not really. They hear what they want, see what's convenient. But if you know where to look, what to listen for..." He trails off, his meaning clear.

I swallow. "And you do?"

His lips twitch. "For the things that matter, absolutely."

The words settle between us, heavy with something I can't name.

It should unnerve me—the way he sees things no one else does, the way he sees me. But instead, it feels... nice. Thoughtful in a way I hadn't realized I craved.

Because with Maddox, I don't have to play the part. I don't have to soften my edges or shrink myself down to fit into someone else's picture of me. He doesn't expect me to smile and nod and carry the weight without complaint.

He doesn't expect me to be easy.

He just wants me to be real.

And against all logic, I'm starting to like being around him.

PHANTOM SHADOW
ARI

THAT NIGHT, AFTER I SHOWER AND SLIP INTO MY oversized t-shirt that Hannah lovingly washed and dried for me, I finally relax for the night. The house is quiet, everyone tucked away in their own rooms. After spritzing some perfume behind my ear—just like my grandmother taught me —I climb into the cozy single bed, staring at the ceiling, my thoughts tangled.

Something about today felt... different.

Like a shift I wasn't prepared for.

As my eyes drift shut, I tell myself to let it go. To stop over-thinking. To forget about the way Maddox watched me during lunch, and then an early dinner of grilled salmon, garlic bread, and zucchini. To forget about the Polly Pocket sitting on my dresser, all wrapped back up in the bubble wrap it came in. To forget about the way Maddox seems to have sized me up in two days flat.

After I finished smoking with him, he left me alone on the side of the house, and I only saw him for meals. I never felt high, but I definitely felt more relaxed as the day went on, which I appreciated. And now?

It's a little past eight at night and I'm feeling completely awake. Picking my phone up, I FaceTime my best friend, Frankie. She answers on the first ring, and I recognize her office as she comes into view.

"Hey," Frankie says, not looking at the screen of her computer, but instead on the baby blanket she's delicately folding. Ever since some influencer shared the link to her baby blanket shop, she's been working overtime on orders. "How's the beach vacay going?"

"It's been... weird," I say slowly.

She finally looks at the screen, and her knitted brows tell me she's concerned. "How so?"

"Well, Asher has an identical twin."

Frankie's mouth pops open. "Really? How come he never told you?"

I smirk. "Because his twin has been in jail."

Frankie snorts. "Your life, man. It's wild. Just like Granny Anastasia. So, what's the twin like?"

"Maddox," I clarify.

"Oh. That's a hot name. He sounds hot. I'm imagining Asher with lots of tattoos, maybe longer hair, and that brooding criminal thing going on."

I bark a laugh. "You're close. He doesn't have long hair, though."

Frankie shrugs, carrying a stack of beige, rainbow-patterned fabric over to her sewing machine on the other side of the room. "Ah, well, I can't be right a hundred percent of the time," she teases, sitting down at the table and beginning to cut the fabric into large squares. "So, why has it been weird? Talk to me."

I glance at the closed bedroom door, wondering if I should say anything out loud when my boyfriend and his entire family are currently under the same roof as me.

"Well, for one, he's all... mysterious," I say, keeping my

voice low so that no one can overhear me. "He took me shopping today because I had a shampoo explosion in my suitcase. He picked out all of my clothes. *And* paid for them. Like I was his sugar baby."

Frankie's head pops up. "That's... Huh. Would it be weird if I said that's kind of hot?"

I chuckle. "And he's just been so... mysterious is the wrong word. It's like he knows me. *Knows* me, knows me. We did a gift exchange today with everyone, and he got me the Polly Pocket I've always wanted."

Frankie drops the fabric she's sewing, her mouth dropping into a large 'O'. "The Jewel Secrets collection?!"

I nod solemnly.

"Holy shit, Ari. You've wanted that set for years."

"I know. And there's another thing..." I hesitate, unsure if I should say anything. But if I don't tell someone, I'll go crazy. "He called me angel."

Frankie pauses, her brows forming a crease. "Wait. Do you think Maddox could be your super-secret stalker?"

I shrug. "Tell me I'm crazy for even having that thought. I mean, I just met him yesterday."

She runs a hand over her mouth as she looks at the computer camera. "Maybe he knew about you in jail. Is he close to Asher?"

I shake my head. "Not really. They seem to have a weird rivalry going on. And there's something else. I think that maybe he came into my room the first night I was here. But I was on Ambien, so maybe I was hallucinating?"

She holds up her hands and laughs. "You know that shit makes you do weird things. You once texted me a five-paragraph analysis of why the moon is probably judging us," she adds, smirking.

I shake my head, feeling oddly unsettled. "This was different."

"Is he... dangerous? Like, are you worried? Because I'll drop everything right now and drive straight to Malibu to pick your cute, little ass up if you say yes."

I laugh. "No, weirdly. I don't feel uneasy around him. I feel like I've known him forever."

Frankie watches me for a moment before nodding. "Okay. Then let's break it down."

"Break what down?"

"Your stalker being Maddox. Didn't the stalker sign his name as 'M'?"

My stomach turns. "Oh my god. I completely forgot that horrifying detail."

"You're welcome," she says dryly, then continues. "Okay, so chances are it's Maddox. Now, we just need to figure out why."

I rub my temples, trying to make sense of it all. "What if it is him? What if this is, like, some weird mind game?"

Frankie's eyebrows shoot up and she walks back to her computer where we're FaceTiming. "But why?"

Frankie's office door creaks open, and Dante, her husband, walks in, carrying a mug of something steaming like some brooding, six-foot-four specter of efficiency.

"One hazelnut latte," he says, handing her the mug.

"Thanks, baby," Frankie mutters, not looking away from her screen as she types at a speed that should be illegal.

"Hi, Dante," I say lazily.

He waves, but he doesn't leave. He lingers, assessing. He's always been like that—too perceptive, too sharp, too powerful in that quiet, unnerving way only men like him can be.

"You should ask him about Maddox," Frankie says, her fingers flying over the keyboard.

My cheeks heat. Dante is... intimidating. Not because he's done anything to me, but because he's too put together, too controlled. A renowned psychiatrist, grumpy to the point of legendary, and filthy rich on top of it. Frankie swears he was obsessed with her long before they got together, and honestly? I believe it.

He watches his wife for a beat, something dark and unreadable flickering behind his eyes before he turns to me on camera.

"Who's Maddox?" he asks.

I hesitate, glancing at Frankie, but she just keeps typing, like she didn't just throw me to the wolves.

I clear my throat. "I—uh. It's nothing."

Dante doesn't blink. He just waits.

That's the thing about him. He doesn't press. He doesn't even move. He just watches you long enough that eventually, you start talking just to fill the silence.

I exhale. "It's probably stupid."

"Most things are," he says dryly, taking a sip of Frankie's coffee and making a face. "Go on."

I shoot Frankie a look, but she's grinning now, entertained. Traitor.

I shift in my seat, and then I tell him everything—from the notes, to meeting Maddox, and the weird things he's said to me. When I finish, Dante lifts a brow but doesn't react otherwise. I hesitate. It sounds ridiculous when I lay it all out loud. I expect him to dismiss me, to say I was dreaming, that I was on Ambien, that I imagined it.

Instead, he studies me, his silence stretching long enough to make my pulse pick up.

"What did the notes say?" he asks finally.

I swallow before relaying the two notes I received.

"You need a security guard or something," Frankie mumbles.

I huff a laugh. "Please. I have pepper spray and questionable life choices. And don't forget about the black belt."

"Ari," Frankie says, her voice reprimanding.

"Also... rage issues. I'll be fine."

Frankie arches a brow. "You're a CPA, not James Bond."

"That's what the government wants you to think." I grin, looking back at Dante, who just sighs. He loathes my conspiracy theory rants, and fortunately, he's used to our deranged banter. Frankie is right, though.

"You think Maddox left the notes?" he asks.

"I don't know," I admit.

Dante exhales through his nose, something sharp flickering in his gaze. "Well, there are two possibilities. And any good detective will tell you that the simplest explanation is usually the right one."

Hearing it put that plainly makes my stomach twist.

"Whoever left it wanted you to know they knew you, but they weren't interested in seeing your immediate response. However, based on what you've told me about the things Maddox has said and done..." He trails off. "There's a good chance he's your guy."

Something cold and heavy settles in my chest.

Frankie frowns. "So you're saying this is, like... some next-level stalker shit? From a guy who just got out of prison?"

Dante doesn't confirm or deny it. He just watches me.

"Maybe. What'd he go to prison for?" Dante asks.

The hair on my arms prickles. "I don't actually know."

"Well, find out," Frankie practically hisses. "And maybe stop ignoring red flags before you become the next *Dateline* episode."

"So comforting," I tell her, my voice sarcastic. A text comes through, and I frown at my screen. "I should go. Asher just texted me. I'll keep you updated, okay? And if they find my body in a ditch... well, tell them I always did have a thing for the villain."

Frankie groans. "Jesus Christ. You're the *exact* kind of girl they make those 'why didn't she just leave?' documentaries about."

I laugh. "Love you."

"Love you, too."

I wave at Dante before the FaceTime disconnects, and before I open my texts, I quickly open a new browser and search Maddox's name.

I should probably figure out what he went to prison for.

An article titled "The Phantom Walks Free" comes up, but just as I click on the link, my phone vibrates with another text from Asher.

ASHER

Hey. Just checking in.

You good?

I frown. Not exactly a *come to my room, I miss you* kind of message, but at least he's acknowledging I exist.

Yeah, I'm fine. Are you going to come and tuck me in? ;)

Three dots appear, then disappear.
Then—

ASHER

I've got an early call tomorrow. I think it's best if we both get a good night's sleep.

And Ari... we talked about this. I don't want us sneaking around like we're teenagers. It's not fair to either of us.

I stare at the screen, heat creeping up my neck. What if I want to sneak around like a teenager? Did he ever consider that?

A whole day of him being distracted, absent, wrapped up

in work and whatever thoughts Maddox's presence is stirring in his mind—and now, when he finally has time, he's choosing not to?

I inhale slowly, steadying myself.

But instead of texting back, instead of coaxing him into giving me crumbs, I put the phone down.

No reply. No invitation. If he wants me, he knows where I am.

And if he doesn't?

Oh well. I refuse to beg for my own boyfriend's attention.

I grab the bottle of Ambien from my bag, dry swallow a pill, and curl under the blankets.

If he shows, he shows. If he doesn't, I'll deal with it in the morning. Pulling my Kindle under the covers, I open my current read—a dark, twisted romance where the heroine is tied to a chair, panting, trembling, while the villain, the one she's been running from for the last eight chapters, trails a knife along the inside of her thigh, whispering filthy things in her ear.

I shift slightly, my thighs pressing together as I turn the page.

It's always the villains. Always.

Something about the way they take. The way they know what they want—who they want—and don't apologize for it.

Thirty minutes later, my eyes grow heavy, and my Kindle slips from my grasp. The last thing I remember is the room fading to black, my limbs turning heavy, my mind sinking into that deep, hazy pull of sleep.

Until—

Something shifts. A click in the quiet air.

A weight in the room.

I stir slightly, caught between wakefulness and dreaming.

It's pitch dark.

And someone is here.

When the Phantom Comes Knocking

Ari

It's small. Barely there.

The faintest click of a door opening.

My breath catches in my throat. "Asher?" I climb out of bed and stand there, unsure of what to do.

Measured, familiar footsteps. My heart slows. The tension eases just enough for me to quell the onset of a panic attack.

Because I know that walk.

It's Asher.

I swallow hard, staring at the shadowed figure standing near the door of the bedroom. Tall. Broad. Too dark to make out anything except the way he fills the space.

His voice is low when he speaks.

"I couldn't stop thinking about you."

The way the words roll off his tongue sends a shiver down my spine. Deeper than usual. Rougher.

"You scared the hell out of me," I whisper, exhaling sharply. He moves closer.

"I know," he murmurs. "I'm sorry. Let me make it up to you."

I should be asking questions, such as why the hell it took him over an hour to come to my room.

But I don't. Because for whatever reason, the space between my legs is throbbing. He steps closer until he's right next to me. My brow furrows as I look up at him, the darkness blurring his features, making everything feel softer, hazier—like a dream.

His touch is warm, firm, as he grips my chin between his fingers, tilting my face up to his.

A slow, shivery exhale escapes me.

Finally.

My body is heavy, warm, pliant. The Ambien has me floating, untethered, sinking into the dreamlike pull of it.

Asher's finally here, finally giving me what I wanted. Isn't he? I blink up at him, the room tilting, shifting around us. A thumb brushes over my lower lip, slow, possessive, and unyielding, as if testing the softness before claiming it.

"Why did you—"

His other hand comes to my throat, fingers curling just enough to make me aware of his strength, his control. Not enough to hurt, just enough to remind me who's in charge. My pulse pounds beneath his grip. His thumb brushes along my pulse point, slow, measured. I break out in goosebumps.

"Shh," he murmurs, the single syllable a warning.

And when he leans in, his breath hot against my lips, I forget how to breathe altogether.

I let him push me back against the wall of the bedroom. Let him part my legs with one knee. Let him control the moment before I even have a chance to understand it.

When his hands find my body—strong, firm, possessive in a way Asher never is—my thoughts splinter.

He touches me like he's never touched me before. Somewhere, deep in the foggy corners of my mind, awareness stirs. A distant voice whispers that something is off. That this doesn't make sense. But it's too quiet, too far away to grasp. The Ambien makes everything slow and liquid, reality slipping through my fingers like silk. The press of his hands, the deliberate way they explore, claim, take, it drowns out everything else.

My breath hitches as his palm skims up my bare thigh, slow and deliberate.

Not hesitant.

Not careful.

Like he knows exactly what he's doing.

Like he's done it before—because of course he has.

A hazy warmth spreads through me, melting resistance into something darker, heavier. The alarm bells muffle, distort, twisting into something else. Something that only spurs my arousal on.

The smooth heat of his hand makes me shiver. I'm only wearing the oversized sleep shirt—no underwear, no bra. I can tell the second his hands pass over my peaked nipples, realizing I'm bare underneath the shirt. A quiet, almost imperceptible inhale leaves him—sharp, restrained—like he's breathing me in, like he's memorizing the way I feel beneath his touch.

When his fingers finally press into my waist, his grip tightens, just for a second, like he can't help himself. A low sound rumbles in his chest—not quite a groan, not quite a sigh—but something in between, something primal.

He drags his hands up, bringing my shirt over my head, and I lift my arms until I'm standing naked before him.

"Fuck, Ari," he rasps, voice frayed, almost like the word scrapes against his throat. His nostrils flare, his chest rising and falling with heavy, uneven breaths, like he's been starving for this—for me.

His tongue drags over his bottom lip, slow, deliberate, like he's tasting the idea of me before even laying a hand on my skin.

"You have no idea what you do to me." His voice is low, almost reverent, but there's an edge beneath it—something dangerous, something claiming.

"Only took you two years to notice," I bite back, trying not to smirk.

I don't want to ruin whatever *this* is.

He doesn't say anything. He reaches for me, his thumbs grazing the sensitive skin just beneath my breasts, and for the briefest moment, his touch stills. His fingers flex, a subtle tremor betraying him before he exhales through his nose, steadying himself.

And I can hardly breathe.

My heart races, and arousal pools between my legs at the way he's taking charge.

Is this part of him trying to read me better?

If so... I'm *all* for it.

His hands roam my body slowly, more sure, more certain than ever before.

And that's the thing.

I've begged for this before—for him to stop being so careful, to stop waiting for permission.

And now?

He finally is.

His fingers skim my thighs, slow and deliberate, a friction that's almost too smooth.

His lips graze my throat, breath warm against my skin. I get a whiff of that same unfamiliar scent. The one from the last time I was on Ambien. It's richer than Asher's scent—more like a forest, more powerful. It wraps around me, and I groan as he runs his hands between my legs.

"You're different," I murmur, my fingers tracing the sharp line of his jaw, the stubble rough beneath my touch.

A sharp inhale. A slow exhale.

"Is that bad?"

I hesitate, my brain swimming in the thick, velvety fog of the Ambien. No. *Yes*. I don't know. I blink up at him, his face blurred at the edges, shifting in and out of focus like a dream that won't stay still.

Not real. *Maybe* real.

My thoughts feel slippery, unsteady, like I'm trying to hold on to water. "No," I whisper. "Just... not like you."

He's still for a moment.

Then... a low hum, a sound that shouldn't send warmth curling through my stomach but does.

"You're tired," he murmurs. Soft. Soothing. A lie wrapped in silk. Maybe he's right. Maybe this is just the Ambien twisting my reality, making everything feel different, making him feel different. Because this is Asher. I'd know his voice, his *feel* anywhere.

He presses his weight against me, and the thought dissolves.

I arch into him, dragging my hands up his arms, over clothed muscle, nothing exposed.

My fingers skim under the waistband of his pants—or at least, they try. But before I can push lower, he catches my wrist. The movement is smooth, controlled—but firm.

I smirk. "Since when are you shy?"

"I'm not," he murmurs, but he doesn't let go.

Instead, he kisses me, deep enough to erase the question, to make it irrelevant. His tongue pushes into my mouth, hot and claiming, and it makes me whimper.

Something is different. The way he holds me—not careful, not hesitant. The way he kisses me—like he's taking, not giving. And then, the taste—not quite right.

Not bad. Just... unexpected.

A hint of something smokier, something sharper, something entirely unfamiliar.

But the thought drifts away as quickly as it comes, swallowed by the haze.

I let my nails scratch against the fine fabric of his shirt. He makes a sound—low, rough, somewhere between approval and restraint. But he doesn't stop me. He just moves faster. Hungrier. His hands pull my waist closer until I'm pressed against him, and I stand on my tiptoes as I grip his shirt, *needing* more.

Then his hand is around my throat again.

Not too tight. Not too soft. Just enough to make me dizzy, to make my pulse stutter.

A slow, indulgent squeeze, like he's testing something. Like he's finally touching me exactly how he's always wanted to.

"God, yes," I whimper, the ache between my thighs settling low and deep, a throbbing pulse of need that makes me shudder.

My skin feels too hot, too tight.

I'm soaked—dripping against my own thighs, making every movement feel slick and uncomfortably wet.

I want him to see. To feel. To take.

I barely have time to gasp before his mouth is at my throat, his teeth dragging along the sensitive skin, his hands gripping my thighs, prying them apart.

His voice is low, dark, starved.

"This is what you wanted, isn't it?"

A shiver unfurls inside me.

It is.

I should question why he finally gave in. Why now, after all this time, he's finally touching me the way I've always begged him to.

But I don't.

Because when his lips trail down my body, when his grip

sinks into my thighs, when he kneels before me, settling himself between my legs, every thought disintegrates.

And then he flicks his tongue against my throbbing clit.

His breath is hot against my inner thighs, his hands spreading me wider, his touch both reverent and obscene.

He licks up my slit once, twice.

I bite my lip, my chest rising fast as a half whimper, half growl escapes my lips. The sharp burn of facial hair surprises me for a second, because Asher doesn't have any stubble.

His grip tightens. "Sit on my face."

Before I have a chance to digest what he's saying, he lies down on the floor.

Lies down—right in the middle of the fucking bedroom.

Asher and I have only ever fucked in a bed. And he has *never* asked me to sit on his face.

"Don't run from me now," he growls, his voice soft like velvet. "I want you to fuck yourself. I want you soaking my fucking mouth."

"Ash—"

"Sit on my face, little warrior."

Little warrior. That's an unusual nickname, and not something he's ever called me.

I hesitate, but he remains lying on the floor, arms at his sides, barely visible in the darkness.

Asher. My sweet, cinnamon roll of a boyfriend who's only gone down on me a handful of times, is asking me to sit on his face?

"I need to taste you again. Right now."

A slow, wicked pause. Then— "Or I might fucking die."

My whole body clenches.

Heat slams between my legs in one long, throbbing beat. I'm already desperate for friction, for his tongue, for anything to ease the ache.

I let out a shaky exhale as I stumble over his large body and straddle his chest. I hesitate briefly—but he doesn't give me time to think. Gripping my thighs firmly, he hauls me up his body and positions me exactly where he wants me. My breath stutters, and a raw mix of confusion and arousal floods through me. I try to lift myself slightly, but his hands lock around me, holding me there.

Despite being on top, I'm completely at his mercy.

"Stay right there," he growls, his voice rough, almost desperate as it feathers against my aching core. His fingers dig into my thighs, keeping me exactly where he wants me— where he needs me. "You don't run from this, Ari. Not when I've been starving for you. Not when I need you more than my next fucking breath."

Then his tongue is on me—

And every single coherent thought disappears.

Throwing my head back, I let him hold my hips against his face as he feasts on me. The rough texture of his scruff only spurs me on, and I groan when he pulls me down further, pressing every inch of me against his mouth—and nose.

"Fuck, yes."

I vaguely wonder if I'm going to suffocate him.

His tongue darts into my cunt, piercing me over and over as the most erotic-sounding noises fill the air.

"Oh—fuck—Asher," I moan.

He goes still.

His fingers dig into the fleshy part of my hips before one large hand clamps gently but firmly over my mouth. The sound dies against his palm.

"Shhh, angel."

My whole body ignites at the contact, at the taste of his skin, warm and salty. The threat of being overheard, the knowledge of who's just down the hall, only makes me wetter. I rock my hips against his mouth, desperate, breath hitching behind his hand.

And then, his voice, low and dark, vibrates against me. "Don't say his name while you're riding my face."

The words sink straight to my core, curling hot and heavy in my stomach.

My breath catches against his palm. When he releases me, I am feral for him. My body moves on its own, instinct overriding thought. My hips rock harder against his face, my skin flushed and electric.

His thumbs brush against the base of my spine, right where I arch for him, right where I start to tremble.

"What should I call you?" I whisper, breathless, a little dazed. I can't deny it—I'm really fucking enjoying this new game we're playing. The intimacy laced with command. The power he takes, and the freedom I feel in giving it to him.

He considers my question for a few seconds. "Call me the Phantom," he says finally, the word slow, smooth, rolling off his tongue like he's testing how it feels.

The word lingers between us.

My stomach clenches—excitement, unease, something I can't name. Recognition, maybe.

Phantom?

Something snags in my mind, but the Ambien doesn't allow me to follow the thought.

I let out a breathless laugh, a weak attempt at brushing it off. "That's... dramatic."

A slow chuckle rumbles against my skin. "Maybe." His voice is low, knowing, just shy of amused. "But I think it suits me, don't you?"

I blink, disoriented at how different he's acting.

"Okay, baby," I whisper feverishly. "Are we doing a little role-play or something?"

He chuckles, low, dark, and dripping with amusement.

"Sure," he murmurs, dragging his tongue over my swollen bud. "Let's go with that."

His hands tighten on my hips, fingers flexing, dragging me forward until I feel the raw strength of him beneath me. The way he holds me there, keeps me exactly where he wants me, sends a shudder through my body.

I should move, should breathe, should say something—but then he groans.

Low. Rough. *Raw.*

The sound vibrates against me, his mouth relentless against me. His tongue flicks, swirls, claims, and I gasp, clutching at his hair, hips jerking forward on instinct. He grunts at the movement, hands hardening, guiding me harder, faster against his mouth. The pressure coils inside me, hot and sharp, and I can barely hold myself up as pleasure overtakes me completely.

"Oh god," I whisper-sob, my back arching as the orgasm rips through me, raw and all-consuming, my body shuddering in his grip. A low groan escapes his mouth, humming against my core, sending another shock wave of pleasure spiraling through me.

The world tilts, my vision blurring at the edges, my entire body coiling, trembling, unraveling all at once. Heat licks up my skin like a flame, my pulse thundering in my ears as the pleasure crests, spilling over, unstoppable, uncontrollable. My thighs quake around his head, fingers gripping his hair like it's the only thing tethering me to reality.

And still—he doesn't stop.

His entire body locks beneath me, his fingers digging into my flesh, his head pressing deeper between my thighs as another ragged, guttural groan rips from his throat. He jerks beneath me, sharp and uncontrollable, a desperate, pleading sound ripping from his throat. The grip on my thighs digs into my flesh—almost bruising—his fingers flexing, shaking. His breath stutters against my skin, hot and uneven, and then I feel it.

The sudden, subtle tremor of his body. The way his body tenses hard beneath me, the deep, velvety groan vibrating through his chest. A second later, a low, shuddering exhale leaves him, his entire body going tight.

Did he just...

The realization slams into me like a shock to the system. He lost control. Completely.

Because of me.

His forehead presses into my stomach, his breathing still uneven. But then—he laughs. Low. Dark. Not embarrassed— *pleased*. Possessive. Fucking insatiable.

The realization makes my stomach knot, makes something dark and possessive twist inside me.

He just came in his pants.

I made him fall apart.

For a moment, the only sound in the room is our frayed, uneven breaths. I feel his chest rising and falling like he's trying to regain control, like he's trying to process what the fuck just happened.

The warm, hazy pull of the Ambien tugs at me suddenly, insidious and soft. My eyelids flutter, heavy, my body begging to give in to sleep. But I fight it. I blink fast, trying to hold on to this moment, to the overwhelming heat of him, to the pulse still echoing through my limbs.

"Fuck," he mutters, his voice so low it sends another shiver down my spine. His fingers flex at my hips, slow and lazy now, like he's memorizing the feel of me.

"I hope you know I'm not done with you."

But then he moves.

A slow, deliberate shift as his hands slide from my thighs, trailing down my legs, leaving a path of heat in their wake. He sits up, his breath still heavy. It's so dark, I can't see him.

I blink, still hazy, my body still buzzing, trembling, needing. "Wait—"

He exhales sharply, like he's at war with himself, then grips my chin between his fingers, tilting my face up. His thumb brushes over my lower lip, his touch rough but deliberate.

"Not yet," he murmurs. He shifts, adjusting his pants, his movements tense, restrained, like stopping now is the hardest thing he's ever had to do.

"Next time, Ari?" His voice is lower now, almost a promise. "I won't be gentle."

And then, before I can find my voice, before I can even fully process what just happened—the Ambien tugs at me, heavy and insistent.

Sleep drags me under, I can't help but wonder if any of this was ever real at all.

PHANTOM'S CLAIM
MADDOX

THE ROOM IS DARK, BATHED IN NOTHING BUT slivers of moonlight spilling through the curtains. The house is silent, the kind of hush that only comes in the dead of night.

And she's right there.

Sprawled out on the bed, tangled in the sheets, her breathing soft and even. Oblivious. *Trusting*.

I exhale slowly, watching the slow rise and fall of her chest, the way the hem of her sleep shirt has ridden up her thighs, teasing me with flashes of smooth, bare skin. Her scent lingers in the air—warm, familiar, laced with something distinctly her. Vanilla, lavender... and me.

My cock twitches at the memory of what I did earlier. How I lost control, how I buried my face between her thighs and made her come apart on my tongue. How she gasped and whimpered and gave in so easily, so perfectly, thinking I was him.

I should leave.

I already made a mess of myself earlier, coming so fucking hard I saw stars. It should've been enough to take the edge off. To keep me satisfied for a little longer.

But it wasn't.

Not even close.

My fingers flex around the glass bottle in my hand, cool and delicate against my palm. Her perfume.

I found it sitting on the dresser, the cap slightly askew like she'd used it before bed, letting the scent linger on her skin.

I bring it to my nose, inhaling deeply, letting it mix with the natural warmth of the room. The familiar fragrance wraps around me, sinking into my skin, into my bloodstream, as if I could absorb her from the inside out.

I walk over and sit down in the chair by the window, watching her and touching myself with one hand while I bring her perfume to my nose in the other.

I lazily stroke my cock. It's already stiff again, straining against my ruined boxers, and a sharp inhale slips through my teeth as I work my hand slow and firm.

Fucking insatiable.

My body still remembers the way she clenched around my tongue, the way she tasted on my lips, the way she shook for me. All mine, and she doesn't even know it yet.

I tighten my grip, leaning back as I bite back a groan. I watch her shift in her sleep, her lips parting slightly, as if she can feel me here. As if, deep down, her body already knows who it belongs to.

I imagine waking her up like this. Sliding beneath the sheets, slipping between her thighs, replacing my hand with her heat.

Sinking into her perfect cunt in one long thrust.

Would she fight it? Would she arch into me like she did before? Would she whisper my name instead of his?

I clench my jaw, my strokes growing rougher, faster, a low growl vibrating in my chest. I look down at the perfume bottle, and a sick thought slithers into my brain before I can stop it.

I smirk, slowing my movements, rolling my thumb over the swollen tip of my cock, smearing precum down my shaft.

What if she carried me on her skin?

Not just in the way she smells.

But deeper.

I let out a harsh breath, my stomach contracting as I squeeze the bottle in my free hand. My mind spins with the idea—of her waking up, getting ready, spraying this perfume on her pulse points.

Unknowingly rubbing me into her wrists, her throat, her collarbones.

A low, guttural groan rips from my throat as the pressure in my spine coils tighter, then snaps. My muscles go rigid, my thighs clenching as heat floods through me in sharp, uncontrollable waves. My cock throbs violently in my grip, and then —I come.

Hard.

Thick ropes spill over my hand, splattering across my stomach as my entire body locks up, jerking once, twice— helpless against the force of it. My fingers crush tight around the perfume bottle, not cracking it, but damn close. The tension coils through every muscle, shaking, brutal, unstoppable. I grind my teeth, the taste of her still lingering, and I don't fucking stop until every drop is spent. When it's over, I'm left gasping, feral and wrecked, knuckles aching from how hard I've clenched the glass, like it's the only thing tethering me to the moment instead of storming across the room and taking what's mine.

Fuck.

The aftershocks roll through me, my skin damp with sweat, my pulse hammering against my ribs. My legs feel unsteady, my chest rising and falling with uneven breaths, but still, I don't move. I can't move. Not yet.

Not while she's right there.

Not while the evidence of my obsession still lingers warm and sticky between my fingers.

I inhale sharply, dragging my hand down my abdomen, smearing the last of my release across my skin. The room feels thick, the scent of sex mingling with her perfume, her warmth —her.

My stomach clenches as my gaze flicks to the bottle in my other hand.

And just like that—that same wicked thought takes root.

I twist off the cap. I should clean up. I should stop.

A satisfied smirk tugs at my lips as I dip my fingers into my own mess and let a few large drops slide inside the bottle, swirling it into the pale golden liquid.

When she wakes up, she'll have no idea what she's rubbing into her skin.

But I will.

And every time she touches her wrist, every time she catches a whiff of that sweet, familiar scent, she'll be wearing me.

Carrying me.

Marking herself as *mine*.

I let out a slow exhale, setting the bottle back down exactly where I found it.

Then, with one last look at her sleeping form, I step back into the shadows.

PHANTOM POSSESSION

ARI

THE SHARP KNOCK ON MY DOOR YANKS ME FROM sleep like a gunshot. My body jerks, and for a disorienting second, I don't know where I am—if I'm still dreaming, if last night even happened, if the heat still simmering between my legs is real or just the lingering effect of a hallucination.

But then—

"Ari?" Asher's voice. Firm, but careful.

I scramble upright, fumbling with the sheets still tangled around my legs. My entire body is thrumming, nerves on fire, skin too tight, a part of me still expecting the ghost of his touch.

"Ari?" Another knock.

I walk to the door and pull it open. My head is still spinning—it must be early. When I look up at Asher, he's looking down at me with a guilty expression.

"Hello," he says carefully, his eyes cataloging me slowly. A rush of heat spears through me.

"Good morning," I reply, crossing my arms and trying not to smile.

He sighs and runs a hand through his hair. "I just wanted

to say I'm sorry about last night. I passed out early and—" He exhales, almost sheepish. "I'll make it up to you tonight, okay?"

That sure as hell wakes me up.

A pulse of realization crashes over me so fast I nearly choke on it. The taste of his mouth. The feel of his hands. The way he touched me like he'd done it a thousand times in his head.

"Don't say his name while you're riding my face."

"Call me the Phantom."

Was it Maddox?

No way. It was the Ambien. It had to be. And it wouldn't be the first Ambien sex dream I'd ever had, so that's the most logical explanation, right?

A sick twist in my stomach coils tight, nausea and panic colliding in my throat. My hands shake as I squeeze my biceps, and I school my face into something I hope resembles disappointment that he wasn't the one in here last night.

Oh god. I need to leave this room. I need air.

"Um, it's okay. I'm going to shower, and then I'll meet you downstairs?" I ask, tilting my head and trying to act nonplussed.

I have no idea if I'm failing or succeeding, but when Asher nods once and kisses me on the forehead before walking away, all I feel is relief.

I wait several seconds before walking back into my room, closing the door, and grabbing one of the dresses that *Maddox* bought me yesterday. After replacing my sleep shirt with the dress as quickly as I can manage, I run my hands through my hair.

I need to find Maddox and make sure I'm not losing my mind. That it wasn't *him*. That it was just a dream, just a trick of my stupid subconscious. It *has* to be.

Yanking the door open so fast it nearly slams against the wall, I storm out into the hallway.

And right into a wall of solid muscle.

Maddox.

His grip is on me before I can react—one strong hand seizing my wrist, the other landing firm against my hip, holding me in place like he was expecting me to come looking for him.

I gasp, barely having time to register the dark heat in his gaze before he's moving.

He pulls me down the hall so fast I stumble, my breath stuttering when he kicks open his bedroom door, drags me inside, and presses me flush against it the second it clicks shut.

The air thickens.

Every single cell in my body goes tight, my muscles locking up as the reality of his closeness—his size, his heat, his scent—crashes into me.

That familiar scent of leather, smoke, and something darker.

Something *familiar*.

Oh god. It *was* him.

He's not holding me gently. No, this grip is possessive. Deliberate. Like last night gave him permission he has no intention of returning.

I slap my palms against his chest, pushing against the wall of muscle, but it's pointless. He doesn't move an inch. Just tilts his head, eyes flicking down my body, his gaze so heavy it might as well be a physical touch.

"Something wrong, little warrior?" His voice is low, taunting, dark with amusement.

I glare up at him, my breath coming in short, uneven bursts. "You—you were in my room last night."

A slow, deliberate smirk.

"And?"

"And?" My pulse jumps violently. "You—you—" I shake

my head, hands fisting in the fabric of his shirt. "That was—God, I thought you were Asher!"

He hums, tilting his head. Unbothered. "I know."

My stomach plummets.

No remorse. No hesitation. Just fact.

"You—" I swallow, my voice shaking. "You let me think—"

His fingers brush my hip bone, barely there but still possessive as hell. "I didn't let you do anything, Ari."

I can't breathe. I can't think.

Because this isn't fear.

It should be.

But it's not.

"You didn't stop me," I whisper, hating how breathless I sound. How raw.

His fingers tighten, pulling me flush against him, chest to chest, hip to hip, and I let out a soft, strangled sound.

"No." His voice drops lower. "I didn't."

His mouth is too close, his body too solid, too warm, too *Maddox*.

Everything Asher isn't.

Everything Asher never will be.

A thrill runs through me—a dangerous shiver of realization. Because the worst part? I don't regret it. Not the way he touched me. Not the way I responded. Not even the way I want more, to feel the way he went rigid underneath me and let out that guttural moan—

I squeeze my eyes shut briefly, as if that will get rid of the mental image swimming around in my mind. He'd touched me the way I've been craving for so long. The way I've been asking Asher to for years. Except with Maddox, I didn't have to ask or direct him.

He just knew.

He must see my thoughts written all over my face because

his smirk deepens, and his fingers skim higher. "You want me to say it, don't you?"

My stomach flips. "Say what?"

His thumb brushes the underside of my breast, teasing. Not touching, but close enough that my breath catches. "All the things you like. All the things he never bothered to learn."

I go still.

He chuckles, his breath warm against my temple as he leans in. "Poor thing. You must be so wound up after two years of missionary and silence."

Heat floods my cheeks, my throat aching. Because *fuck him,* he's right.

"Shut up," I snap, jerking my head back, desperate for space, for clarity, for something that isn't the dizzying effect of him.

Maddox just grins. "Tell me I'm wrong."

I press my lips together. Because I can't. And he knows that too. The drag of his gaze is unbearable, suffocating in its intensity. Like he's reading me, seeing everything I try to hide.

So I say the only thing I can. "I'm not yours."

His eyes bore into mine, but he stays silent. And then a slow, wicked smirk breaks out on his beautiful face.

"Yeah?" He leans in closer, his voice barely a whisper. "Then tell me why you're wearing the clothes I picked out and bought for you... why you smell like me..." His thumb drags over my hip, where last night's bruises are starting to bloom. "...and why I can feel you shaking beneath my touch, like you can't fucking wait for me to do it again?"

I let out a sharp, uneven breath, but I have no answer.

Because he's right. *Again.*

"I should call the cops and report you," I hiss, heart hammering in my chest.

It was Maddox.

It was Maddox.

Oh God, I sat on my boyfriend's twin brother's face while he ate me out.

"Probably."

My brows knit together, and somehow, his casual indifference only makes me angrier. "You think this is funny? That you can just—just sneak into my room like some kind of deranged stalker and—" I choke on my words, my pulse fluttering against my throat. "Oh my god. It was you. The letters... Blythe seeing a guy that looked like Asher..."

I look at Maddox like I'm seeing him for the first time.

"Just to warn you, I have a black belt and I'll kick your fucking ass if you try and hurt me—"

"Hurt you?" His voice dips lower, edged with something rough, something almost... offended.

He leans closer, his body pressing into mine, solid, unyielding, the heat of him sinking into my skin like a brand. My pulse stutters, betraying me.

Then, his lips brush my ear, his breath hot against my skin. "Angel, the only way I'd ever hurt you is if you begged me for it. If you got on your knees, looked up at me with those pretty, desperate eyes, and asked me nicely."

A sharp, traitorous shiver dances across my skin.

"And even then?" His fingers skim my jaw, tilting my chin up until my breath is trapped between us. "I'd make sure you loved every second of it."

I can't breathe. I can't... think. This is all so wrong, but why does it feel so... inevitable?

Like I was always meant to end up here, trapped between him and the door, drowning in the storm of his presence, his words curling around me like smoke.

"I can feel it, you know," he murmurs, his fingers tracing the barest line down my throat, not applying pressure—just reminding me that he could. That I'd let him. "The way your pulse is racing. The way your breath shudders every time I get close."

I swallow hard, my throat working against his touch. "You're imagining things."

Maddox chuckles, low and knowing. "Mmm." His lips brush my temple. "If that's true, Ari, then why are you still here? Why haven't you screamed—or run?"

Because I don't want to.

The realization crashes over me like a wave, and *fuck*, I think he sees it, too.

"Do you have any idea what you've done?" I ask, my voice a frayed whisper. "I'm not a cheater. That's not who I am."

That smirk is back, sharp and unrepentant, cutting through me like a blade. And now, in the unforgiving daylight, I see it.

The difference.

Asher is polished, all smooth edges and effortless charm, a man who's never had to fight for anything in his life. His face is untouched by hardship, unmarked by anything more than the mild inconvenience of a delayed dinner reservation or a difficult client. But Maddox...

Maddox is carved from something rougher, honed into something sharper. A man forced to become a predator to survive.

It's in the way he moves—controlled, deliberate, always calculating. It's in the way his body holds tension, coiled like he's always waiting for the next fight. Even his features, so identical to Asher's in theory, have been molded into something else entirely. The same sharp cheekbones, the same strong jaw, but harder. *Harsher*. His blue eyes don't just see, they assess, stripping me bare with a single look. His dark blond hair, just a little too long, gives him a casual recklessness Asher would never allow himself.

And I feel it now, too—the way his presence alone shifts the air, turning it heavier, thicker. More dangerous.

"Is that so?" His voice is smooth, a razor wrapped in silk. "Because from where I was standing—" His hand trails lazily down my hip, thumb brushing against the hem of the dress *he* picked out for me. "—you weren't just a willing participant. You were desperate for it."

I suck in a sharp breath, my body betraying me as heat flares between my thighs. "I didn't know it was *you*," I snap, ignoring the way my pulse jumps at his touch.

His smirk deepens, predatory. "Maybe not." His fingers press lightly against my waist, right where he held me against his face last night, fingertips over the two bruises I'm sure will bloom by later today. "But tell me, Ari—if you really believed it was Asher, then why did it finally feel right?"

"I should put you back in a cage, where you belong," I grit out, trying to pull out of his grasp.

Maddox hums, tilting his head, his blue eyes glinting with something dark. "You won't."

I let out a breathless, humorless laugh. "You really think I won't? Watch. Me."

His lips twitch, amusement flickering over his face like this is some kind of game, like I'm an irritable little fly that amuses him. Like I'm not threatening to send him back to prison for life.

"You won't. Because you liked it."

I go rigid. "Fuck you."

"You already did." His voice is low, smug. His thumb brushes my lower lip. "Well... my mouth, at least."

Heat floods my face, a mix of fury and something far more dangerous. I shove at his chest, and this time, he lets me go, taking a step back and gesturing to the door, as if to say, *Go on and run, but I'm going to catch you eventually.*

"And next time? You'll be fully awake for it."

His response sends shivers down my spine, and arousal drips down the inside of my thighs. I gulp air as I open his door and storm back to my room, closing the door and locking it before I sit down on my bed and press my thighs together, as if that will do anything to erase the way my body still thrums, still aches for something it shouldn't.

My pulse is a frantic, stuttering thing, hammering against my ribs. I press my palms to my face, trying to will away the heat, the dizzying aftershocks of what just happened.

It was Maddox. It was *Maddox*.

And the worst part?

I can still feel him—his breath against my skin, the touch of his hands, the gravel in his voice when he made that promise.

"Next time? You'll be fully awake for it."

A choked sound escapes me, something between a curse and a whimper.

Because even now, locked away in my room, separated by walls and reason and common fucking sense...

I think I want there to be a next time.

PHANTOM IN THE FLESH

MADDOX

THE NIGHT IS QUIET, EXCEPT FOR THE DISTANT crash of waves against the shore. From my seat on the patio, I watch the water stretch out toward the horizon, the moonlight fractured across its surface like shattered glass. Ari's been avoiding me all day—which is cute. Like she really thinks ignoring me will change anything. Like she thinks it'll rewrite last night.

What's already been set in motion.

The cigarette between my fingers is unlit. I don't smoke, not really. But I like the feel of it. The reminder that I could if I wanted to. Freedom feels unsteady, like I've spent so long drowning that I forgot how to breathe air.

I could've gone anywhere after San Quentin. Any city, any direction. Left it all behind. But I didn't. I came here.

To her.

I pull the picture out of my pocket, the edges soft from over a year of constant handling. *Ari*. Her smile in the photo is small, unsure, her fingers curled in like she doesn't know what to do with them. My mom sent it over a year ago, tucked in with a few others. A casual update. She said Ari was the girlfriend Asher never really talked about. In the original picture, she was standing next to my brother, but I ripped him out a long time ago.

I bet Asher never noticed the way her eyes crinkle when she forces a smile. The way she looks like she's trying to take up less space. But I did.

For over a year, locked in a cell, I traced the lines of her face. Memorized every shadow, every soft curve. I built her in my head, piece by piece, until she became more than an image.

She became my reason. A reason to stay sharp. A reason to get out. A reason to win.

And then I did.

I walked out of prison, and the first thing I did was find her. I watched her move, watched the way she carried herself, watched the way Asher didn't see her at all. Didn't see what I saw.

Ari spent her whole life holding the world together. Carrying a weight no one else can see. I saw it the first time I looked at her picture—that tension in her shoulders, the way she stood like she was bracing for something. Like she's always preparing for the next expectation, the next demand, the next thing she has to fix. That's not something you learn overnight. It's something ingrained, beaten into you over years.

I know it because I've seen that look before.

Every time I looked in a mirror.

And once before—on someone I loved.

Someone I *lost*.

Someone who used to smile just like that—bright, but a little too careful. Someone who never put herself first, who gave and gave until there was nothing left.

Ari's never been allowed to put the weight down. And when I take her, when I peel her apart piece by piece, she'll finally understand what it's like to be free.

And fuck—last night...

The way she broke apart for me...

The way she whimpered a plea in the dark, thinking I was my brother...

A slow breath leaves my lungs as I drag my thumb over the worn edges of the photo.

Of course she'll fight it. She'll push. She'll tell herself she's loyal, that she's in love with Asher, that she doesn't want this.

And maybe she'll even believe it. But I don't need her belief.

I need her *surrender*.

And that? That's only a matter of time.

She's not like Asher. She's not polished, predictable, or boring. She's a warrior. And Asher? He's just another thing she's been carrying. Another weight she's been told to hold. He doesn't appreciate her. Doesn't deserve her. He thinks he can keep her tucked into his perfect, polished life without ever noticing that she's slipping through his fingers.

But I see it.

I've been watching it happen.

The last month since I got out of prison has been a blur of surveillance feeds and silent tailing—tracking her through alleys, watching when she thought she was alone. Her security system was laughably easy to breach. Disabling it at night? Child's play.

I started in the Marine Corps, then moved into private security—contractor work that paid better and asked fewer questions. By 25, I was in deeper than most ever get. Encryption, black hat networks, corporate espionage. Some thought I was a criminal. Others saw me as a ghost in the machine, taking down corrupt suits and helping out veterans and families left behind.

They never proved I had anything to do with Whittaker's death. But I was there. I got into his building the night he died, no question. The charges didn't stick for murder, but twenty years for conspiracy and obstruction? That held. They said I was part of a coordinated effort to intimidate corporate leaders. Maybe I was.

Prison didn't slow me down. I ran my operation from the inside, kept my team sharp, the money flowing. Now I'm out —and richer than ever. Slid right back into the role like I never left.

And Ari's defenses?

They never stood a chance.

I know her schedule better than she does. I know when she gets her coffee, how she taps her fingers against the counter when she's impatient, the way she worries her bottom lip between her teeth when she's deep in thought.

I know how she sleeps—curled on her side, arms wrapped around a pillow like she's holding herself together.

I know the way she moves through the world, careful but unaware of how many eyes are on her. Of how mine have never left.

Ari's tired. She's been holding everything up for so long, she doesn't even realize she can let go.

That's what I'll do. I'll make her let go. I'll show her she doesn't have to make the decisions, or be the strong one, or take care of everyone else.

She's mine to take care of now.

Even if she doesn't realize it yet.

THE PHANTOM'S WEB
ARI

THE THIRD MORNING AT THE HOUSE IS WORSE THAN the first.

I wake up groggy, my body too warm, my limbs stiff with a tension I can't shake.

Frustration.

I spent last night alone—and I don't know why that bothers me.

It shouldn't. It should be a relief.

I swallow hard, trying to push the thought aside as I throw the covers off my body, but the discomfort lingers, itching beneath my skin.

He didn't come back last night.

I tell myself I should be grateful that he didn't come to my room again. That it means maybe—*maybe*—I can pretend it never happened. Maybe I imagined the way he had held me down, had groaned into my skin like he was worshipping me —like he was starving.

I stare up at the ceiling, breathing through the dull, frustrating ache between my legs. He's screwing with me. Getting inside my head. And it's working.

I grab my laptop off the nightstand and pull up a search engine before I can second-guess myself.

Maddox Cross.

I hesitate before pressing search, but my finger moves before my mind can stop it.

And then—

A headline.

The blood drains from my face as I skim the first few lines. My pulse jumps, each beat a hammer against my ribs.

The unexpected passing of Daniel Whittaker, president of GoldStar Health, has certainly sent shock waves through the corporate community and ignited important conversations. At just 53, his life came to a tragic end in his downtown San Diego penthouse this past Sunday. While there are whispers of foul play, law enforcement is still gathering details.

Oh my god.

I keep reading, my breath hitching as the words blur together.

The investigation took a dramatic turn when Maddox Cross, 25, a former Marine turned security contractor, was arrested on charges of conspiracy and obstruction of justice. Cross allegedly accessed restricted areas of Whittaker's office building on the night of the president's death.

Prosecutors claimed Cross was linked to an anonymous vigilante group targeting corrupt executives. Though there was insufficient evidence to convict Cross of murder, he was sentenced to 20 years in prison for his involvement in what authorities described as a "coordinated effort to intimidate corporate leaders."

Twenty years.

The article is old, but the shock isn't. I knew Maddox was in prison, knew Asher never spoke about it. But this?

I skim the last lines, my hands trembling.

While Whittaker's death remains unsolved, public opinion remains divided. Some view Cross as a dangerous criminal, while others have branded him a modern-day Robin Hood, pointing to his history of aiding veterans and disadvantaged families. People have even given him a nickname: the Phantom.

I can't breathe.

I scroll down, my fingers shaking as I click another article, one buried deeper in the search results. This one isn't about Daniel Whittaker—it's about Maddox.

A brief profile of his life before the arrest.

And that's when I see it—a photo.

The article is twenty years old, the quality grainy, but it's him. A younger Maddox, standing in uniform, holding a little girl.

My stomach drops.

She can't be more than two, her tiny arms wrapped around his neck, her head resting against his shoulder. She looks like she's Lucia's age. *Oh, god.* His expression isn't the one I've come to know—the sharp smirks, the taunting grins. He's softer here. His lips pressed to the little girl's hair, his eyes closed like he's breathing her in.

The caption hits me like a punch.

Maddox Cross, 23, pictured with his late daughter, Lila Cross, 2, during his final deployment.

Late.

Daughter.

A rush of blood roars in my ears.

There's another photo—a woman this time. She's beautiful. Warm brown eyes, a bright, easy smile. Her hand rests on Maddox's chest, fingers curling over his heart.

Elaine Cross, 23, beloved mother and wife, tragically passed away three weeks after her daughter in 2005.

Holy. Fuck.

My stomach twists, a painful, disorienting thing. All at once, the things he's said to me start rearranging themselves in my mind.

"You remind me of someone."

I think I'm going to be sick.

I type in Elaine Cross, and multiple articles on tabloid websites pop up.

Lila Cross. Four years old. Denied treatment by GoldStar Health. Passed away in a pediatric hospice. Elaine Cross. Found dead in her home three weeks later. Ruled a suicide.

My vision tunnels.

There's another picture of the three of them, buried beneath a wall of text—an old family photo taken before everything fell apart. Maddox is younger in it, clean-shaven, dressed in his Marine Corps uniform, looking at the camera with the quiet, sure confidence of someone who still had a future. Elaine stands beside him, her arm looped through his. And then there's Lila.

A baby with chubby cheeks and Maddox's sharp blue eyes.

I stare at the screen until my vision blurs.

I don't know how long I sit there, my breaths coming too fast, my chest too tight. Because suddenly, Maddox isn't just Asher's dangerous older brother. He isn't just the criminal, the convicted felon, the man who snuck into my room and ruined me in the dark.

He's a father who lost his daughter. A husband who buried his wife. A man who had everything ripped away from him before being locked in a cage for two decades.

My stomach twists violently. I swallow against the lump in my throat, but it doesn't move.

This changes everything.

This means I don't know him at all.

And yet a part of me wonders if I ever really knew Asher, either.

I force myself to close the laptop, but the damage is done.

Because now, when I look at Maddox, I won't just see the

smirking, cocky ex-felon who taunts me with promises he shouldn't be making.

I'll see the man who buried his whole world.

And I don't know if that makes him more dangerous... or more human.

As I shower and get ready, stepping into a yellow linen skirt and shirt combo that's both elegant and casual, I tell myself that I need to keep the information to myself. Especially as I blow-dry my hair straight and pull it back into a ponytail, I don't let my eyes skim down the outfit that Maddox chose for me. I don't let my mind think of the way his eyes drank me in from the moment we met.

But knowing this? Knowing what happened...

It changes something.

After spritzing some perfume on my neck, I wander downstairs. Asher is already at the dining table, half focused on his laptop, half picking at his breakfast.

Hannah beams at me when I enter, already sipping her coffee from her usual spot.

"Good morning, sweetheart."

I manage a small smile, but something feels off. The dull ache of the newly acquired information hangs heavy in my chest, and for some reason, the quiet normalcy of breakfast only makes it worse.

I make my way toward the kitchen, intent on pouring myself some coffee, but freeze when I step through the archway.

Maddox is there.

He's shirtless, a damp towel draped over his shoulder, sweat still clinging to his skin from whatever workout he just finished. His tattoos ripple over taut, lean muscle as he moves, stretching his arms overhead before reaching into the fridge for a bottle of water.

The sight of him unsettles me.

Not because I'm afraid.

Because something hot coils in my stomach before I can stop it.

My body remembers too easily—how firm he had been beneath my hands, how his breath had felt between my thighs.

His sharp blue gaze flicks toward me as he cracks the water bottle open. A slow smirk curves his lips as he catches me staring.

"See something you like, angel?"

Heat slams into my cheeks, but I lift my chin. "You wish."

Maddox's smirk is lazy, knowing. He sets the bottle down deliberately, like he has all the time in the world, like he's already won. Then, he tilts his head just slightly, his voice low, smooth—a quiet threat wrapped in velvet.

"Do I?"

The words curl through the space between us, sinking into my skin like heat.

My stomach drops.

I should leave. I should say something cutting, something to shut him up. But my tongue is heavy, my brain useless. Plus, I can't stop picturing the younger version of him. The happier, more carefree version.

As if sensing my struggle, Maddox steps closer. Too close.

The scent of him wraps around me—clean sweat, something woody, something distinctly him.

I take a step back, he takes another forward.

My breath hitches, my pulse unsteady.

And then—

"Ari?"

I jerk at the sound of Asher's voice from the dining table. Maddox's lips twitch like he's amused at how easily I jumped.

I clear my throat and step around him, grabbing my coffee without looking at him again.

———

I watch him during breakfast, but Maddox doesn't look at me. Doesn't smirk, doesn't push. But I feel him, the space between us thick with unspoken things.

After breakfast, Otto suggests going into town. There's a nearby overlook with a small marketplace within walking distance, an easy way to kill a few hours. While we walk over, I stay close to Asher—not because I want to, but because Maddox is watching me again. It's as if he's messing with me on purpose—ignoring me when I give him my attention, but only watching me when he knows I can't look back.

I'm used to avoiding him now. I did it perfectly yesterday, and he didn't push. A pang of disappointment clangs through me as we meander through the stalls.

It doesn't matter—I'm not his, despite what he claims.

The air is crisp, and the market is lively—vendors selling fresh fruit, handmade jewelry, little souvenirs. The overlook stretches into a breathtaking view of the ocean, the drop-off a sheer cliff.

I reach for Asher's hand, squeezing it three times as we walk to the overlook along the ocean a few hundred feet away. Hannah and Otto are telling me all about the islands visible in the distance, but I'm not really paying attention.

The whole time, I can feel Maddox's eyes on my back—waiting, watching, letting me stew in my own awareness of him. I pull my hand away from Asher and step close to the edge of the cliff. The breeze whips at my skirt, my heart skipping as a gust of wind nearly knocks me over.

"Ari," Asher's voice cuts in sharply behind me.

I glance back, catching his glare. "What?"

His jaw tightens. "Be careful."

I roll my eyes. "I'm not going to fall, Asher. I'm just looking."

Turning back to the ocean, I inhale deeply, letting the salty air fill my lungs. The air is heavy with brine and warm sand, and I suddenly feel so relaxed. I've always loved the ocean. Not just because it's beautiful, but because of what it represents. It feels... endless. Uncontrollable. *Wild*. All things I was never allowed to be. Growing up, I had to be steady for my younger sisters. I had to be reliable. The calm in every storm. There was no room for chaos. No room for mistakes.

No room for me to just... be.

But the ocean? It doesn't care about expectations.

It crashes. It swells. It devours and gives and takes without asking for permission.

Maybe that's why I always felt drawn to it.

Because no matter how much I had to be in control everywhere else, here? Here, I can finally breathe.

I open my eyes just as another large gust of wind catches me off guard—

And then I slip.

The dirt beneath my feet crumbles faster than I can react, my balance vanishing as gravity yanks me forward.

I scream, but the fall never comes—

Because Maddox grabs me.

His hands lock around my waist, yanking me back against his chest with a sharp, commanding strength.

My pulse slams against my ribs. My whole body trembles. I suck in an uneven breath, my chest heaving as I cling to his forearms.

For a second, neither of us move.

Then Maddox exhales, a slow, measured breath against my neck. "You really need to be more careful, angel."

I shudder, and his grip locks around me.

Over my shoulder, I hear Asher huff. "Jesus, Ari. Can you not almost kill yourself for one second?"

I pull away from Maddox, my breath still shaky as I turn to face Asher. "I didn't do it on purpose," I snap.

Asher scowls.

Maddox just smirks.

And as I stand between them, my heart still hammering, I realize it wasn't Asher who saved me. It wasn't Asher who reacted first, who moved without thinking, who caught me before I could hit the jagged cliffs below.

It was Maddox.

Asher was too busy scolding me.

Maddox was too busy making sure I was safe.

Phantom Hunger

Maddox

I watch Ari move around her bedroom from my place on the lower deck. Lucky for me, this vantage point gives me a pretty decent view into her bedroom. If I were at home, I'd have hidden cameras with a perfect three-hundred-sixty-degree high-resolution feed, capturing every flick of her fingers, every shift of her weight. The grainy, black-and-white security footage most people are familiar with? That's amateur work. My setup is military-grade. Untraceable. A closed network that no one—not even the CIA—could breach.

Alas, I'm here, so I have to use my own two eyes.

I see her grab a towel, and knowing her routine at night, I know she's going to take a shower.

I could have planted a small, portable camera in there. A simple, undetectable one, disguised in the LED lighting strip or inside the vent.

But I didn't.

Because even I have lines I don't cross.

Morality isn't something I cling to, but privacy? That's different.

After twenty years in a maximum-security hellhole, I

know what it means to have your every movement watched, your dignity stripped away one humiliating inch at a time.

Some things you just don't take from a person.

I exhale through my nose, rolling my shoulders, shaking off the memory.

I stare out into the dark abyss until movement in her window catches my eye.

Ari walks back into the bedroom, skin dewy from the shower, a small towel barely clinging to her curves.

Heat coils in my stomach, sharp and immediate. I'm already fucking hard, and I haven't even touched her yet tonight.

Looking down, I give her sixty seconds to get dressed, and it's the longest sixty seconds of my life.

The light in her bedroom turns off, so I stub out the joint I'm smoking and make my way back into the house. Knowing her, she's reading on her Kindle, and I'm bored as fuck, so once I'm back in the bedroom I'm sleeping in, I log into her account from my phone.

A small perk of being one of the best cybersecurity specialists to ever exist.

My lips twitch into a smirk as I see what she's reading.

"*Thirsty for the Terrible Monster,*" I say out loud.

A monsterfucker romance. I shake my head, amused, and immediately sync my page to hers.

Might as well read along, right?

I settle back in the bed, one hand idly resting against my thigh as I skim through the next few pages.

Then, I hit the line that changes everything.

"Bend over, mortal."

I gasp as his large hand comes around my neck, claws digging into the sensitive skin just above my pulse point.

Thor's tongue slithers out, and he bends down so that it flicks against my cheek, and I squirm as he tightens his grip around my neck.

"Wondering what my tongue can do, pet?"

"N-no," I say quickly, trying to cover my growing arousal.

"I can smell your slick, and I want to taste it."

Fuck.

Is she touching herself to this?

Is it bad that I want to know?

Quietly, I set my phone down and exit my bedroom. I'm barefoot, and, fortunately, all those years in the Corps taught me one thing—*stealth.* Walking up to her door, I twist the handle slowly, already knowing it's not going to creak thanks to my technique.

The door opens just a crack, and I wait for my eyes to adjust. And when they do...

Ari shifts in bed, the glow of her Kindle lighting up her face and neck. Her eyes flicker across the page hungrily, legs pressing together.

Then—her hand slides beneath the sheets.

I inhale silently, my fingers clamping down on the frame of the door.

Is she—

A soft moan slips from her lips. My cock jumps. *Jesus Christ.*

I can just make out the way her expression shifts, the subtle arch of her hips, the tension in her thighs.

She's touching herself. To this. To claws, to monsters, to being devoured. The idea of someone taking control of her.

I don't think, don't hesitate. I reach down, lowering my sweatpants, and my aching cock springs free into my palm.

My pulse pounds at the base of my throat, my breathing silent as I stroke myself slowly. Her breathing picks up. Faster. Needier. It feels like we're sharing this, even if she has no idea that I'm watching her.

I lick my palm, my hand wrapping around my shaft, twisting slightly as my hips rut forward.

I should be inside her.

I should be tasting her, making her come on my tongue until she's sobbing, wrung dry, and desperate.

Instead, I'm here. *Watching*.

I tighten my grip, matching her pace, my strokes falling into perfect sync with the slow, needy rhythm of her fingers. My breath hitches when she bites her lip, her body tensing, her movements becoming more desperate. My own strokes speed up, sliding slick and rough over my aching length, feet lifting from the floor as the heat coiling in my gut pulses, sharp and unrelenting.

I can't stop watching her. Can't stop picturing how she'd look if I were the one between her legs instead—if it were my fingers, my mouth wringing those perfect little sounds from her throat.

My free hand dips into my pocket, fingers brushing over the stolen scrap of lace I'd stolen earlier when she was downstairs.

Her panties.

I bring them to my nose, inhaling deep as I stroke faster, matching the way her breath catches, the way her thighs tremble, the way she's falling apart for me without even knowing it.

Her body stiffens. Her back arches. Her head tilts back.

And when she moans—soft, needy, completely broken—

I fucking lose it.

A silent groan vibrates in my chest. My body goes rigid, tension winding sharp and hot before it snaps—electric, uncontrollable, like a live wire. Hot spurts of cum coat my hand, my hips jerking up in desperate, uneven thrusts as her name slips from my lips in a reverent whisper.

Goddamn her.

She turns over and continues reading, facing away from

me. I clean my cock and hand up with her panties before placing them back inside my pocket. Slowly, quietly, I walk down the hall back to my room. Once inside, I fall back onto my bed, my body still vibrating with tension. It's not enough. Not even close. I should feel sated. I should be done for the night.

But I'm nowhere fucking close.

Because watching her isn't enough.

I need to feel her. *Breathe* her in. Taste her.

I decide that I'm done watching her, because right now, all I want to do is consume her, body and soul.

PHANTOM AT MIDNIGHT

ARI

LIGHT, EARLY-MORNING SLEEP ENVELOPS ME, allowing me to sink deeper into the warm duvet. I feel like I'm floating in that calm, halfway space between being asleep and being awake, where time seems to disappear. The place where hours feel like minutes, and everything feels cozy and comforting. At first, I assume it's the duvet brushing against my skin, awakening my senses just slightly.

But then something pulls the duvet down my body slowly, and something grazes the curve of my hip, tracing slow, deliberate lines that pull me from the comfortable depths of sleep. My breath catches, the fog in my mind thinning as awareness creeps in.

I shift, my body instinctively responding, even as confusion flickers at the edges of my consciousness. The sheets feel different. The air feels charged. And that touch—possessive, unhurried—isn't my own.

A shiver rolls through me, my pulse kicking up as my senses fully awaken. The bed dips beside me, a slow shift in weight. Not an accident.

Someone is here.

And I can't move. Not out of fear—not entirely. But because somewhere, deep in the marrow of my bones, I know who it is.

My skin burns where he's touched me, a ghost of heat lingering even as his hand stills.

His breath fans against my cheek, and I catch the faintest trace of Maddox's scent. Leather. Musk. The slightest hint of pine.

I swallow, my breath hitching, my body tensing beneath the heavy weight of realization. A tremor rolls through me, and as if sensing it, his fingers flex against my skin, pressing just a little harder. He grips me with a slow, possessive squeeze against my hip.

The heat of his breath ghosts over my temple, and then—a whisper. "Shh."

A single syllable, barely audible, but I feel it more than I hear it.

I blink into the darkness, my body frozen in place, halfway between fear and something dangerously close to excitement.

I try to steady my breathing, to slow the rapid drum of my pulse.

But then his fingers move again.

A slow, measured drag over the exposed skin of my thigh that will be the death of me. Not pushing. Not taking. Just reminding.

I exhale shakily, my body betraying me. My thighs clench together as my breath stutters. He shifts beside me, solid and inescapable, the heat of his body pressing against my spine.

His presence isn't just close.

It's everywhere.

A calloused finger traces the dip of my waist. Lazy. *Unhurried*, like he has all the time in the world. As it slowly dives lower, through my dark curls to the pulsing bud I need him to touch more than my next breath, a ragged whimper escapes my lips.

And just like that, reality cracks through the haze. *Asher.*

The reminder stings, sharp and sudden, slicing through the heat curling low in my stomach. I shouldn't be doing this. I shouldn't want this. But then Maddox's finger dips lower, circles exactly where I need him most, and the guilt?

It shatters.

It drowns beneath the ache of how much I want to see what happens. The pressure coils tighter, hotter, until there's nothing left but need.

No logic.

No rules.

Just *him*.

A satisfied hum rumbles in his chest. "Good girl. So needy for me. Now, turn around."

Twisting my body out of his grip, I turn around as I try not to get tangled in my sheets. When I do, my breath hitches when I see him laying down next to me.

Tonight, he's dressed in black. A hoodie. Dark jeans.

My pulse quickens, heat curls low in my stomach.

The bedroom isn't pitch dark tonight. I forgot to close the curtains. The soft glow of the streetlight outside filters through the window, casting just enough light to see him. My eyes catalog the familiar blue eyes. The sharp cheekbones. The faint crease between his brows.

The tattoos... the *wicked* smile.

My brows knit in confusion as his hand comes to my mouth. His thumb presses against my lips, insistent, until I part them without thinking. The salty taste of his skin floods my senses, and shame curls hot and sharp in my chest.

The audacity.

The sheer, unrelenting arrogance of him.

And yet my tongue presses against his thumb as if it's welcoming it into my mouth.

I glare at him in the dark as I suck his thumb deeper into my mouth—not because I want to give him the satisfaction, but because I want to defy him in the only way I know how. A silent, dangerous dare.

My body betrays me, hungry for him, even now. Even when I should be disgusted. Even when I should be thinking about Asher and the fact that he and his parents are just down the hall.

I should pull away. I should bite down. I should shove him off me and tell him I am done playing whatever game this is.

But I don't. Because I'm tired.

Tired of doing the right thing. Tired of choosing the safer option. Tired of pretending I don't want more.

But tired doesn't mean weak. Not tonight.

My heart pounds, furious and desperate all at once. Because he didn't come last night. And I hate that it bothers me. I should be grateful that he stayed away. But instead, I tossed and turned, restless, aching for something I'm not supposed to want.

The guilt is sharp, but it isn't sharp enough to make me stop.

His thumb slips from my mouth, and when he drags it down the center of my throat—slow, possessive—I shudder like it's the first time anyone has ever touched me there.

"You missed me," he says low, his breath warm against my temple. "Didn't you?"

I don't answer. I *can't*. If I speak, I'll unravel.

Because I did.

I really fucking missed the way he makes me feel small—protected. *Desired*.

But that familiar pang of guilt crops up again. I'm

supposed to be loyal. Good. Reliable. The strong one. The one who never lets her guard down.

But here, with him, I'm allowed to be selfish. Allowed to want.

"I didn't," I try, but the words are too soft, too unsure.

"You don't have to lie," he murmurs, brushing his nose along the shell of my ear. "I get it. You didn't want to miss me." He pauses as his hand flattens against my rib cage, warm and anchoring. "But you did."

My breath hitches. He says it like it's not something I should be ashamed of, and if I wasn't so pissed, I might find that refreshing.

His fingers trail down to my waist, his palm splaying over my hip.

"Tell me no," he whispers. "And I'll walk away."

Silence stretches between us. My pulse pounds against his fingertips; he must feel how violently my heart is betraying me, how hard I'm trying to stay still, to keep control.

But there is no control. Not with him. Not here. Not when every inch of me is screaming to let go.

The worst part? He knows it. His smirk tells me so. His touch tells me so. And when his thumb brushes lower, just enough to feel the trembling anticipation on my lower hip, I snap.

"Fuck you," I hiss, the words tumbling out sharp and helpless, laced with frustration, hunger, and something dangerously close to surrender.

And that scares the fuck out of me.

I rip my wrist from his grasp, moving back like I can put distance between us, between this pull that refuses to let up.

But his hand shoots forward, gripping my wrist.

The movement is smooth—effortless.

He's not holding me back, exactly. It's more like he's reminding me who's in control.

"Let go of me," I growl.

Another dark chuckle. Richer this time, like he's enjoying this. Like he knows exactly how this is going to end.

"I'll let go..." He leans in, his breath warm against my cheek. "...if you can prove you're not already soaking for me."

The bastard.

I shift my hips and squeeze my thighs together, and I can *feel* how soaked I already am.

My lips press together, and he smiles again.

"Thought so."

"Screw you—"

But before the words fully leave my lips, his hand is on my mouth.

Firm. Possessive. Daring me to *bite*.

I stare up at him, my breath coming in short, sharp pants. His fingers flex against my jaw, a slow, indulgent press of control.

"You can try to fight me, little warrior." His voice is low, rough velvet, dragging over my skin like a promise. "I know that's what you do. What you've always done." His other hand traces my collarbones, trailing lower, his fingertips skimming my bare skin. "Always carrying everything. Always in control. Always making the decisions. Always settling, melding yourself into what other people expect of you instead of fighting for what you deserve."

A slow, calculated drag of his knuckles down my throat.

"But you don't have to do that with me."

My chest rises, lungs straining to hold in the oxygen. I suddenly forget how to breathe. He leans in farther, his lips barely brushing the shell of my ear.

"You don't need to fight me, Ari. And I know you don't want to." A shiver rolls through me. "You don't need to think." His grip locks just enough to make my pulse stutter. "Not with me."

I swallow hard, my body caught somewhere between surrender and defiance.

His mouth grazes the curve of my jaw, his next words slow, precise, devastating.

"Let me take care of you."

Phantom Control
Maddox

She's still fighting it. Fighting *me*.

Her breath is shaky, her body tense next to mine, but I can feel the way her pulse flutters against my fingertips. The way her thighs squeeze together, trying to chase friction. The way her body knows what it wants, even if she won't admit it yet.

I move on top of her, pressing my weight against her, slowly, deliberately, until she's pinned beneath me. I reach down and spread her legs so that I'm settled between her soft, bare thighs.

Lifting her sleep shirt up, I growl when I look down at her perfect cunt.

"Wait—" Her hands go to my chest, pushing—but there's no real strength behind it.

Just resistance for the sake of resisting.

I let her pretend for a second.

I let her feel like she has a choice.

Then I roll my hips against hers, my hard cock pressing against her hot core. I inhale sharply, imagining that I'm actually sinking into her tight heat.

Not tonight, but soon...

My movements are slow—*purposeful*.

She gasps.

Her nails dig into my shirt, and I let out a low, knowing chuckle.

"Are we still pretending you don't want this, angel?"

She inhales shakily, her breath catching in her throat. I roll my hips again, just enough for her to feel me. The hard length of me presses against her core again, separated only by the fabric of my pants.

She shouldn't be this wet already.

But she is. I feel it through my jeans—the warmth of her, the damp heat seeping through the fabric, clinging to me like a brand.

Her body is betraying her in every way possible.

Her hips shift up against my cock—instinctive, desperate for more. I grip both of her wrists and press them into the pillow above her head, holding her there with one hand.

Not to restrain her.

Just to remind her who's in control.

She squirms, her breathing uneven now, and as I dip my head to hers, I smirk against her neck. I drag my tongue up the right side of her throat, slow and deliberate, tasting the heat of her skin. And then—I bite.

Not hard. Just a slow, perfect press of my teeth against her pulse point.

She gasps, body jerking against mine. "Jesus—" she hisses, but the sound doesn't hold any anger.

I smirk. "Not quite, angel. Try again."

Her chest pushes against me, but it doesn't do anything.

"I never said you could touch me," she rasps.

I chuckle against her throat, grinding against her again.

"You never told me to stop, either."

She lets out a breath, shifting beneath me, glaring even as her body betrays her.

"I don't belong to you," she spits, voice tight, forced, like she's trying to convince herself.

Perfect. Keep trying, angel.

I tilt my head, dragging my nose along her jaw, inhaling deeply. "You can lie to yourself, but you can't lie to me."

She tenses, her mind fighting the truth her body can't deny.

I nip at her throat again, just to hear that little gasp, just to feel the way she twitches beneath me.

"You can fight me all you want, little warrior." I lean in, pressing my weight into her. One of my fingers trails up her side, slow, teasing, stopping just beneath her ribs. The other holds her hands above her head. "But your body already knows who it belongs to."

She sucks in a sharp breath and her hips shift, seeking friction.

Then she lets out a quiet laugh, shaking her head. "You're so full of shit."

I grin against her skin. *God, I love her fight.* Her hips shift, almost like she's trying to get away. But in doing so, she just rubs against me harder.

She realizes it at the same time I do.

Her eyes go wide, her breath stalling.

I hum, low and pleased. "Fighting me only makes you want it more, doesn't it? You've dreamt of being taken like this before, haven't you? The thought of me doing this is one of your deepest, darkest fantasies. And you've been waiting for my brother to fuck you senseless, just the way you want. Isn't that true?"

Her lips part, either to deny it or curse me out. I don't let her. Instead, I press against her again, letting a low moan escape my lips.

And then her body fucking *gives*, allowing me to settle between them completely.

I grind against her, slow at first, teasing. Just enough for her to whimper. I feel it through my whole fucking soul, the way she starts to tremble. Either from fear, defiance, or... complete and utter arousal.

The heat pools low in my stomach, the slow, brutal ache of wanting her for so damn long sinks into me, until all I can think about is finding my release. *Again.*

She tilts her head back, exposing her throat.

A silent surrender.

But I want more.

I move against her again, rolling my hips, pressing her deeper into the mattress. Her thighs tremble and her breath stutters.

I murmur against her skin, my voice dark and possessive. "Every time you squirm, every time you fight me, you just press that sweet little pussy harder against my cock."

She squeezes her legs around my waist as her body arches against me. I don't rush it. I just keep moving. Grinding against her.

Slow.

Deep.

I roll my hips against her, letting her feel how hard she's made me. How fucking desperate I am.

A groan claws up my throat, raw and shattered. She's so fucking drenched for me. Already mine in every way that matters.

She lets out a shaky moan, her fingers twisting against my hand above her head.

My control frays at the edges, unraveling with every slow, torturous roll of her hips. A tremor racks through me, muscles locking tight as I drop my forehead to hers, grinding harder now, chasing friction, chasing her.

Heat surges through me, a sharp pulse of pleasure building too fast, too strong. My breath shudders, a ragged sound against her lips, and I can feel it—the edge, the fucking precipice—I'm right there. My cock throbs, the pressure unbearable, the slick warmth of her making it impossible to hold back.

A low, quiet, guttural sound rips from my throat, my hips jerking of their own accord. I'm going to come. Fuck, I'm going to come just from this—just from her. From the way she clings to me, from the way her body moves like she already belongs to me.

And I don't know if I want to stop it.

Her head tilts back against the pillow, her eyes squeezing shut.

She gasps, her whole body locking up.

And then—she falls apart beneath me.

Fuck.

I feel it happen. The soft, pulsing grip of her thighs around me, the way her body spasms. I grind against her harder, chasing my own release, letting myself fucking drown in her. And then it hits me.

Hard. Violent. Uncontrollable.

A rough groan tears from my throat as my body locks up. Pleasure crashes through me, pulsing, hot, and raw. My muscles tense, my cock throbbing as I spill into my jeans, untouched, just from feeling her like this.

I barely hold myself up as my body shudders, every ounce of restraint ripped from me.

She feels it.

She knows.

And fuck me if that doesn't make it even hotter.

For a moment, the only sound in the room is our uneven, heavy breathing. I let my forehead rest against hers once more, my fingers still wrapped around her wrists. Then I pull back just enough to look at her. Her lips parted, her eyes still hazy, her breath still shaky. I run my thumb over her cheek.

I adjust myself, letting out a sharp exhale, glancing at her one last time. She stares at the ceiling, dazed, breathless, completely spent. I press my lips to her temple, lingering. Then, I shift away, rolling off her and sitting up.

"Are you okay?" I ask, pulse stuttering at the thought that perhaps maybe I hurt her, or...

"I'm fine," she says, sitting up now. Her voice is clipped, almost defiant. She doesn't look at me. Just adjusts her shirt and tosses her hair over one shoulder like it's a shield, blinking like she's trying to process what the fuck just happened. Her gaze darts to the door, to the dark, empty hallway beyond it. I can practically hear her thoughts racing. Her voice wavers. "But we shouldn't have done that."

And then I stand, adjusting my hoodie, my voice low and firm. "Probably not."

I wait for her to say something else, but she doesn't, so I attempt to make light of the situation.

"That's twice now, angel."

My voice is gravelly, strained, still catching up to the wreckage of what she just did to me.

Her brow knit together, her breathing still unsteady. "Twice?"

I smirk. "That I've come in my fucking pants because of you."

A blush crawls up her throat, and I fucking love it.

Then, she lets out a breathy laugh—light, too light. "Don't let it go to your head. You're not the first guy who couldn't keep it together with me."

The words are casual. Careless. But they land flat. Her bravado doesn't reach her eyes. Not when they finally meet mine. There's a flicker of something behind them—panic, maybe. Or guilt. Or fear of what she just let happen.

And fuck, I feel it. The tremble in her fingers as she wipes her palms on her bare thighs. The way her legs won't quite hold still.

She's unraveling. She just doesn't want me to see it.

I don't move. I let her have the illusion of space. Let her pretend she's still got a grip on her world, even as it's slipping through her fingers.

But then?

Her eyes flick down to where I'm still adjusting myself, the dark stain on my jeans undeniable. A shaky breath leaves her, and the smallest smirk tugs at the corner of her mouth, wry and sharp despite the turmoil still written all over her.

The blush is still crawling up her throat. Her bravado is thin, a shield barely holding against the storm raging behind her eyes, but it's there. And fuck if it doesn't make me fall a little harder.

Surprise lashes through me. I lean in, letting her feel the heat of my breath against her swollen lips as I grip her hips firmly.

"I won't be nearly this patient again, little warrior." I pause, just long enough to let the words sink in, just long enough to feel her shiver beneath me. "And next time?" I press my thumb against her slick, trembling lips, dragging it down her chin. "You'll beg me not to be."

With that, I lower my mouth to her ear, voice dipping into something low and lethal. "Sleep tight, angel. Don't you dare dream about anyone else but me," I murmur, my fingers brushing over her throat, a slow, dangerous caress.

A sharp inhale. A flicker of something dark and conflicted in her gaze.

Good. I *want* her to question everything. I *want* her to crave me.

I tilt my head, trailing my nose along the column of her throat before pressing one last kiss there. Then I pull back, standing upright, adjusting my hoodie. Before I leave, I glance down at her—still on the bed, her body wrecked, her breaths uneven.

And I grin as I walk out of her bedroom, still feeling wholly out of control and completely insatiable when it comes to Ariana Clarke.

PHANTOM OF THE PAST
ARI

ASHER, OTTO, AND MADDOX ARE ALL GONE WHEN I meander into the kitchen the next morning, the house quieter than it's been since we arrived.

According to Hannah, Maddox and Otto are working out.

And Asher?

He's dealing with a work thing on the computer in the home office just off the kitchen. The door is closed, so I can't see him, but I can hear him speaking to someone on a video call.

He's yelling, so I know it's not a good call.

Hannah sighs as she pours herself more coffee, her fingers drumming against the side of her mug. She looks like she wants to say something, but I don't press her.

I pull a cup from the cupboard, deliberately not asking. Because it's not my problem. Then again, I'm technically dating one of her sons and messing around with the other.

God, I'm so fucked up.

I glance toward the back patio, where the faint clink of weights echoes from the home gym outside.

Maddox.

I swallow hard, turning back to my brewing coffee.

"I hope everything's okay with Asher and his work," I say casually.

"Me too," she says quietly. "Sounds like a big deal. Something about his firm's sensitive client information being hacked. Millions of dollars are at risk, apparently."

"That sucks," I say, taking a seat next to her.

She shakes off her worried expression. "So, are you having a good time, Ari?"

I nod enthusiastically. "I am. It's beautiful here."

"It is." She sets her coffee mug down and clears her throat. "Asher works too much, doesn't he?"

I huff a laugh. "I'm used to it."

Hannah studies me for a moment, something warm and knowing in her gaze. Then, she sighs, picking up her coffee mug again. "You know, sweetheart... you deserve someone who makes time for you. Who puts you first."

I blink, surprised by the sudden shift in conversation.

"We love Asher," she continues, her voice careful, measured. "He's always been driven. Focused. But... well, relationships need more than just good intentions." She takes a sip, her eyes soft as they meet mine. "We like you, Ari. And we would understand if—" She pauses, choosing her words carefully. "If it ever felt like too much. If you ever needed more than what he's willing to give."

A sharp pang twists in my chest.

I force a small smile, ducking my head. "It's not like that. I know Asher cares about me in his own way."

Even as the words leave my mouth, I feel the lie settle heavily between us. Because it is like that. Maybe it always has been. I've just never had anyone else to show me the difference.

Not until Maddox.

I feel like I'm standing at a cliff's edge, too scared to jump, too ashamed to admit I already have.

But what am I supposed to say to Hannah? That the problem isn't just Asher's distance or his busy schedule, but that I've already let someone else touch parts of me Asher never has? That I wanted her other son? That I want Maddox, not Asher?

"I have no doubt that he cares about you," she agrees easily. "But words and effort aren't always the same thing."

Something heavy settles in my stomach.

Before I can respond, another voice cuts through the air. "Interesting conversation," Maddox drawls, stepping into the kitchen, his blue eyes locking on to mine. "What are we discussing?"

Hannah sighs but doesn't say anything. She just gives me a look. One I can't quite decipher.

Maddox smirks, but I ignore the way he's looking at me.

"I was thinking we could go to the Santa Monica Pier today," Hannah suggests, changing the subject again before winking at me.

I nod, forcing a smile, but my stomach still feels unsettled. Hannah's words latch on to something inside me, something I don't want to examine too closely. But before I can dwell on it, Asher enters the kitchen, already dressed in a crisp button-down, checking his phone like the conversation in the room doesn't exist.

"I'll drive," he says absentmindedly. "I need to take a call on the way."

Maddox chuckles under his breath. "Of course you do."

I glance between them, but Asher doesn't seem to notice the jab. He just grabs his coffee and takes another call on his cell as he walks out of the room, already distracted.

Hannah leaves, presumably to get ready.

Maddox's gaze flicks to mine, and that smirk tugs at his

lips again. "You heard my mother," he murmurs. "You deserve better."

Heat flushes up my neck, and I push past him, rolling my eyes as I head upstairs to get ready.

————

The sun glows warm over the pier, casting long shadows across the boardwalk. The air is thick with the scent of sea salt, fried food, and sugar—funnel cakes, cotton candy, caramel corn. A rush of nostalgia washes over me. I haven't been here since I was a kid, and for a second, I let myself enjoy it. The chaos, the color, the buzzing crowd of people, the street performers, the flashing arcade games, the spinning neon rides... the sounds of laughter and crashing waves blending together into the perfect cacophony of summertime.

Hannah, Maddox, and Otto walk ahead, pointing at different food stands while Asher hangs back with me, already on another call. His fingers loosely lace with mine, and despite being in a romantic spot, this feels so *unromantic.*

I'm restless. Uneasy. Every time I look at Maddox, I feel something coiling tighter inside me. The shadow of last night lingers on my skin—the way he touched me, the way he made me fall apart. And the worst part?

I'm starting to crave him.

I don't want to care, don't want to acknowledge the ache of it. But I can't help it.

And maybe that's what scares me the most. Not the craving itself, but the lack of guilt.

I'm walking hand in hand with Asher, our fingers entwined, and all I can think about is another man's mouth on my body. His voice in my ear. His scent still lingering on my skin.

Shouldn't I feel sick with shame? Shouldn't I feel ruined by it?

Of course there's guilt. A low, constant hum beneath my ribs. But it's not for what I did; it's for what I let fade into complacency. Isn't that what Frankie said? That I was just with Asher because it was easy?

Two years, that's how long I've been with Asher. That's how long I've spent telling myself this is what stability looks like. That love means compromise. That I didn't need fireworks, just consistency.

But Maddox?

Maddox is a maelstrom of fire and electricity.

For the first time, I've been shown what's possible—and how it *should* feel when you're fully, sexually satisfied.

I've never gotten off without helping. I always have to use my hands, or a toy.

But that's twice now that Maddox has made me come all by himself.

The worst part—the part I'm still trying to make peace with—is that I feel more seen in five minutes with Maddox than I have in two years with the man I thought I'd eventually marry.

What does that say about me?

I thought I was building a future with Asher. I thought I knew the shape of what my life would hold. There were the soft edges of his routine. The predictability of his life, his ambition, his expectations. But now, I'm wondering if I've been shrinking quietly for months, tucking away pieces of myself just to keep things peaceful. Just to keep him from leaving.

I should walk away from Maddox. I should breathe, regroup, figure out what the hell I'm doing.

But all I want to do is go back to last night and let him ruin me again.

We stop near the entrance to the Ferris wheel, one of the pier's biggest attractions. A soft ocean breeze rolls in, cooler than the heat of the afternoon sun.

"Who's riding with who?" Otto asks, eyeing the winding line.

Hannah loops her arm through his. "We'll go together."

Maddox exhales through his nose, shoving his hands into his pockets. "I'll skip this one," he mutters, almost like an afterthought. His gaze flicks toward the towering Ferris wheel, and for the first time, I see something unreadable flicker across his expression.

"You don't like heights?" I ask, tilting my head.

His jaw hardens. "I like being in control of my surroundings."

The words are quiet, almost lost in the chatter of the boardwalk, but they land heavier than they should. Something tightens in my chest.

I glance at Asher, already anticipating that he'll be the one in the seat beside me. He hangs up his phone and grins down at me.

"You're with me," he says, his voice soft, smiling as he rests his hand on the small of my back.

I don't miss the way Maddox's jaw tics, and his eyes flick to where Asher's hand is on my back.

I nod at Asher and swallow, suddenly feeling guilty about... everything.

I'm not a cheater. I don't cross lines. I don't betray the people I love.

So why does my stomach twist with something dangerously close to regret?

Why does my skin still tingle where Maddox touched me? Why can I still feel the weight of his body on top of mine, his scent wrapping around me like a second skin?

I swallow hard, forcing myself to smile at Asher as he leads me toward the Ferris wheel. This is what I wanted, isn't it?

To be safe. *Secure*. With someone predictable.

But... why does it feel like something inside me is unraveling?

Asher's phone rings, and he gives me a small, regretful smile. A work call, then. He looks at the screen, grimaces, but for once, he doesn't immediately answer.

I barely notice, too lost in my thoughts, eyes tracking the slow turn of the Ferris wheel ahead. We're only a couple groups away from the front of the line now.

When the phone rings again—sharp, persistent—he curses under his breath. This time, he doesn't hesitate.

"I'm sorry, I have to take this," he says, already stepping away. "Go ahead and ride without me, okay? I'll meet you guys after."

I stiffen. "Wait, but—"

"Sorry, babe," he calls over his shoulder, phone pressed to his ear. "I won't be long."

And just like that, I'm left standing there, my chest aching.

A presence shifts beside me.

Maddox.

I don't have to look to know he's watching me.

"Guess that means you're with me, angel."

My stomach clenches.

Before I can argue, Hannah is already ushering us toward the line. "Go, go. It'll be fun!"

I glare at Maddox as we step forward, but he doesn't smirk this time. His usual easy arrogance is absent, replaced by something more controlled, more calculated. His shoulders are tense, his jaw locked tight.

Not fear, exactly. But something close.

As if he's forcing himself to do this.

As if being trapped in a small, swaying gondola, suspended high above the pier, is the last thing he wants.

But when he catches me watching him, his mask slips back into place. The smirk returns, slow and deliberate.

Like this was inevitable.

Like I'm the only thing keeping him from turning around.

A minute later, we climb into the small gondola, and the safety bar locks in place across our laps. The Ferris wheel lurches forward, slow and steady, lifting us high above the pier.

Maddox shifts beside me, and suddenly, I'm hyperaware of everything.

His scent hits me first: clean soap, leather, and something darker that curls low in my stomach. His arm brushes against mine, a seemingly accidental touch, but the heat of it is scorching. It spreads beneath my skin like wildfire, making every inch of me tense and overly aware.

I keep my eyes on the view, but all I can feel is him.

It's barely noticeable at first—a subtle tension in his shoulders, the way his hands flex against his thighs. But when we climb higher, the wheel rocking slightly with the wind, I feel it again. His chest rises and falls a little too fast, his knuckles paling against the metal bar.

The tightness in his posture.

The long, deep, steadying breaths.

Maddox Cross isn't afraid of anything.

But this? This unsettles him.

The view is breathtaking—the vast sprawl of the ocean, the golden sand stretching along the coast. But all I can feel is the heat of Maddox beside me.

I keep my gaze forward, arms crossed tight.

"You're mad," he muses, voice low, edged with amusement.

"I'm not mad."

"You are."

"I just—" I exhale sharply, hating how unsettled I feel. "It's not a big deal. I just... thought I was riding with Asher."

Maddox chuckles, deep and low, but there's something forced about it. "Thought you'd be safer with him, huh?"

My pulse jumps.

That's not it. Not even close.

The truth is, I wanted Asher to show up for me for once. I wanted the Ferris wheel, the sun, the stupid photos, and the lazy kisses at the top like something out of a cliché date. I wanted a memory with him.

I swallow hard, blinking out at the ocean as disappointment presses heavy on my chest.

But Maddox watches me like he already knows all of it. Like I'm transparent, easy to read. Like he knows it's not about safety at all—it's about me still clinging to the hope that Asher might finally make me feel like I come first.

The gondola sways slightly as the wheel stops to let passengers off below. Maddox's jaw tightens. His fingers grip the edge of his seat, just for a second, before he releases.

"You've been avoiding me all day," he says, tipping his head slightly, his blue eyes sharp, assessing. He's wearing a white t-shirt, black pants, and a black leather jacket that looks *way too fucking good* on him.

I stiffen.

Of course he noticed that I spent my morning on the beach with my Kindle. And any waking moment as far from him as possible.

"You think ignoring me is going to change anything?" he continues.

The gondola sways again, and I see it this time—the way his body goes rigid for half a second. The way he exhales slowly, like he's forcing himself to stay relaxed.

Maddox Cross, unshakable ex-Marine, doesn't just not like heights. He's *terrified*.

The realization catches me off guard, and I study him out of the corner of my eye.

I swallow. "I don't know what you're talking about."

Maddox smirks, but he doesn't push it. He just watches me, something knowing in his gaze.

A gust of wind rolls through, chilling my bare arms. I'd pulled on the new pair of jeans and a cropped t-shirt earlier because it was warm and sunny, but now that we're so high up, it's much colder. Plus, the fog is beginning to roll in.

I shiver before I can stop myself.

Maddox notices. Of course he does. Before I can react, he shrugs off his leather jacket.

"Here," he murmurs, leaning forward and draping it over my shoulders.

I freeze. "I don't need it," I say, but I don't move to take it off.

"I don't care," he murmurs, his voice a slow, dark promise. His fingers brush the collar, a deliberate, possessive touch. "Let me take care of you the way you deserve to be taken care of."

My breath catches. Maddox watches me, his fingers still lingering near the collar of the jacket, his blue eyes flicking over my face like he's memorizing every reaction. But when the wheel creaks and sways again, he shifts, rolling his jaw. He glances out at the open air around us before looking back at me.

Something shifts between us.

A pull. A weight.

And then my phone buzzes. I flinch, fumbling to pull it out of my pocket. A message from Frankie.

FRANKIE

Look at this!

(Linked article) Justice or Revenge?
Maddox Cross: The Man Behind the Most
Controversial Case of the Decade

I swallow hard, my fingers hovering over the screen as I glance at the headline of the article she just sent me. I quickly type out a reply. I'd kept her apprised of the situation—minus the midnight rendezvous—and we'd slowly been going through the hundreds of articles about Maddox. I'd found his wedding photo to Elaine and even her old LiveJournal page.

It felt like a violation, but somehow, I want to know more about her—and *him*.

Maddox notices the way my whole body tenses. And then he speaks, voice quiet, knowing. "You looked me up, didn't you?"

My head snaps up, and his eyes are on my phone. *Fuck.*

I swallow. "I—"

He smirks. "Did you find what you were looking for?"

My chest squeezes. I don't answer. Maddox tilts his head slightly, studying me. Then his smirk fades. Just a little.

He's been so sure the entire trip, and this is the first time I've seen anything that resembles vulnerability.

And... I don't hate it. The idea of him being scared of something—of having a hard past—softens everything between us, and I feel something akin to empathy bloom in my chest.

Or perhaps... affection.

What the hell?

"Lila was four," he says, voice lower now, rougher. "She was sick for months. They kept denying her treatment." A beat. A sharp exhale. "She died waiting for an answer."

I stare at him.

His jaw rolls. "Elaine couldn't live with it," he continues, quieter now. "Three weeks after we held our daughter for the last time, she put a bullet in her head."

My stomach lurches.

Oh my god. It's a hundred times worse hearing it from him.

For the first time, Maddox isn't teasing. For the first time, I see something raw in his expression—something heavier, something dangerous in an entirely different way.

A man who lost everything.

And maybe, just maybe, he's never stopped looking for something to make up for it.

The Ferris wheel jerks slightly as it slows, and Maddox shifts beside me, his knuckles tightening against the metal bar.

This whole ride...

He's been uncomfortable the entire time, hasn't he? But not once did he say a word about it. Not once did he let it show.

And suddenly, I remember—he wasn't even going to ride. He was going to sit it out entirely, being the odd man out.

But the second Asher stepped away and I was left standing there, alone, Maddox didn't hesitate. He stepped forward, wordless, taking the empty seat beside me without giving me a choice.

He'd rather face the lurching fear of the Ferris wheel than let me go up alone.

It hits me, sharp and soft all at once.

I swallow, my chest constricting as I glance at him—the tension in his jaw, the way his fingers are gripping the bar, the careful way he keeps his gaze locked ahead. I hadn't noticed it at first, not with the way he was teasing me, pushing me, watching me like he always does. But now? I see it.

The slight tremor in his fingers. The way his knuckles go taut when the gondola rocks slightly. The way his breath is a fraction slower, more measured, like he's forcing himself to stay calm.

I frown, shifting slightly in my seat. "Why did you come with me?" I ask softly, keeping my voice even.

Maddox doesn't look at me right away. His gaze stays fixed on the horizon, the ocean stretching out in an endless sprawl below us. For a second, I don't think he's going to answer. Then his throat bobs, and his fingers flex against his thigh.

"Would've been worse watching you go without me," he mutters, his voice rougher than usual.

My chest aches, and warmth floods through me, tangling with something else, something deeper. I shouldn't feel this way. Shouldn't let this affect me.

But it does.

Maddox swallows, finally shifting his gaze to mine. His blue eyes are sharp, assessing, but there's a rawness beneath the surface.

An unguarded expression, just for a second.

"Are you going to tell me I'm an idiot for that?" His voice dips lower. It's meant to be teasing, but I can hear the weight behind it.

I shake my head and try to swallow through the thickness in my throat. "No," I whisper. "I—"

I, what? I appreciate it? I feel something dangerously close to admiration for the man who should be my enemy? I don't know what to say, so I do the only thing I can.

I shift closer, closing the space between us just enough that our knees brush, that the heat of him seeps into my skin. Maddox's gaze drops to my lips, just for a second, before he exhales and looks away.

The ride slows as we near the bottom, but I don't move. Neither does he.

When the gondola finally comes to a full stop, he glances

at me again, something unreadable in his expression. Then he tips his chin toward the exit.

"Come on, angel," he murmurs. "Let's get you back on solid ground."

I haven't been on solid ground since we met, I think.

And even as I step out of the ride, even as I spot Asher waiting for me a few feet away, arms crossed, phone still in hand...

I don't take Maddox's jacket off.

I should. I know I should.

But I don't.

Phantom Temptation

Maddox

I KNOW SHE'S COMING OUTSIDE TO JOIN ME ON THE patio that night before she does. I can see her shadow hesitate in the hallway, and the slow inhale followed by a long pause telling me she's deliberating.

Like she's talking herself out of it before finally giving in.

I smirk as I take a slow drag from the joint between my fingers, letting the warm burn of smoke curl into my lungs. The door creaks open behind me, and I hear her soft footsteps behind me as she pads closer.

I don't turn around.

Instead, I exhale a long, lazy stream of smoke and wait. The hesitation is short-lived this time, because she speaks as soon as she joins me against the railing overlooking the ocean.

"Are you hiding from the rest of us? Or just waiting for the government drones disguised as seagulls to report back?"

Her voice is softer than I expected. Not accusing. Just observing. But that sharp little bite? I like it.

I huff a laugh, lifting the joint to my lips again, taking my time before responding. "Maybe I like the view. Maybe I like the quiet," I add, shaking my head. "And maybe the seagulls are onto something."

She makes a quiet sound, something like half-amusement, half-exasperation.

"Are you going to share?"

I grin at that, finally turning to face her. She's standing a few feet away, arms crossed, the moonlight casting silver shadows over her skin. My jacket still hangs off her shoulders. She hasn't given it back. And by the way it's draped over her, I suspect she has no plans to give it back anytime soon.

I spread my legs slightly as I extend the joint toward her. "That's twice this week. Didn't take you for a bad girl, angel."

She rolls her eyes but steps forward anyway, plucking it from my fingers. "I'm not."

I hum, watching as she brings it to her lips, the tip glowing orange in the dim light. Her throat moves as she inhales, and fuck, why does that make my dick twitch?

She exhales, her lips parted just enough to let the smoke curl out slowly. "But I don't think I have to be good all the time, either."

A slow, wicked grin pulls at my lips. "Oh yeah?"

She doesn't answer. Just takes another drag before handing it back to me.

I keep my eyes on her as I take it, letting my fingers brush hers. Her pulse jumps at the contact. I can see it flutter against her delicate neck.

I smirk. "So tell me something, Ari."

She leans against the porch railing, her gaze flicking toward the ocean. "What?"

"What do you want?"

She exhales sharply, a short laugh escaping her lips. "What do you mean?"

I take another slow drag, exhaling before tilting my head at her. "I mean, what do you actually want? Out of life. Out of yourself. Out of him."

I don't have to say Asher's name. We both know who I'm talking about.

Ari stills, her fingers tightening around the railing. "Those are loaded questions."

I chuckle. "I can handle it."

She exhales, her expression shifting, like she's debating whether or not to give me a real answer.

"I want peace."

The admission is so quiet, I almost miss it.

My smirk fades slightly. "Peace?"

She nods, her gaze still locked on the waves. "I want to wake up one day and not feel like the world is sitting on my chest. I want to stop thinking about everyone else before myself. I want to..." She hesitates, then shakes her head. "I don't know. I just don't want to be responsible for everything all the time."

I stare at her. And for a second, I see it—the exhaustion, the weight pressing against her, the years of being the strong one, the reliable one.

She continues. "My dad was strict. We weren't allowed frivolous things. I had to be a good example for my sisters. I went to college, got a master's degree right off the bat. I never had a chance to just... *breathe.* My mom's life revolves around my dad. Whatever he wants, she wants. She was never truly on our side, you know? She was a good mom, but she's not prone to thinking for herself. We're not that close." She exhales, shaking her head. "But the worst part? I don't even know who I'd be without all of it. If given time to be myself instead of who my father expected me to be... *who* would I be right now?"

I stay silent, watching her, letting her give me this piece of herself.

She lets out a humorless laugh. "It's like I was raised to be useful before I was ever allowed to just... exist. Forever the lieutenant's daughter."

The anger that stirs inside me is sharp, immediate.

"That's bullshit." My voice is rough, edged with something raw. "You're not just some tool for other people to use, Ari. Not your dad. Not Asher. Not anyone."

Her gaze flicks to mine, searching. I don't know what she's looking for, but I want her to find it. I want her to understand.

"You don't have to be strong all the time." I reach out, brushing my knuckles against her cheek. Softly. Slowly. "You don't have to carry everything alone."

She swallows hard, her breath shaky. "And who's going to carry it for me?"

I don't hesitate. "Me."

She blinks up at me for a second before scoffing, turning her face away. "Yeah, that's what they all say. Men are all the same."

I watch her for a few seconds—watch the way she builds that wall up so high she thinks I can't possibly climb it. "Your dad did a real number on you, didn't he?"

She tenses. "I don't want to talk about him anymore."

"Too bad." I shift closer, my voice dropping. "I bet he made you think you had to be perfect. That you couldn't ask for help. That love was something you earned by being useful."

Her breath catches, but she doesn't look at me. "You don't know anything about me."

"I know more than you think." I reach out, brushing a lock of hair from her face. She flinches, but she doesn't pull away. "And I know you're tired, angel. I can see it. You're exhausted down to your fucking bones."

Her lips part slightly, her throat working against a swallow. "I should be with Asher." Her voice is quiet, but there's something hollow in it. Like she's convincing herself. "He's stable. He's safe. That's what I was supposed to want."

I scoff, shaking my head. "How's that working out for you?"

Her jaw hardens. She turns away, but I don't let her. My fingers grip her chin, forcing her to meet my eyes.

"I don't know why you're doing this. You can't have me."

I smirk, leaning in so our noses almost brush. "Watch me."

Ari shakes her head, the struggle written all over her face. "I can't do this."

"Yeah, the fuck you can." My grip tightens slightly, not enough to hurt—just enough to make her feel it. Make her feel *me*. Make her *believe* me.

Her breath shudders. Her pupils are blown wide, lips parted. She's fighting herself, and we both know it.

"I'm dating your brother," she whispers, a final attempt at logic.

I let out a low, dark chuckle. "I don't fucking care."

She sways toward me. Her fingers twitch at her sides like she wants to grab me. Wants to pull me in.

My thumb drags along her jaw, my grip firm. Her pulse is a rapid beat against my fingers. She exhales shakily, her tongue darting out to wet her lips.

"You're impossible."

I tilt my head, my voice dipping lower. "I'm inevitable."

A heavy pause. The world goes quiet around us, the ocean roaring in the distance, but all I hear is her breath. All I feel is the warmth of her skin beneath my fingers, the heat radiating from her body, the magnetic fucking pull that's been drawing us closer from the moment I saw her.

I could kiss her right now. She knows it. I know it.

But then... she steps back.

She inhales sharply, blinking like she's waking up from a trance. "I should go inside."

I let my hand drop, smirking slightly. "Run while you still can, little warrior." I watch the way her breath catches, betraying her. Leaning in, I let my lips hover just above her ear, close enough that she can feel the heat of my breath. "But we both know you won't get far."

Her body is stiff, rigid with tension, but she doesn't move. I drag my knuckles down her arm slowly, reveling in the way she shudders at my touch. The air between us is thick, electric. She's waiting for me to make the next move, because in her mind, she's not pursuing me. She's the victim, and I'm the villain.

And fuck, whatever she needs to think to give in is fine with me.

"When you're ready to stop lying to yourself, you know where to find me." My voice is low, steady, laced with the kind of certainty that doesn't leave room for doubt. I brush my fingers over her jaw, the touch deceptively soft. "But I'm getting real fucking tired of watching you pretend you don't want this just as much as I do."

A muscle in her jaw tics, but she still doesn't pull away.

That's what I thought.

I tilt my head, studying her, letting the shroud of my words sink in. "So keep running, if that's what you need to do. But don't kid yourself." I grip her tighter, just enough to make sure she's listening. "Because when you finally give in?" My voice dips into something dark and possessive. "I'll be right here. Waiting."

She glares at me, but there's no real venom in it. Just frustration. And heat.

Without another word, she turns and walks inside.

I take another slow drag from the joint, watching her disappear through the doorway, and I can't help the grin that pulls at my lips.

She's unraveling. And I can't wait to watch it happen, because as soon as she does...

She's mine.

Wholly.

Completely.

Forever.

No Escaping the Phantom

Ari

Maddox doesn't come into my room again, which is fine.

It's fine.

I fall asleep quickly, and when I wake up, the morning light filters softly through the curtains. For a second, I expect to feel something different. A hand gripping my thigh. A voice murmuring in my ear. A body too solid, too familiar, too Maddox.

But when I blink up at my surroundings, my stomach knots.

Because it's not Maddox sitting at the edge of my bed.

It's Asher.

He smiles down at me, his blond hair still damp from a shower, already dressed in khaki shorts and a fitted polo. Crisp. Put together. Safe.

A deep ache settles in my chest.

"I thought we could take a walk?" he asks, his voice soft and careful. Like maybe he's making an effort.

I nod, checking my phone. It's just past eight. He waits for me downstairs and I quickly get dressed in white linen shorts and a black tank top before brushing my teeth. I walk downstairs into an empty house, and Asher is leaning against the front door waiting for me. Grabbing an oversized sweater and stepping into my sandals, I follow him out the door and down the narrow pathway to the beach.

The sand is still cool beneath my feet, the early morning breeze lifting my hair as we walk along the quiet shoreline. My sandals are slung in one hand, and my other hand is tucked into my sweater to keep warm.

It's beautiful out here. The fog is starting to lift, and the blue sky pokes through the light gray mist, warming my skin whenever it shifts enough to let the sun through. There's almost no one on the beach, and it's so tranquil. It should feel nice. But something sits heavy between us.

Asher is quiet at first, his hands stuffed into his pockets, his gaze flicking toward me like he's searching for the right words.

Finally, he exhales sharply. "I've been thinking about us."

I glance at him, my pulse jumping. "Yeah?"

He nods, his jaw tight. "I know I've been distracted lately. Work has been... a lot."

I say nothing.

"I don't mean to neglect you, Ari," he continues, his voice measured. "It's just... this data breach is screwing with my head. And I know I don't always give you the attention you deserve."

The words should make me feel something. Hope. Relief. Maybe even gratitude. Instead, a strange, familiar numbness settles inside me. It's not the first time he's said something like this. In fact, it's sort of a pattern—pulling me closer, promising to do better, to stay the night and act more like a committed partner—before work gets in the way again.

Before he pulls away again.

I nod, waiting. He pauses, kicking at the sand. Then, a small, almost bitter laugh.

"I guess I just assumed you understood." He looks at me then, his brow furrowing. "You've always been independent. Strong. You don't need me hovering over you all the time, right?"

A sharp pang twists through my stomach. "I don't need you. But that doesn't mean I don't want to be wanted. Not just when it's convenient. Not just when it's *easy*." I swallow, unsure of how to say what I'm really thinking. "I guess I'm just wondering where this is headed."

Something flickers in his expression, but I don't know if it's guilt or frustration. "Yeah. I've been wondering the same thing."

"So, what are you saying?" I ask, my voice careful. My heart pounds, my fingers tightening around the sleeves of my sweater.

Asher exhales, running a hand through his hair. "I'm saying that I want to be better, Ari. I do. But my job is—" A pause. A helpless shrug. "It's always going to come first. I hope you understand."

A dull, resounding thud echoes in my chest. There it is. Honest. Blunt. *Final.* The classic nail in the coffin.

I don't know why I'm surprised.

It's always like this, isn't it? My dad was the same way—work first, family second. I grew up watching my mom shrink herself into the background, molding her wants and needs around his schedule, his priorities. And me? I was trained early. The eldest daughter, the responsible one, the fixer. I learned that love wasn't something freely given, it was earned. Fought for. Pursued.

And I'm so fucking tired of chasing it. I'm so *fucking* tired of pretending that's okay.

I look away, staring out at the waves, swallowing past the

lump forming in my throat. "I don't think that's fair to me," I murmur, my voice barely audible over the crashing surf.

He stiffens. "What do you mean?"

I inhale slowly, steadying myself. *I deserve better.* And I don't mean Maddox. I don't. This isn't about him. This is about *me*. About the fact that I've spent two years molding myself into the perfect, easygoing, supportive girlfriend. About the fact that I never ask for too much. That I never demand more than what he's willing to give.

Because somewhere deep down, I knew. I knew he would never choose me.

So I made sure he never had to.

The realization makes my stomach twist, but Asher doesn't look upset.

I let out a shaky breath and meet his eyes, finally. "I guess I always just hoped you'd wake up one day and decide I was enough to come first."

He just nods, like I'm confirming something he's always suspected. Something that, deep down, he already knew, too.

"I never wanted to hold you back," he says after a moment.

I let out a small, bitter laugh. "No. You just wanted to keep me waiting on the sidelines."

His lips press into a thin line. "That's not true."

I lift a brow. "Isn't it? I think we both know where this is headed," I say softly. "We're just too afraid to say it out loud."

He nods. "Yeah. I suppose you're right. So... what? This is it?"

I swallow hard, then nod. "Yeah. This is it. I'm done trying to fit into a life that was never going to make space for me, Asher."

He looks at me warily, as if he's trying to decide if I'm angry. So I reach out for his hand, trying to show him that I'm not mad.

I'm just *done*.

My fingers curl around his, gentle and steady. "No hard feelings," I say, offering a faint, sad smile. "I just can't do this anymore."

Before I can say anything else, his phone buzzes. He glances at it, then sighs, pulling his hand from mine.

"I have to take this," he mutters. "We'll talk more later, okay?"

I don't answer. Because we won't.

As he steps away, phone pressed to his ear, I wrap my arms around myself. The ocean stretches endlessly before me, waves lapping at the shore.

———

Hannah suggests we go out to eat at one of the restaurants along the cliffside for dinner. I presume Asher hasn't told his family about us breaking up yet, because no one says anything. And after tucking myself away on the beach all morning and afternoon, it feels good to shower and get dressed.

The car ride is short, just a five-minute drive along the coast.

And the restaurant is stunning—floor-to-ceiling windows overlooking the ocean, candlelit tables draped in crisp linen, the low murmur of conversation weaving through the clinking of wineglasses and silverware.

I should feel happy to be here. Instead, all I feel is off-kilter. Because Asher isn't different. He's never going to be different. And as I look at him, clean-shaven and proper, I know he's not what I want anymore.

Across the table, Maddox is watching me. I catch the slight tilt of his head as I sit down, eyeing the dress *he* picked out for me days ago—a dark red cotton dress with thin straps and a square neckline.

And when Asher's phone buzzes for the third time during dinner, I don't even flinch. I just lift my wineglass, holding Maddox's gaze as I take a slow, deliberate sip.

Because if Asher wants to be distracted? Then maybe I do, too.

Maddox is cleaned up. *Too* cleaned up. It's fucking unfair. I'm used to him in black hoodies and tattoos, used to the way he carries himself like a predator in waiting.

But tonight?

Tonight, he's in a crisp black button-down with the sleeves rolled up to his forearms, showcasing his ink. The top button is undone, the open collar exposing a sliver of golden skin and the sharp ridges of his collarbones. His hair, usually an unruly mess, is brushed back in a way that makes him look almost respectable.

Almost.

But his eyes still give him away.

They burn under the dim lights, a searing, unrelenting blue that pins me in place every time I make the mistake of looking at him—which is often.

Because, fuck me, I can't stop looking. It feels ironic to be sitting here next to Asher, who was my boyfriend until about eight hours ago, eating a sixty-five-dollar steak, in a dress Maddox chose.

His smirk tells me he knows it, too.

God, I *hate* him.

I'm too distracted to enjoy dinner. Asher is to my left, half absorbed by his work, nodding at something Otto is saying. Hannah is talking about a winery she and Otto visited last year. The conversation is perfectly polite.

Perfectly safe.

And across from me?

Maddox.

Silent. Watching me.

I refuse to look at him, keeping my focus on my wineglass. The deep red swirls in the light as I turn it between my fingers, trying to ignore the heat licking at my skin.

It's fine. *It's all fine.*

Until Asher's phone vibrates on the table again.

He sighs, glancing at the screen. Then at me. Already apologizing before he even says a word.

"I have to take this."

Of course he does.

"Go ahead," I murmur, taking another sip of my wine.

He leans in to kiss my temple. I flinch before I can stop myself. His eyes widen, confused, but I say nothing. I don't need to. He gives me a pleading look, and I realize he's expecting me to play along.

Expecting me to continue to pretend to be his girlfriend, despite ending our relationship on the beach earlier today.

All for show.

His lips press together into a thin smile, and then he slips out onto the patio to take the call.

Otto and Hannah are recounting their time in Italy two years ago, completely unaware of what transpired, but I'm hardly paying attention.

My skin is burning, and I can feel Maddox looking at me.

I last all of ten seconds before I finally glance his way.

Maddox leans back in his chair, elbow propped on the armrest, his fingers resting against his jaw. He doesn't speak; doesn't need to.

That smirk? The one playing at the corner of his lips? It says everything.

My grip squeezes around my wineglass. "What?"

He tilts his head, studying me. "Just wondering how long you're going to let him treat you like an afterthought," he whispers.

A sharp pang lodges in my ribs. And immediately, the memory from this morning hits me like a wave.

I see the shoreline again—the soft fog lifting, the bitter realization curling in my chest as Asher told me, plain as day, that work would always come first. The gravity of those words still presses down on me now, heavy and relentless.

I should say something. Anything. But what would I even say? That I knew it was true? That I've known it for a while? That I'm still here anyway?

I hate the way my stomach clenches. The way my thighs press together under the table like my body is betraying me—not because of his words alone, but because Maddox sees it. He sees all of it.

Not just that Asher forgets me. But that I've let him.

His voice dips lower, just for me, just like on the Ferris wheel. "Careful, Ari. If you keep looking at me like that, I'm going to start thinking you want me to ruin you right here in this restaurant."

And the worst part? I do.

The heat in my belly spreads like wildfire, licking up my spine, knotting in my throat. I should be used to his taunts by now, the slow, deliberate way he strips me down with nothing but words. But I'm not. I never am.

My fingers tighten further around the wineglass. I force myself to look away, to focus on something—*anything*—other than the man across from me and the way my pulse trips over itself every time he speaks.

I need a second. A breath. Some space.

I push my chair back, grabbing my clutch. "I'm going to the restroom."

Maddox doesn't say a word. But when I glance at him, his smirk is lazy, like he already knows something I don't. Like he's letting me go just to see what I'll do next.

Bastard.

I make my way toward the bathroom, head high, spine straight, like I have everything under control. But the second I step inside, my grip locks on the edge of the sink, my breath coming too fast.

I shouldn't feel like this. Not here. Not now. Not because of him.

My reflection stares back at me—flushed skin, wide, wild eyes, lips parted.

I look shattered. And it's not from the wine.

My phone buzzes.

> (858) 667-9960
>
> Are we playing a little game of cat and mouse?
>
> Because I think we've established that I'll always catch you.

A sharp exhale leaves my lips. My fingers hover over the keyboard. I shouldn't respond. I *shouldn't*.

But my fingers move before my brain catches up.

> You're all talk. Let's see if you can walk the walk, big guy.

I hit send before I can think better of it.

A pause. A beat of silence where the only thing I hear is my own pulsing heartbeat in my ears and the clinking of porcelain from the restaurant.

Then—

> (858) 667-9960
>
> Game on, angel.

My fingers tremble over the screen. I didn't expect him to hesitate, but it does something funny to my insides. I appreciate him checking in, but it somehow makes it feel more real. Less of a fantasy.

Am I sure?

Asher's out there, working. Distracted. Prioritizing every-thing but me. *Like always.* For two years, I've been patient. I've been understanding. I've been *good.* And for what? A man who will always put me second? A relationship that felt more like an expectation than a choice?

Besides, we broke up this morning. Or, at least we *mostly* broke up. He's been too busy to really talk it over since this morning.

Maddox is none of those things. He's chaos. Uncertainty. Hunger. But he's here. *Seeing me.* Wanting me with a ferocity that terrifies and thrills me all at once.

And for once—*just once*—I want to take something for myself.

I'm waiting.

I don't even get a response.

Fifteen seconds later, the bathroom door crashes open.

MARKED BY THE PHANTOM

ARI

I CLOSE MY EYES, BREATHING THROUGH MY NOSE TO calm my racing heart. Before I open them, before I see him in the reflection, I feel him.

A slow pulse of heat at my back. *Maddox.* My spine locks up, my breath freezing in my chest. I snap my eyes open, meeting his gaze in the mirror—dark, unreadable, burning with something I can't name. His neck, covered in tattoos. Black button-up giving him the appearance of a gentleman.

But I know better.

He doesn't say a word, just closes the door behind him and locks it.

When he's done, he takes a step closer.

"Answer me one thing," I say quickly, glaring at him in the mirror.

His eyebrows shoot up, and he looks at me with amusement. "I'll try my best."

"It was you," I say simply. "The notes in my house. You wrote them."

He tilts his head as he walks closer. "It was, and I did."

"But we hadn't met," I say slowly, watching his reflection

as he comes up behind me. "Did you know I was dating Asher?"

He smirks, and when his hands settle on my hips, my breath comes out in short pants.

"I knew. I've known for a long time."

"How'd you get past my security system?"

"That's more than one question, Ari."

"Tell me," I breathe. My skin is *on fire.*

"I disabled your security system in less than a minute. Is that what you want to hear? Once you're back in that house, I'll be ensuring you have a more robust system set up."

I.

Can't.

Breathe.

"Now I have a question for you, angel." Goosebumps erupt along my bare arms. "Why did you resist it for so long?"

I swallow, gripping the counter so tight my knuckles ache. "I didn't—"

"You did." His lips twitch, like he's amused by the lie.

The tenor of his voice is low, dark, edged with something sinful. He moves again, stepping closer so that he's caging me against the sink, his warm body pressed up against my back.

"I don't know," I whisper, my voice too breathy, too affected.

He lifts a brow, tilting his head. "Are you done lying yet?"

I should tell him to fuck off. But all I can think to do is stare into the mirror, watching him watch me. My reflection looks different. I see myself through his eyes. I see the way he's looking at me.

Like he already owns me.

Like I've been his from the moment he first came to my house.

He works a finger up my side, trailing my bare forearm. A shudder racks through me.

He notices, and his smirk sharpens. "If this isn't what you want, tell me to leave."

My pulse hammers, and the words catch in my throat. I *can't*. His finger drags slowly back down my arm, calloused skin against smooth, bare skin, heat licking at my stomach.

"Tell me to stop," he murmurs.

I swallow hard, my lips parting, but nothing comes out. A dark chuckle rumbles in his chest.

"That's what I thought."

Then his hands grip my hips again, and he twists me around.

Pinning me against the vanity, he steps into my space and presses his body against mine. He's warm, and that familiar, intoxicating smell hits my nostrils. Leather and some kind of expensive cologne.

"Wait," I whisper, putting a hand against his chest.

To my surprise, he inches back, giving me space. A crease forms between his brows as he looks down at me. His presence crackles with something raw and unrelenting, an energy that demands attention without a single word. His light blue eyes, so much like Asher's, should make me feel safe. Instead, they unsettle me. They strip me bare, exposing thoughts I haven't even fully admitted to myself. My pulse stutters, a mix of nerves and something far more dangerous threading through me.

"Did you kill him?" I ask, my voice raspy. "Did you murder that insurance guy to avenge your wife and daughter?"

He chuckles, and the sound sends a flash of hot energy through me. "Yes. I killed him." I can hear the pulse rushing through my veins, but before I can react fully, Maddox takes a step back. "Does that scare you?"

His question and the way he seems to know to give me space catches me off guard. I expected him to take what he wanted from me, but instead, he seems unsure of what my answer will be.

"No," I say quickly. "But... why me? Is it just because I remind you of your late wife?"

Maddox's gaze is steady, unwavering, as if he's deciding just how much truth to give me. He studies me for a beat longer, then exhales, shaking his head like he's amused at himself.

"Not really. You have the same fight as her, but you're different than she was. Do you want to know the truth?" I nod, and he swallows, like the truth will cause him pain. "When my mom sent me a picture of you, I couldn't stop looking," he finally says, his voice low, rough around the edges. "I kept staring, wondering what you'd be like—how you'd move, how you'd speak. There was something in your eyes, something strong. But the picture didn't do you justice. It never could."

He steps closer, not touching me, but close enough that I feel the warmth radiating from him, feel the thrum of his presence pressing into me like a force I don't know if I want to resist.

"I've always been drawn to strong things," he continues, his voice quieter now, almost thoughtful. "Not just anything with power, but things that endure. Things that have been broken and still piece themselves back together." His lips curve into something that's not quite a smile, something more like understanding. "Things like me."

A shiver runs through me, but I don't step away. I can't.

His gaze flickers over my face, lingering like he's memorizing me. "And you... you're stronger than you realize," he murmurs. "Maybe that's why I couldn't look away. Maybe that's why I already know I won't be able to stop."

His jaw tenses, and something unreadable flashes in his eyes. "Because I can feel it already—the pull, the need. And it has nothing to do with the way you look, though I must admit, you're even more beautiful in person." His voice drops even lower, almost a whisper. "It's you. And I think I've been looking for something like you for a long time."

His words catch me completely off guard, and before I realize what I'm doing, my fingers curl around the back of his neck, pulling his lips down to mine. He doesn't hesitate. His mouth claims mine in a kiss that's deep and consuming, stealing my breath, unraveling me with every flick of his tongue. He tastes like something dark, something forbidden, something I know I shouldn't crave—but I do.

Maddox growls against my lips, his hands sliding down my waist, gripping my hips like he's anchoring himself to me. His fingers press into the fabric of my dress, bunching it up, dragging it higher. I barely have time to register what's happening before he lifts me onto the vanity, stepping between my legs, his body flush against mine.

"Ari," he groans against my skin. Soft. *Pleading.*

I tilt my head back as his lips trail down my throat, his hands spreading my thighs wider, his grip firm, commanding. Heat pools low in my stomach, and when his fingers skim up my inner thigh, teasing, testing, I gasp, my nails biting into his shoulders.

A low, satisfied hum rumbles from his chest. "If I wasn't mistaken, I'd say the fact that I killed someone arouses you. Because your cunt is weeping for me, little warrior."

"Shut up and fuck me," I hiss, rolling my hips against his hand.

He chuckles, moving my underwear to the side. He works me like he's done this a thousand times before, like he already knows how to pull me apart, how to push me right up to the edge. Every touch, every press of his body against mine, is deliberate, dominating. The sound of his belt coming undone echoes through the small bathroom, and I gasp as the thick head of his cock presses against my entrance, stretching me just enough to send a shudder rolling through my body. Then, my mouth drops open in a silent scream as he thrusts into me with one hard push—deep, unrelenting, filling me completely.

"Oh, *fuck*," I whimper, my hands gripping the edge of the vanity for dear life. My nails dig into the cool marble, desperate for something to hold on to, something to anchor me against the sheer force of him.

"I knew you could take me," he mutters, his voice reverent, almost disbelieving. His fingers flex against my hips, possessive, grounding himself, like he needs something to hold on to before he loses himself completely. His breath stutters, a low, hoarse groan rasping against my ear. "You feel so much better than I imagined."

A spark licks up my spine, pooling low in my belly. I've never been this full, this *taken*. There's no hesitancy in his movements, no uncertainty—he fucks me like he's done this a million times before, like my body was made for this, made for him.

Asher never touched me like this. Never *moved* like this.

Maddox doesn't just take—he claims.

His hands slide up my waist, spreading me open wider, angling my hips just right. And then, with a deep, punishing thrust, he presses into something devastatingly perfect inside me—so deep, so precise, so fucking good that a strangled moan tears from my throat.

A sharp inhale. A satisfied chuckle against my neck.

"There it is," he murmurs, voice dark, smooth, laced with something lethal. "That's what I wanted to hear."

My thighs tremble as I brace myself against the vanity, trying to hold myself up as the pleasure rips through me, fast and all-consuming. His strokes are deep, deliberate, dragging over every sensitive part of me with unbearable precision.

"Fuck, you're squeezing me so tight," he groans, his forehead dropping briefly to my shoulder. Like it's too much. Like he's barely holding himself together.

Then, he pulls out slowly, letting me feel every inch of him, making me *ache* with the loss before driving back in hard and deep, forcing me farther back on the vanity. The impact sends a sharp, bright jolt of pleasure straight to my core.

My breath shatters. "Maddox—"

"I know," he growls, fucking into me again, harder this time, his hands tightening around my waist. "I fucking *know*, angel."

I gasp as his fingers slide down between my thighs, finding my clit without hesitation. He doesn't fumble. Doesn't second-guess. Just circles it with ruthless precision, his movements confident, controlled, like he already knows exactly what I need.

And that's what's different.

Maddox doesn't just fuck me, he *reads* me. Learns me. Pulls me apart piece by piece like he's always known my body better than I do.

Asher has a big dick, sure. But he used it like a fucking accessory. Like he expected *that* to do all the work.

Maddox, though? Maddox *wields* it.

He watches me like a man hunting weakness, like he won't stop until I come undone completely. Until he ruins me for anyone else.

"Twenty years," he rasps against my neck, his voice strained, almost pained.

His thrusts grow sharper, more urgent, his control fraying at the edges. I can feel it—the way he's unraveling, the way his body trembles, the way his fingers dig into my skin just a little harder.

But I don't want him to hold back. I want to feel all of it.

"It's been twenty fucking years."

Something raw and desperate breaks in his tone, and the

weight of those words hits me like a force. He's been starved for this. For touch. For warmth. For something real. And now he's here, inside me, and it's undoing him from the inside out.

Then—a knock at the door.

I freeze, my entire body going rigid beneath him. Maddox doesn't stop.

"What if it's Asher?" I whisper, panic threading through my voice. But before I can even think of pulling away, Maddox's free hand is on my mouth, silencing me.

His lips brush my ear, his voice low and sinful. "Then I dare you to make a sound while he's right outside this door."

I shake my head, pleading with my eyes, but he just smirks, slow and knowing. He wants this, wants to see how far I'll go, how much I'll take. And the worst part? So do I.

Outside, Asher's voice is muffled, confirming my worst fears. "Ari? You in there?"

Maddox presses deeper, his other hand gripping my hip, holding me in place. I try to hold back the desperate moan threatening to escape, my nails digging into his shoulders.

"Don't make a sound," he warns, voice like a blade against my skin. "Let him stand there, clueless, while I ruin you."

I whimper against his palm, my body shuddering around him. He knows I'm close. He can feel it.

His hand slides from my mouth to my throat, a gentle squeeze, grounding me as he whispers, "I know what you need. I know how to give you everything you've ever wanted. And I bet my brother never fucked you like this."

My head falls back against the mirror, my lips parting under his grip, and he feels it—the exact moment I give up the fight.

I nod, surrendering, giving myself over to him completely.

"I'm sorry for taking the call, Ari." Asher exhales sharply outside the door. "Let me know when you're done in there."

Maddox chuckles darkly, never stopping. "That's right,

sweetheart. Let him walk away without knowing how completely mine you are right now."

"There's nowhere else I'd rather be," I tell him truthfully.

Because *fuck*, I've never had sex like this.

His rhythm falters for a split second, like he's struggling to keep himself together. Like he's never felt anything like this before.

His teeth graze my shoulder, sending a shudder dancing along my nerves. A shaky exhale escapes him, his body pressing deeper, harder, his control slipping.

His fingers never stop circling my clit, and when he presses down harder, I feel my climax draw up closer and closer and *closer* with every movement. It's like he's somehow able to draw the pleasure out of me like a fucking vacuum.

"I can't—" His grip tightens, his hips stuttering, like he's barely holding on. "I'm not going to last..."

He thrusts again, rougher this time, and his groan is guttural, almost tortured. "Fuck. You feel..." He trails off, like words aren't enough, like nothing could ever capture what this moment means to him.

I clench around him, pleasure twisting inside me like a live wire. My body is on fire, burning from the inside out, but I need *more*. Need him to push me over the edge.

He feels *so* good—too good. Deep, thick, perfect, dragging against every sensitive part of me with a precision that makes my head spin. And his fingers against my clit... the obscene sounds of wet skin meeting wet skin fill the air, mingling with my gasping breaths, and his ragged groans...

Fuck.

His thrusts slow, but they don't lose their intensity. Each one lands deep, sharp, hitting *that* spot inside me that sends a hot shock wave through my core. I whimper, my thighs shaking, my fingers gripping the vanity so tightly my knuckles go white.

Maddox notices. Of course he does.

A dark, satisfied chuckle rumbles against my shoulder. "That's it," he murmurs. "Take it, angel."

I bite my lip, trying to hold back a scream. It's too much. It's not enough. My body is *begging* for more.

Maddox exhales sharply, his hand on my clit slowing down deliberately, like he has all the time in the world, like he's savoring every reaction.

A broken moan rips from my throat, my head falling against his shoulder.

He groans. "Fuck, I *love* that sound."

His touch is merciless, slow but devastating, sending sparks of pleasure through my veins. He knows exactly what he's doing. Exactly what I need. His fingers match the rhythm of his thrusts, teasing, coaxing, unraveling me one perfect movement at a time.

I arch against him, rolling my hips, chasing it.

"Good girl," he rasps, but there's something rougher underneath it. Darker. His voice so broken, so raw with need it makes my stomach clench and my thighs tremble. "I knew you'd be perfect for me."

A desperate sound slips from my lips as pleasure coils, sharp and unbearable, knotting tight inside me.

"That's it," Maddox murmurs, almost cruel with how soft he says it. His hand then delivers a sharp, deliberate slap against my clit.

I jolt, a strangled sob escaping me as the sudden sting blooms into molten pleasure.

I'm gone.

Completely undone.

"There you go," he snarls, dragging the words along my skin like a promise. "Let go for me. Give it all to me."

His hand flexes around my throat, not tight, but enough to make sure I stay exactly where he wants me. The weight of it grounds me, pins me, but it's the desperation in his voice that shatters me wide open.

"I need you to come with me," he growls, the words low, rough, barely restrained. "I need to feel you fall apart first."

And I do.

Pleasure crashes over me like a tidal wave, brutal and all-consuming, stealing the breath from my lungs. My thighs snap tight around his hips, locking him to me as my entire body bows beneath the force of it. My back arches, a helpless, uncontrolled reaction as molten heat explodes from deep inside me and ripples outward in relentless, shattering waves.

My walls flutter around him, gripping him like a vise, pulling him deeper, demanding more. A sob catches in my throat as sparks race skitter across my skin, my vision going hazy, my thoughts slipping completely out of reach. My nails carve into his shoulders like they're the only thing tethering me to reality.

And that's when he breaks.

Maddox growls, a frayed, almost tortured sound, and then he's rutting into me harder, chasing the inevitable. His body trembles above me, locked, desperate. His cock throbs deep inside me as he loses it, pulsing, emptying himself until I swear I can feel every last drop.

A deep, fractured sound tears from his chest as he comes —twenty years of hunger and need crashing down all at once. His grip is relentless, fingers bruising, holding me like if he lets go, I might vanish.

"You're mine," he hisses, cracked and reverent, every syllable seeping into my bones. "My perfect little angel. That's my girl."

I can barely breathe, barely think as he presses his forehead against mine, panting hard against my lips. His praise, his possession, his desperation—they're the only things anchoring me through the aftershocks.

And I fucking love it.

When it's over, when he finally stills, his breath ragged and his body trembling against mine, he doesn't pull away. He just stays there, inside me, his face buried in the crook of my neck, his arms wrapped around me as if letting go isn't an option.

And maybe it isn't.

"Fuck," I whisper, feeling his cum leak out of me. "You're lucky I'm on the pill, asshole."

Maddox smirks, his fingers gripping my hips possessively as he pulls out and watches his release spill from me. His thumb drags through the mess between my thighs, pushing it back inside with slow, deliberate pressure.

"Lucky?" he murmurs darkly, his gaze burning into mine. "I don't think so. If I had my way, you wouldn't be on the pill at all." He leans in, his breath hot against my ear as his fingers press deeper, making sure none of it goes to waste. "I'd fill you up again and again until you were dripping with me. Until your body knew who it belonged to."

A shiver rolls through me, and he chuckles, low and knowing. "And the best part?" He brushes his lips against my jaw, his voice like sin. "You'd let me."

Fuck him. I push him away from me as I hop onto my feet. He tucks himself away with ease, and just as I reach for some toilet paper to clean myself up, his hand tightens around my wrist, firm but unhurried.

"Don't." His voice is low, commanding, laced with something dark and possessive.

I scowl, tugging against his hold, but he doesn't let go. "Don't what, Maddox?"

His smirk is slow, deliberate. "Don't wipe it away. I want my cum dripping down your thighs when you're sitting next to Asher at our family dinner."

Heat coils in my stomach, my pulse stuttering. "You're unhinged."

Maddox tilts his head, eyes flicking between my parted lips and the mess still dripping between my thighs. "Maybe," he murmurs, his thumb dragging lazy circles over my pulse point. "Or maybe I just want you to remember exactly who you belong to."

I let out a shaky breath, and his smirk deepens.

"Every step you take back to that table, every shift of your thighs, you'll feel me." He leans in, his breath warm against my ear. "And later, when you're pretending like nothing happened, I want you to know, *this* is still mine."

Holy fuck.

His fingers move down under my dress, pressing against my core, slow, possessive. "And the next time you try to forget?" His voice dips into a gravelly whisper. "I'll just have to remind you all over again."

A shiver rolls through me, traitorous and undeniable.

I yank myself free, my heart pounding as I glare at him. "You're a fucking bastard."

Maddox just grins, lazy and satisfied, stepping back as he tucks himself away. "And yet, you let me ruin you anyway."

"Fuck you."

He laughs. "You already did, little warrior."

Before I can get another word in, he turns around, unlocks the door, and leaves me standing there with flushed cheeks and his cum still dripping down my thighs.

My breath comes in sharp, uneven bursts.

What have I done?

And the worst part is... I don't regret it.

Not even a little.

PHANTOM IN HER VEINS

MADDOX

I CAN'T EVER WALK AWAY.

I've known it for a while now, but sitting here at this pristine, candlelit table, watching Asher glance between Ari's empty seat and me, the truth settles deeper, taking root in a way that gives me a sense of pride.

This was never going to be temporary, and I think a very large part of me always suspected that.

Asher thinks he knows her. He thinks he's got her all figured out, all wrapped up in the polished, predictable life he's created for himself. But Asher doesn't see her, not the way I do. Not the way I have from the start.

He doesn't see the fire simmering beneath the surface, the way she hides behind forced smiles and careful restraint. He doesn't see the woman she really is—the one who just let me take her against the sink, who clenched around my cock with a helpless little whimper, who let me fill her up so completely that I know she's still feeling me now and probably will for days.

The one who probably likes the idea of my bruised fingerprints on her hips.

The one who likes it *rough* and wants someone who won't treat her like a goddamn gentleman.

The wine in my glass tilts as I swirl it, pretending to give a damn about my dad's commentary on the seafood. I don't care. I'm waiting.

The soft click of heels against tile makes my breath slow, makes my grip tighten around the delicate stem of my glass.

My eyes flick up to Ari as she slides into her seat across from me, her expression perfectly composed, her movements effortless. But I know better.

I see it—I see *her*.

The too controlled breath, the flush still lingering on her throat, the way her fingers grip the napkin just a little too tightly as she places it in her lap.

She feels me all over her just like I feel her all over me.

Every step she took from that bathroom to this table, every movement, every shift of her thighs—she feels me. My cum inside her, slick and warm and undeniable.

A ghost of me still owning her.

Heat curls in my balls, low and insistent, my cock twitching beneath the table as I imagine her squirming, trying not to give herself away. Trying to act like she's not dripping for me right now, in the middle of this fancy fucking restaurant, next to the man she's supposed to belong to.

Asher looks over at her, probably wondering what took her so long in the bathroom. "You okay?"

Ari stiffens. I smirk as I watch her hesitate, searching for words, something neutral, something safe. Instead, she downs the entire glass in one go.

"Fine."

I chuckle into my wine.

Asher blinks. "Uh. Are you sure?"

Ari clears her throat, setting the glass down with a clink. "Just thirsty."

I stretch my legs out under the table, letting my knee brush against hers. Subtle. Possessive. She inhales sharply, but she doesn't pull away.

She grips her fork instead, knuckles white. I take a slow sip of wine, watching her over the rim. She's unraveling, piece by piece, right here at this table, in front of all of them. And no one but me can see it.

That's the best part about all of this.

Asher carries on, oblivious, talking about some client, something mundane, something that doesn't fucking matter. I don't care. I barely hear him.

Her fork scrapes against the plate when I shift, slow and deliberate, making sure she feels me. The way she grips the edge of the table tightly with her other hand, like she needs something—anything—to hold on to.

I lean back in my chair, casual, stretching my arms behind my head. I could say something. I could ruin her right now, right in front of everyone.

I could murmur something just for her.

Something about how well she took me.

Something about how I'm still inside her.

Instead, I settle for this—this slow, quiet destruction.

She exhales, shaky and uneven. And I can't help but smile.

She knows it. I'm not just under her skin now, or something she can excuse away as a bad dream or harmless flirting.

I've burrowed deep, carved myself into her bones, left a mark no man will ever erase.

And now, with every step, every breath, every slow, aching shift of her thighs, she feels it.

Feels *me*.

A reminder that she's already been claimed in the most unforgiving way.

Phantom Reminders

Ari

I wake the next morning with my skin burning. Everything feels used and bruised, but in the best way. When I think back to what Maddox and I did, my whole body thrums with the remnants of last night. The memory of his hands, his mouth, his *claim*, lingers in my bones.

I shift under the covers and feel it. The tenderness between my thighs. The soreness he left behind like a brand. I squeeze my legs together and my breath catches at the sensitivity, at the undeniable reminder of what we did. How is it that I'm already ready for more?

I should feel guilty, but I don't.

I stretch lazily, exhaling slowly, my body still tingling from the aftershocks of him. When I'm done, I slowly get out of bed.

It feels like I've run a marathon, which is funny because I determined a couple of years ago that I don't have the endurance to be a runner.

As I check myself over in the bathroom mirror, my hand moves absently over my stomach, trailing up to my neck—

And then I freeze.

A faint bruise. *His* bruise.

I suck in a sharp breath, my fingers tracing the mark as heat curls low in my stomach. A brand, a silent reminder of how he touched me, how he whispered my name like it was the only thing he believed in. I should feel ashamed. I should be panicking. Instead, I feel owned.

And I don't hate it.

A knock at my door startles me. I yank my sleep shirt higher to cover the bruise, pulse skittering as I clear my throat and walk out of the bathroom.

"Yeah?"

The door creaks open just enough for Asher to step inside, a coffee mug in his hand.

"Morning," he says softly, offering a small smile as he crosses the room. "I figured you could use this."

Guilt slams into me so fast I nearly choke on it. Not because I regret Maddox. But because I don't. Asher made me coffee, and I've been standing here admiring the bruises his brother left on my skin.

"Thanks," I murmur, taking the cup from his outstretched hands. My fingers brush against his briefly. And I think back to when we first started dating—if I *ever* felt a spark between us. But... no. I didn't. And now? There's no warmth. Just a hollow emptiness that I can't ignore.

He sits on the edge of the bed, looking tired. Looking like he's forcing himself to be present. "You disappeared early last night." His voice is careful, and the tone is definitely more observant than affectionate. "Everything okay?"

I force a small smile, bringing the coffee to my lips to stall for time. "Yeah, I was just tired."

He nods, but there's something defeated in the way he looks away. It's like he knows. Knows that no matter how many cups of coffee or late apologies he offers, I've already left him—we just haven't said it aloud yet.

There's a beat of silence as his blue eyes scan my face, and my heart throbs when his eyes rove down to my neck.

"I haven't told my parents about us." His gaze flickers over me, searching, but luckily for me, he doesn't notice the small bruise. "But I want you to know that I hope we can be friends. You still mean a lot to me, Ari."

I swallow, gripping the coffee mug a little tighter. Perhaps something in him senses the shift, the fracture spreading between us.

"Sure," I lie. "But we should tell them soon."

He nods. "Okay. I'll tell them once everyone's home. I don't necessarily want any drama on our last day, you know?"

I smile. "Sure."

He rubs the back of his neck. "Well, my dad made break-fast, if you want to come down. It's nearly eleven," he adds, giving me a wry smile.

My eyes bug out. "Shit, I didn't realize how late I slept."

He stands up. "You must've needed it."

You could say that again.

With another soft smile, he leaves me alone to change into yet another outfit that Maddox picked out for me. Today, it's a dark green, silk romper that ties at the waist with flowy shorts, a sweetheart neckline, and flutter sleeves. It makes me feel very feminine, and despite changing my underwear, I haven't show-ered—so the evidence of Maddox is still very much there. I *smell* like him, and the worst part is, I don't want to wash it off.

I rub some perfume on my neck and walk out of my room.

When I get downstairs, the kitchen is humming with quiet conversation. The scent of coffee and freshly baked croissants lingers in the air, but I don't have an inkling of an appetite.

Hannah smiles when she sees me. "Morning, sweetheart. Did you sleep okay?"

Before I can answer, Maddox speaks. "She seemed content after dinner," he muses, swirling his coffee lazily, his gaze never leaving mine. Something akin to pride flashes across his face. "Must've been a satisfying meal if she slept for fourteen hours," he drawls, his blue eyes locked on to mine, knowing.

I choke on my sip of coffee.

Asher scrunches his brow, glancing between us. "I'm sure Ari doesn't need you to notice every single thing about her."

If only Asher knew...

Maddox smiles, pulling his lower lip between his teeth as he leans forward. "I'd have to be dead not to notice her, Asher," he murmurs.

I hate him.

And I hate how my stomach flutters at his words anyway.

I force myself to sit down, ignoring the way Maddox's knee brushes against mine under the table, the heat of his body seeping into my skin.

I'm halfway through forcing down a piece of toast when Maddox gets up. He walks over to the counter and grabs something I can't identify, something green and blue and small. Setting it down next to my plate, I freeze, my stomach twisting as I glance down—

A flower.

A *forget-me-not.*

I don't touch it, don't react, but my pulse pounds in my ears.

My phone vibrates against the table, and I nearly jump. I tear my gaze away from the flower, casting a quick glance around. Asher is focused on his parents, nodding along as Hannah discusses the day's plans. No one is paying attention to me. No one sees the war raging beneath my skin.

I lower my gaze to the screen.

(858) 667-9960

I don't need to remind you, do I?

A slow, involuntary shiver unfurls inside me. My pulse stumbles. I glance up, and Maddox is already looking at me, his expression unreadable, his fingers curled around his phone like he has all the time in the world.

Heat prickles at the back of my neck.

I force myself to take a sip of coffee, my fingers squeezing around the ceramic.

My phone vibrates again.

(858) 667-9960

You're thinking about last night. Right now.
Even with him sitting right next to you.

A sharp inhale lodges in my throat. My entire body tenses. I flick my eyes up again, but Maddox is already looking away now, his expression smooth, his posture casual. Like he didn't just reach into my mind and pick apart my thoughts with surgical precision.

Asher leans over slightly, oblivious to the tension that has me locked in place.

"You good?"

I swallow thickly, forcing a nod. "Yeah. I should go shower."

Hannah smiles kindly. "Well, today should be nice and relaxing. A perfect beach day. And tonight, we're doing a bonfire. I can't believe it's the last night," she adds, smiling at all of us warmly.

"That sounds perfect," I reply, pushing my plate away as I stand.

My phone buzzes again.

(858) 667-9960

> You should really get some more rest,
> angel. You're going to need it.

I feel Maddox's gaze follow me as I leave the kitchen, arousal licking at the base of my spine.

The forget-me-not stays on the table.

THE PHANTOM WAITS
ARI

THE AFTERNOON SUN SHINES AGAINST THE glittering Pacific Ocean, sending golden light into the living room. The house is bustling with movement while I sip my wine, and I stay curled up on the couch with my Kindle. I'm tired from the sun, but I somehow feel... content.

Hannah and Otto are already making plans for the evening, debating the practicalities of setting up a bonfire on the beach. It's the last night before we all return to reality, and while I should feel some sort of unease about what's transpired here, I can't bring myself to worry.

My reality has already shifted, whether I like it or not.

I'm almost... relieved. After tonight, I won't have to keep pretending.

And Asher seems to know it, too.

I help Hannah carry two large pieces of wood down to the beach, and the others follow us. After offering to help and being turned down, Otto, Maddox, and Asher begin piling the wood and using the larger pieces to form the outer, tall shape for the bonfire. Hannah is busy dictating where each piece goes, and I sit back on my hands, watching everything unfold.

Once Otto gets the bottom part lit, and the rest catches fire quickly, thanks to the warm wind. Asher hands me a beer, coming to sit down next to me as Maddox sits closer to the shore with his parents. They seem to be in deep conversation, and it's the first time I feel like I physically crave Maddox's attention.

How ironic.

"Hey," Asher says softly.

I turn to face him, feeling the gravity of his gaze. He studies me the way he has all day today. Like I'm just out of reach, like he's holding on to something that's slowly slipping away from him.

"Hey."

He exhales loudly. The silence stretches between us, broken only by the rhythmic crash of waves against the shore and the crackling of the bonfire.

"Were you happy? With me, I mean." His voice is almost *too* quiet. The words are soft, but they land like a punch. My stomach knots, my pulse picking up speed. I stare at the horizon, feeling the ocean breeze sweep over my skin, and I say the only thing I can.

"I was... at first."

Asher stiffens beside me, but I don't look at him. I can't.

The wind shifts, carrying the distant sound of Hannah's laughter. Asher exhales sharply, rubbing the back of his neck. When he speaks again, his voice is lower, tinged with something that sounds a lot like quiet defeat.

"I feel like I kept trying to make this work, but it just didn't. No matter how hard I tried."

I bite the inside of my cheek, swallowing down the sharp response that threatens to rise.

Did he try, though? Because all I saw were words without action. Empty promises. Half-hearted gestures after the damage was already done. He listened, sure, but he never really heard me. And maybe for a long time, I pretended that was enough. That if I stayed patient, if I stayed quiet, things would magically shift.

But they never did.

My throat constricts. I press my fingers into the warm sand like it might steady me.

I want to deny it. I should deny it.

Because, yes, Maddox is part of this. His attention, his touch, the way he sees me, it's all tangled up in this mess.

But he isn't the only thing. Not even close.

This quiet unraveling between me and Asher started long before Maddox ever stepped foot inside that beach house. The missed calls. The distracted dinners. The way he never really listened when I told him what I wanted.

Maybe Maddox was just the spark.

Maybe... I was already gone before Maddox ever touched me.

Still, the thought makes my stomach twist. A cold feeling of dread works through me. This thing between Asher and me... I think it's been fading for months. We just ignored it, both of us too comfortable, too unwilling to confront the truth.

And now, there's nothing left to ignore.

I turn to face him, my chest aching. "I don't want to hurt you."

He gives me a small, resigned smile, but there's no real heartbreak in it—just acceptance. "I think you've been hurting for a while now," he says quietly. "And maybe I've been too comfortable to notice. Or maybe I just didn't want to." He lets out a shallow breath. "We had a good run, Ari."

A sharp pang twists in my ribs. I reach for his hand, squeezing gently, and for the first time in a long time, we're not pretending.

We both know how this ends.

He sighs, running his free hand through his hair before looking over at me, searching my face. "So what now?"

I swallow hard, glancing back at the water. "I don't know," I whisper.

Asher stares at me, something unreadable flickering across his face. "I guess we go home and figure it out from there."

It's not dramatic. It's not a fight. It's not an explosion of emotions.

Which, I suppose, is exactly like our whole relationship. Safe. *Steady.* No real passion or drama. It just... is.

When I look up toward the bonfire, my eyes catch on a familiar figure leaning back on his hands, watching me.

He doesn't move, doesn't react, doesn't try to intervene.

He doesn't have to.

Because he knows Asher is letting me go.

My stomach erupts with traitorous butterflies at the idea of what he'll do now that I'm officially no longer tethered to his brother.

And then I instantly feel guilty for thinking it, so I ask for another beer and try to drown my nerves with alcohol instead.

TOUCHED BY THE
PHANTOM

MADDOX

THE KNOCK ON MY DOOR LATER THAT NIGHT IS SOFT. *Hesitant.* Like she's not sure she should be here.

Like perhaps... if she crosses this threshold, there's no going back. Because there isn't. Not really, anyway.

I don't answer right away. I savor the heat of the moment. The way she came *to me* this time, like she knew she'd have to make the first move.

Climbing out of bed in only black sweatpants, I pull the door open slowly.

Ari stands in the dim glow of the hallway light, fresh from the shower, her damp, long hair curling slightly at the ends. She's wearing nothing but that loose t-shirt my mom washes for her every day, the hem brushing mid-thigh, her bare legs smooth and tan from the days spent under the Malibu sun.

Her gaze flickers up to mine, and fuck, it's different now. It's open, and vulnerable, and... something that makes my whole body prick with longing. And not just physically, but with everything I have. Everything I'm willing to give her, which is every piece of my soul.

There's no more defiance, no more pushing back, no more pretending. She's already made her decision. I can see it written all over her face.

But still, she hesitates. There's a small part of her that's still unsure.

"I—I just wanted to talk," she says, voice barely above a whisper.

I lean against the doorframe, crossing my arms over my chest, letting my gaze trail over her, slow and deliberate. "Yeah?"

She nods, her fingers twisting together like she's bracing for something. "I need to say this before anything else happens."

Before anything else *happens*.

My smirk is lazy, amused, but beneath it, my pulse is already hammering. "Go on."

Her throat works as she swallows. "I need time, Maddox. This thing between us—it's huge. It's more intense than anything I've ever experienced. And I just—" She exhales sharply, looking away. "I need to figure myself out first."

My chest burns.

But I don't argue. I *knew* this was coming. I knew it wouldn't be simple, that she'd need to reconcile the heaviness of what we are, especially now that Asher is out of the picture.

Because of course I asked my brother what they talked about at the bonfire earlier. And while I know we'll never be close again, I think he appreciated the fact that I asked if he was okay.

And now Ari is trying to do the right thing.

The problem is, I don't fucking care about the right thing.

I care about *her*.

I watch her for a long beat, letting the silence settle between us, thick and heavy. Then, I step back, opening the door wider.

"Come in, angel."

She hesitates.

I arch a brow. "Unless you think standing out here is going to make this easier."

Her lips part, something flashing in her gaze, and then she steps inside. I close the door behind her, locking it. The room is dark, only the faint light from the moon spilling through the balcony doors, casting long shadows across the floor. She moves toward the center of the room, arms crossed, as if physically trying to hold herself together.

"You want time," I say, stepping closer. "I get that." She turns, her eyes meeting mine. My voice drops lower, rougher. "But I'm not a patient man, little warrior."

She sucks in a breath, eyes widening.

I continue. "And I know you," I murmur, my fingers trailing up her arm, light, teasing, but possessive. "I know the way your body responds to me. I know you're still feeling me inside you right now, no matter how hard you try to fight it."

A shaky exhale leaves her lips.

I tilt my head. "And I know that you didn't come here just to talk."

Ari clenches her jaw, but I can see her resolve cracking.

So I push. "Tell me," I murmur, stepping even closer, our bodies nearly flush. "Tell me that you don't want me, right here, right now, and I'll step back and watch you walk away."

Her breath hitches. I reach up, brushing my knuckles along the side of her throat, feeling her pulse jackrabbit. She's *so* responsive to my touch. Always has been. It's addictive, watching the way she reacts under my scrutiny. I'll never get enough of it.

"Tell me, Ari," I whisper. "I'll give you as much time as you need. I'll stop the letters, the texts. I'll wait. Because while it's fun to toy with you, I want you to be *all in*. I need you to be. Because I am. I want this, and you, forever. I decided before I even met you. So…" I arch a brow, waiting.

"That's not fair," she whispers, eyes flicking between mine. "You, standing here, looking like…" She swallows, her delicate throat bobbing.

"Like I said, I'm not a patient man," I tell her, my voice a dark purr. "But I don't do halfway," I finish, my voice low, steady. "If you want safety, if you want easy—you already had that. With me? It's every ugly and real thing. It's chaos and passion. It's heavy, but it's *real*. I want all of you, and not just the polite or palatable parts. I want every breath, every bruise, every broken piece you try to hide. I want it all."

I pause, my thumb brushing her pulse again, savoring the frantic beat beneath her skin. Just knowing my words are having an effect on her…

"I'll wait," I murmur, softer now, but no less certain. "But when you come to me, Ari… it has to be with your whole fucking heart. Because once you're mine, that's it. No going back. No pretending this didn't happen. No pretending I don't own every part of you."

Her lips part like she wants to argue, like she *needs* to. But she doesn't. Because she knows I'm right. The silence is thick and charged. For a second, something unsure flickers behind her beautiful brown eyes, and something cracks in my chest.

I'm not an insecure man. I know my worth. But Ari? She makes me feel like I'm constantly walking a tightrope with no net beneath me.

Because no matter how confident I am—how *certain*—I know one word from her could level me. She's the one thing I didn't plan for, not really. Not *like this*. She's the chaos I didn't see coming, the storm I thought I could tame, but now? I don't want to. I just want to stand in the middle of it and *burn*.

She swallows again, her gaze flicking to my mouth like

she's thinking about kissing me. Like she's remembering *exactly* how I taste.

And maybe, just maybe, she's finally realizing what I've known all along.

We don't get peace, she and I.

We get *fire*. We get *ruin*.

We get each other.

I step closer, my voice dropping into something unraveled, barely human. "Say the word. Tell me to back off, and I will. But if you don't? I'm going to kiss you like it's the last thing I'll ever do."

She breathes in, shaky. Lips parting, and then she stands on her tiptoes as her mouth crashes into mine.

It's not soft. It's not hesitant. It's everything we've been holding back, everything we've fought against, everything we've denied ourselves for far too fucking long.

I groan into her mouth, my hands finding her hips, yanking her against me so hard she gasps.

And fuck, *this*.

This is what I've been waiting for.

No more games. No more pretending.

Just *us*.

I spin her, pressing her back against the edge of the bed, my lips dragging along her jaw, down her throat, nipping, tasting, *claiming*.

Her hands tangle in my hair, nails scraping against my scalp as she tilts her head back, baring her neck for me.

"That's what I thought," I murmur against her skin, my voice dark and strained.

Ari shudders. I grab the hem of her t-shirt, yanking it over her head, exposing smooth, bare skin and the tight peaks of her nipples. I groan, running my palms over her ribs, her waist, every fucking inch of her I can get my hands on.

"You're mine now," I growl, pushing her onto the bed, crawling over her. "Do you hear me?"

Her breath stutters, but she nods. I fucking love how submissive she becomes with me—fiery during the day, and soft as silk beneath me when she lets go. It's fucking *beautiful*, watching that fire in her dim just enough to flicker into something else entirely. Something raw. Vulnerable. *Mine*.

Because that's what this is. Her surrender isn't weakness, it's trust. It's her knowing, deep in her bones, that I'll never take more than she's willing to give. That I'll wreck her only in the ways she wants to be wrecked. That I'll give her *everything* she didn't even know she needed.

I lean down, kissing her collarbone, biting softly as I murmur against her skin, "I've got you now, angel. And I'm never letting go." My fingers slide down her stomach, slipping between her thighs. *Fuck, she's so wet.* My cock throbs as I delicately run my middle finger down her seam before inserting it inside of her. "Say it, Ari."

She whimpers, her hips lifting, her body desperate for my touch as she cants her hips against my hand.

And then, so fucking soft I almost miss it—

"I'm yours."

My heart fucking stops.

I press my forehead to hers, my fingers flexing against her cunt. She *means* it. And for the first time in twenty years, I realize—I finally fucking *won*.

But before I can respond, she cups my face, her touch gentle. And the words slip out before I can stop them.

"Elaine would have loved you."

Ari stills beneath me. I don't know why I say it. Maybe because she should know. Maybe because she deserves to understand the depth of what she's just given me.

I don't expect her to respond. But then her fingers trace along my jaw, so light, so fucking *careful*.

"I'm sorry," she whispers.

And it fucking wrecks me. Because she means that too.

I kiss her slowly... deeply. And this time, it's not about claiming or taking or proving anything.

And fuck if that isn't the scariest thing of all.

Ari's fingers curl into my jaw, holding me there, her lips parting with a soft sigh that's equal parts surrender and need. She tastes like trust, like fire and sweetness tangled together. My free hand sweeps down her side, relearning the map of her body now that everything has changed—now that she's mine in more than just the ways I've taken.

She arches into me, gasping softly as I press my palm to her chest, right over her heart.

"Feel that?" I whisper. "That's mine now."

Her eyes flutter open, wide and shining. "You already had it."

The words knock the breath from my lungs, but I chuckle. "Is that so?"

She huffs a laugh. "You didn't really give me any choice in the matter."

Smiling, I lower my forehead to hers, breathing her in, trying to make sense of what the fuck she's doing to me. And maybe that's the point—there is no logic in the room with us.

I slide my free hand down, slow and reverent, until I'm spreading her legs and pressing her further onto the bed. She scoots up my mattress and I knock her knees apart as I slide down her body. Without another word, I lean down and smell her, moaning at the sweet smell of *her*. Before she can protest, I lean forward and flatten my tongue against her clit, pressing down slightly and reveling in the way it makes her twitch.

"Fuck, Maddox—"

A second later, I add a second finger inside her heat and curl them as I flick my tongue against her swollen bud. I'm not gentle—I nibble, pinch, and suck. I didn't shave this morning so I'm sure my scruff burns as I feast on her. But she doesn't seem to mind. She arches her back as I continue, and when she lets out three shaky, quick breaths, grabbing for my hair, I thrust my fingers into her harder.

God, the fucking sounds...

I can feel my cock leaking as I work her to her climax. Watching her come undone beneath my touch is addicting, and I have to keep my hips still so that I don't come in my pants again.

Ari's thighs tense around my head, her mouth falling open in a soft, shuddering moan as I fuck her with my fingers rhythmically, reading her body like scripture. Thankfully my room is in the back of the house, far away from everyone else—otherwise I might have to tell her to be quiet. Her breath stutters every time I circle her clit with my tongue, hips chasing me, trying to pull me closer.

Her fingers rake down the back of my neck, nails scoring skin. "Maddox," she whispers, desperate. "Please. I'm so close."

I stand up and brace myself above her, gaze locked on hers. "I know," I murmur. "You don't have to ask."

I remove my fingers and quickly suck on them. She watches me with half-hooded eyes, her pupils nearly black as I stare down at her wet seam. The dark curls look so pretty against her golden skin, and I know her cunt will look even prettier with my cum leaking out of it soon.

Stepping out of my pants, I fist my cock a couple of times before climbing on top of her. She's so small compared to me, and I feel massive on top of her. Lining my cock up, my brow furrows.

"Ari—"

"Take it, Maddox. You know you want to."

I let out an uneven breath as I press the head of my cock against her entrance. She gasps when I push into her, and I begin to shake with all the reverence of a man finding home. She pants, her legs wrapping around my hips instinctively. Slowly, I push in inch by inch, her mouth dropping open when I'm fully seated.

"*Fuuuck*, little warrior."

"Told you," she snarks, smirking as I pull out, admiring the way my cock is slick with her arousal.

We move together, slow at first, letting it build, letting it burn. I kiss every part of her I can reach—her neck, her jaw, her lips, her shoulder—as if my mouth can make up for all the months I spent dreaming of this moment.

I'm going to have to build up a tolerance to fucking her, because right now, I'm seconds from coming. She feels too good, like she was made for me. The way her cunt grips me, the warm, tight heat, the feel of her body beneath mine, the feel of her light brown nipples as I play with them, the look on her face when I slam into her—

Yeah.

She's my own personal drug, and I will never be able to get enough.

Especially when I can smell her perfume, knowing she's always wearing a small part of me...

I'll tell her about that.

One day.

She digs her heels into my back, gasping as I thrust deeper. Her body trembles, fluttering around me, so fucking perfect I think I might lose my mind.

"Look at me," I rasp, brushing a strand of hair from her cheek. "Come with me, angel."

Her mouth drops open as I roughly thrust into her. My grip bruises her hips, my rhythm relentless, filthy. The air is thick with sweat and skin and need. The bed groans underneath us, and despite being far away from the others, some sick, primal part of me *hopes* someone hears how roughly I'm taking her, wants them to hear the wet slap of flesh and how wild I get with her clenched tight around me.

I'm losing the thread of who I am. Right now, I'm nothing but raw nerve and need, seconds from breaking apart inside her.

Aliens could descend from the ceiling and I wouldn't give a shit. All I can think about is the feeling of being inside her, tight and warm and impossibly wet. Every time I thrust, her walls clench around me, dragging me closer to the edge, milking me like her body already knows I belong there.

It's heaven and hell, the way she wraps around me. Hot silk and slick heat, the kind of pleasure that scrapes down my spine and makes my vision go black at the edges. My balls are tight, drawn up painfully, my whole body coiled like a fucking live wire. I feel every tremor of her, every gasp and whimper and desperate hitch of breath as she clenches again—*so fucking close.*

I grit my teeth, hips snapping harder now, chasing the rush building low in my gut like an explosion waiting to detonate.

"Fuck, Ari," I growl, my voice shattered. "You feel so goddamn good, so fucking tight, I—"

She moans, trembling beneath me, her fingers clawing at my shoulders as I drive into her again and again, deeper, rougher, every thrust a promise that I'll never leave her wanting again.

Her hands slide into my hair, tugging, grounding. Her body arches beneath me, hips rising to meet every thrust like she's just as desperate—just as wrecked.

I drop my forehead to hers, breaths mingling, bodies locked together, skin slick with sweat. I'm right there, so close to losing my mind again.

"Touch yourself," I rasp, my voice nothing but gravel. "I want you to come with me."

Her eyes flutter, lips parted, and she obeys without question, her fingers sliding between us, finding her clit. The sight alone nearly undoes me.

"Good girl," I breathe, teeth clenching as her inner walls start to flutter, pulling me deeper. "That's it, angel. Let me feel you."

Her back bows.

Her mouth drops open in a silent cry.

And then she breaks.

She comes hard, her body convulsing around me, crying out my name like it's a prayer and a curse all in one. Sudden, rhythmic, wet heat drags a raw sound from my throat. It feels like I'm being swallowed whole, tightening with every pulse until I can barely hold on. My muscles lock, every inch of me straining, burning with the pressure, the need. It's blinding— that split second before I come, when I'm caught between agony and bliss, and all I know is her.

It sends me over the fucking edge.

I slam into her one final time, groaning her name as I come —hot, deep, raw—every drop spilling into her as my body locks up, pleasure crashing through me like a fucking tidal wave. My cock pulses inside of her, hard and fast, filling her with everything I have. I ride it out slowly, thrusting once, twice more, like I never want to leave her warmth. Like I could stay buried inside her forever.

And maybe I will.

When I finally still, my chest heaving, I press a kiss to her lips.

Brushing a sweaty strand of hair off her cheek, I cup her face in my palm. "You okay?"

She nods, dazed. Spent. Glowing. "Yeah," she whispers, and there's a shaky smile on her lips now.

"Did I hurt you?" I ask, almost afraid of the answer. I didn't hold back, and physically it's so easy to overpower her.

"No, you didn't hurt me, big guy." She smiles and holds a hand against my cheek. "Are you okay?"

I laugh under my breath, dropping one last kiss to her temple. "Ask me again when I can feel my legs."

She laughs too—quiet, breathy, real.

And I know without a doubt that I'll spend the rest of my life chasing that sound.

PHANTOM IN THE REARVIEW

ARI

THE BEACH HOUSE IS QUIETER THAN IT'S BEEN ALL week. Suitcases sit by the door—mine packed with all new clothes, thanks to Maddox, and the Polly Pocket tucked away safely on top. The kitchen smells like freshly brewed coffee and nostalgia. By the time I grab my phone charger and purse, everyone is waiting out front to say goodbye.

Asher's already at his car, shutting the trunk. When he sees me, his mouth lifts into a tired smile that doesn't quite reach his eyes.

"Got everything?"

I nod. "Yeah."

There's a moment. Just silence. Just us. And it's strange how something so steady can still feel so foreign.

He exhales, rubbing the back of his neck. "I guess this is goodbye."

I'd arranged Frankie to come pick me up, and she was more than happy to do it. I figured a three-hour car ride with Asher would only lead to more awkwardness.

"Guess so." My voice is quieter than I mean it to be.

"I hope you find what you're looking for," he says. No

bitterness. No resentment. Just... the kind of grace that hurts more than anger ever could.

"I hope you do, too."

We don't hug. We don't linger.

And somehow, that feels like the most honest part of all of it.

I wave at his car as he pulls out. Hannah steps up to me a moment later. Her smile is soft, knowing. I don't think Asher told her, but my guess is she knows. Mothers always know.

She reaches out and hugs me tight. "Take care of yourself, sweetheart. I hope we can see you soon."

I nod into her shoulder, swallowing the lump in my throat. "You too."

Otto pats my shoulder from behind. "Don't be a stranger, okay?"

"Thank you again for having me. I had a wonderful time."

We all hug again, and then they leave, the tires of their SUV crunching against the white gravel driveway.

Frankie should be here any minute. Wrapping my arms around myself, I sit on top of my suitcase and take in the warm sun. When I hear the front door of the house open, I look over my shoulder to find Maddox walking to his car, sunglasses low on his nose.

He doesn't say a word. He doesn't have to. He just watches me like I'm already his, like the goodbye I just said was the last barrier between us. There's no awkwardness, nothing to make me feel like we're about to say goodbye.

After falling asleep in his bed last night, it's like every pretense has been stripped from this thing between us. I want him, and he wants me. It's as simple as that. With Asher, there was so much of the *will he or won't he?* But with Maddox, it's like our story was already written into the universe, like he'd already decided our fate and I never stood a chance.

It feels like everything I've ever wanted is snapping into place.

He drops his bag in the trunk of his car and then he walks over to me. "You sure you don't want me to drive you?" he asks, voice low.

"I'm sure. Thank you for the offer."

Maddox nods once, but I can tell he doesn't like it. Not because he doesn't trust me to make my own decisions, but because letting me go, even for a little while, is going to be hell for him.

His hand comes to rest lightly on my hip. Just the weight of it makes my breath catch.

"Text me when you get back," he says, voice rough.

"I will."

"And, Ari?" His fingers squeeze harder, just slightly. "You don't have to pretend with me. About anything. Not anymore."

I nod, throat thick.

He leans down, brushing his mouth against my cheek—barely a kiss, more like a claim whispered into my skin. "I'll see you soon."

It's not a question. It's a promise.

Then he steps back, but not before his fingers graze mine one last time, like he's not quite ready to stop touching me. Like he needs to carry that last piece of me with him for the road.

But just as he turns, he glances back. "Oh, and when you get home," he says, voice dropping into that low, teasing rasp, "make sure to work on that fan fiction you've been writing for me."

I blink. My heart plummets. "What?"

His smirk deepens, clearly enjoying the stunned look on my face. "Don't worry. I didn't read it. I wouldn't invade your privacy like that." His head tilts slightly. "But I do know about it. And for the record? I think it's fucking cool."

My cheeks burn. I want the floor to swallow me whole. "It's not—it's not for you. It's just—"

He steps back in before I can escape, catching my wrist gently. "Hey." His thumb brushes over my pulse point. "I'm sorry if I embarrassed you. I wasn't trying to. I mean it. The fact that you've written a story that big, with that much heart, that people actually care about?" His voice softens, earnest. "That's badass."

I swallow hard, my throat tight as I stare up at him.

"And," he adds, softer now, "I'm dying to know what happens to Murtagh and Nasuada..." He gives me a devilish grin, naming two characters from my story. My eyes widen. "Yeah, I did read a little bit. Couldn't help myself. You're kind of famous, you know that?"

I gape at him. "You internet searched me?"

"I searched everything about you," he says unapologetically. "How do you think I found your wish list?"

I sigh. "Psycho," I mutter under my breath.

He chuckles, his whole face brightening. "Hey. You should be proud." He brushes his lips against my cheek again, more reverent this time. "Don't ever be ashamed of being passionate about something."

And just like that, he walks away, leaving me standing there, completely undone—but warmer than I've felt in a long, long time.

I'm pulled out of the moment with the sound of another car coming down the driveway. *Frankie.* Waving at Maddox, I watch as he slips into the driver's seat and starts his car. I know if I asked him to stay, even for just five more minutes, he would.

But I don't, because right now, I need my friend.

Maddox's engine hums to life, and I watch the way his eyes

linger on me through the windshield—burning, possessive, like he's memorizing me all over again. Then, with a final nod, he pulls out of the driveway and disappears down the winding hill.

I exhale, only just realizing I was holding my breath.

The sound of Frankie's door slamming pulls me the rest of the way back to reality. She's already halfway to me, oversized sunglasses on, a giant iced coffee in hand.

"Bitch," she calls out, all grin and sass. "You look like you've just had the best sex of your life."

I laugh, the sound coming out too fast, too frayed.

"Because I did."

Her brows rise above her sunglasses. "Okay, I'm not sure the three hours back is going to be enough. You have to tell me *everything.*"

I shake my head and pull her into a hug, grateful for the grounding weight of her tall, mother-like presence.

As I inhale the familiar scent of her shampoo, I glance down the road where Maddox disappeared, my chest still fluttering.

"This is for you," she says, handing me the coffee. "Figured you could use it."

I take it and gulp the life sustenance down. "Thank you, bestie. And thanks for coming all the way out here to get me."

"Six hours of childfree time? It's like a reward."

I huff a laugh and help her with my suitcase. Once we're in the car and back on the road, she reaches for the volume and lowers the music, then glances at me like I'm a puzzle she's trying to solve.

"So," Frankie says, nails clicking against the steering wheel, "I'm just going to take a wild guess. You dumped golden boy for his ex-con brother."

I groan. I hadn't told Frankie anything that happened over

the last few days because I wasn't sure how to broach the subject.

"I cannot keep a single secret from you, can I?"

"Absolutely not. I'm your best friend. It's literally in the contract."

"Technically... yes. But I cheated on Asher, Frankie." The guilt surfaces fast, hot in my chest. "And Maddox is... intense."

She snorts. "You say that like it's a *bad* thing."

"It kind of is!"

She eyes me sideways. "Okay, walk me through this. Did he coerce you? Threaten you? Drag you off somewhere against your will?"

"No. I mean... maybe a little, but I wanted it. All of it." I pause. "He did eat me out like a starving man and make me see God."

Her mouth drops open. "Oh my god."

I just laugh, and we sit in the comfortable silence for a few seconds.

"Look, if you're talking about a man who looks just like Asher but knows how to please you in bed, *with* tattoos and no boring job? Come on. If you *didn't* ride his face, I'd have to stage an intervention."

I cackle. "I missed you."

She grins, unapologetic. "I missed you, too. In all seriousness, Ari... yeah, you cheated. And I know that eats at you. But that doesn't mean you're a terrible person, it means you were deeply fucking unhappy and didn't know how to get out."

I stare out the window, her words sinking in like ink on paper.

"Do you still love Asher?" she asks, voice softer now.

"I think a part of me always will," I murmur. "But I wasn't *in* love anymore. I think I just... held on because I was supposed to. Because he was safe."

Frankie nods. "Safe isn't always what you need, babe. Sometimes it's just the thing keeping you stuck."

I shift in my seat. "It's not that simple."

"Sure it is," she says, reaching into the bag between us and pulling out a croissant. "You picked the hotter, dirtier, more dangerous brother. You are now living the plot of *every* fan fiction I read in high school. Honestly, I'm living for it."

I can't help the laugh that bubbles out of me.

"But seriously," she says between bites, "I get that Maddox is a lot. Prison time, the smirking, the stalker-ish 'you're mine forever' energy—"

"Super intense," I mutter, nodding.

"—but also? I bet he looks at you like he'd burn the whole goddamn world to the ground just to make you smile. And I say this as someone who married a man with a similar vibe, it's fucking terrifying. But it's also the most powerful thing in the world when it's real."

I blink at her, emotion prickling at the backs of my eyes. "You think it's real?"

"I think *you* think it is. And that's enough." She pauses, watching me. "But also? You're scared shitless."

"I am," I whisper, and it feels like a confession.

She grabs my hand and squeezes. "Good. That means it matters. The right kind of love doesn't always feel safe. Sometimes it feels like a hurricane you can't survive. But maybe that's the point. Maybe it breaks down all the bullshit so you can finally build something real."

I swallow hard, throat tight.

Then my phone buzzes in my lap.

(858) 667-9960

(Sent with car voice note) I'm still thinking about the way you tasted last night. And the way you whispered my name when you thought I was asleep.

I slam the screen down quickly, cheeks burning like wildfire.

Frankie doesn't even flinch. "Let me guess," she says dryly. "The criminal."

I nod, dazed.

She takes a long sip of her water, calm as ever. "You're so fucked."

And somehow, I've never been more okay with that.

Phantom's Sanctuary

Ari

I LIE IN MY BED, STARING AT THE MESSAGE MADDOX just sent me.

> STALKER
>
> You're not sleeping either, are you, angel?

He always knows. It's both irritating and... oddly comforting. I bite my lip, hovering my fingers over my phone.

> Nope.

A few seconds pass before he responds.

> STALKER
>
> Come to me.

My heart stutters.

> You don't even ask anymore?

> STALKER
>
> It's like you don't know me.

I bite my lip to keep from smiling. He can be such an asshole. And yet... I love it. I love that we can banter and that he can meet me head to head. Still, I'm cozy in my bed.

STALKER

Ari. Just get in the car.

I don't reply right away. I stare at the glowing screen, my stomach knotting with nerves. It's been just over twenty-four hours since I've been home. I'd finally caved and put him in my phone as 'Stalker' and last night, I'd asked for some space. I clarified that I wasn't running away, but I just needed a night back at my house to clear my head. And despite spending nearly twelve hours today catching up on work, I'd spent way too long thinking of Maddox.

I close my eyes.

He'll ruin me. I know it.

But I suppose he already has, hasn't he?

Send me the address.

Two seconds later, it pings through.

STALKER

550 Front Street. 35th floor. Ask for Cross.

And just like that, I'm grabbing my keys and slipping into leggings and a black hoodie. I don't even stop to ask myself what I'm doing.

Because I already know.

I'm just as addicted to him as he is to me.

The drive to Maddox's place is quick. It's just after eleven at night, and while downtown San Diego is usually pretty busy, it's a Tuesday night and most people have work in the morning. I pull into the basement level parking structure of

Maddox's building, rolling my eyes at the exorbitant hourly rate.

I should send him an invoice.

Walking into the lobby of the building, I stop in my tracks. *Oh, this is fancy.* I stare at the marble floors of the high-rise lobby, taking in the freakishly shiny walls, the modern art, and the fig tree that's about thirty feet tall situated in the corner.

What the hell have I walked into?

The concierge greets me like he already knows who I am.

"Mr. Cross is expecting you," he says, sliding a key card across the desk and motioning me to the private elevator.

As the elevator ascends, I clutch my phone like a lifeline, heart thudding. Every floor we pass ratchets up the nerves. I don't know why I thought his place would be some dark, shadowy corner of the city.

I didn't think it would be a penthouse.

I didn't think it would be... this.

When the doors slide open, I step into the kind of apartment that belongs on a magazine cover. Glass walls, warm lighting, sleek lines. It smells like leather and expensive cologne. It smells like him.

"Maddox?" I call, my voice catching.

And then I see him.

Barefoot. Shirtless. Low-slung black sweatpants that hang off his hips like he knows exactly what they're doing to me. Damp hair pushed back from his forehead, tattoos on full display—ink climbing his arms, chest, and neck.

Holy shit.

"You came," he says, his voice that low rasp that always makes my stomach twist.

"I said I would," I manage, trying to look anywhere but at the line of muscle cutting down his torso. "You didn't tell me your place looks like a Bond villain's apartment."

He smirks. "Is that a compliment?"

"It's just unexpected," I say, spinning around and admiring the sweeping view of downtown and the ocean beyond it. Floor-to-ceiling windows stretch the length of the room, the dark sky making the nearby lights pop. "But I can't deny it's stunning."

He shrugs, like none of it really matters. "I like it. It's quiet. Private."

"You must've made good money in cybersecurity," I say, arms folding across my chest. "You know, before you turned into a full-time stalker."

Maddox takes a slow step toward me, that infuriating smirk still tugging at the corner of his mouth. "I did," he replies easily. "Fortunately for me, I had friends in high places who kept my money safe."

I tilt my head. "Legal money?"

He chuckles, the sound low and rich, like I've said something he enjoys. "Mostly. Enough that the IRS isn't knocking on my door. Let's just say I had contingency plans... and a few people who believed I'd make it back."

"Home," I muse, glancing around again. "This is home?"

His gaze shifts, like he's really looking at the space for the first time. "It's walls and glass and silence," he says after a moment. "But it's not home without you in it."

That stops me cold.

"Maddox—"

He shrugs again, but there's no indifference this time. Just something raw and open in the lines of his face. "I like things that are mine. Things I can control. But this?" He gestures around at the modern furniture, the dimmed lighting, the sleek stone countertops. Then his gaze cuts back to me. "This place doesn't mean shit without someone real in it with me."

His voice is even, but the presence of it presses against my chest.

"I used to tell myself that this penthouse was the goal. That if I had a view like this and no one breathing down my neck, I'd finally feel free," he says, softer now. "But it turns out freedom means fuck all if you're just sitting alone in a glass box at the top of the city, wondering who's going to remember you when you're gone."

Something in my chest aches for him, for everything he lost. His daughter. His years spent in prison. The quiet loneliness that still follows him like a shadow.

I reach out without thinking, my hand brushing across one of the tattoos on his chest—a pattern of black ink that looks like the inside of a kaleidoscope, fractured but symmetrical.

"You don't have to be alone in it anymore," I whisper.

His breath catches—barely—but I feel it in the tension between us, in the way his muscles go taut under my touch.

His hand covers mine, holding it flat against his chest, grounding us both. "I don't want to be."

His other hand lifts, fingers sliding to the back of my neck, thumb brushing behind my ear with a devastating gentleness. Like he's memorizing the shape of me. Like he's afraid I might vanish if he doesn't anchor me.

"You nervous?" he asks quietly.

"A little," I admit. "Not of you. Just... this."

"This?" he echoes.

"Us," I clarify. "Now that we're not hiding. Now that we have to be out in the real world with Asher and your past and... everything else."

He studies me, his blue eyes dark and unreadable, that dangerous edge to him surfacing like it always does. But it's tempered by something softer now. Something deeper.

"You think this hasn't been real all along?" he asks, voice rough. "I've been dying for you for over a year, angel. I've built my fucking world around the idea of you. That's real."

I try to breathe, but it feels like there's no air left in the room.

He leans down, his forehead resting against mine. "You're here now. That's all I need."

Then, his tone shifts, tender and uncharacteristically hesitant. "And just so you know... I don't expect anything from you. I know what your house means to you, what it meant to move into a space that belonged to your grandmother."

My eyes sting, and before I realize what I'm doing, I blurt out the first thing that comes to mind. "She was the first person who made me feel like I didn't have to earn love. She made it feel like home no matter what was going on outside the walls."

His hand flexes on the nape of my neck. "I get it. That house is part of who you are. I'd never ask you to give that up."

I blink fast, trying to clear the emotion clouding my vision.

"But I'd follow you anywhere, Ari," he murmurs. "Anywhere. I'd live in a one-bedroom apartment with cockroaches and no fucking hot water if it meant I got to wake up next to you."

I let out a shaky breath, and he leans in, brushing his lips against mine.

"I'm not trying to trap you," he whispers. "I'm trying to show you you're free. As long as you'll let me worship you wherever that freedom takes you."

My hands curl into his skin, and this time when he leans down and kisses me—slow, reverent, nothing like the greedy kisses from before—it feels like something entirely new is beginning. His mouth moves over mine, slow and careful at first, like he's afraid he might break something delicate between us. But it's not delicate. It's not fragile. It's a wildfire —ravenous and consuming and impossible to stop.

I kiss him back with everything I have, my fingers grabbing the hard muscles of his back, tugging him closer. He groans softly, the sound vibrating in his chest, and then his arms are around me—tight, claiming, anchoring. The foyer of his penthouse is silent except for our breathing, and I swear the walls lean in to watch.

He lifts me without warning, strong hands gripping the backs of my thighs as I wrap my legs around his waist. My back hits the cool marble wall behind us, but the chill barely registers because he's there—his mouth at my throat, dragging open-mouthed kisses along the pulse pounding just beneath my skin.

"Maddox," I gasp, clutching at his shoulders. "Here?"

His voice is rough, almost pained. "I need you. Right now. I don't give a fuck where we are."

The desperation in him floors me, in the way his hands hold me like I might disappear, the reverence in his touch, both delicate and needy all at once.

His mouth finds mine again, hungrier now. His hips roll against me, and I can feel how hard he is beneath his sweatpants—thick, straining, hot. I grind against him instinctively, the friction sparking through me like lightning. I feel him everywhere—his breath in my lungs, his heartbeat against my ribs, his hands tracing every inch of skin they can find beneath my clothes.

"You have no idea," he mutters between kisses, "what it does to me... to have you like this. To know you're mine."

"I'm yours," I breathe.

A low, broken sound escapes him. "Say it again."

"I'm yours, Maddox."

His head drops to my shoulder with a groan, his body tightening against mine. "Fuck, Ari." He kisses my neck again, slower this time, his tongue tracing the curve of my jaw. "I could die a happy man just like this. With your body wrapped around mine and the taste of your lips on my own."

"Please," I whimper.

"I have a confession," he murmurs, his tongue feathering against my pulse point as he inhales the scent of my perfume. "At the beach house, I put some of my cum in your perfume bottle."

I go still. "Why?"

"So you'd always smell like me."

A bolt of heat goes through me. "Fuck. I hate that I find that so hot," I mutter, pulling his face up to mine and kissing him fully.

When he pulls away slightly, one of his hands slides beneath my sweatshirt and bra, the rough pad of his thumb brushing over my nipple, and I cry out softly, the sound swallowed by his mouth. His other hand slides down between my thighs, pressing against the thin barrier of my leggings.

"You're soaked," he rasps, moving his hand under my leggings and dragging the fabric of my underwear to the side. Then he slips his fingers into the wet heat of me. "God, you're always so fucking ready for me."

He presses two fingers inside me, slow and deliberate, his forehead resting against mine like he needs the connection just as much as the release.

"I need you," I whisper, grinding down against his hand, needing more. Needing everything.

His breath shudders out against my cheek as he draws his fingers out and back in, curling them in just the right way. His thumb finds that sensitive bundle of nerves and starts to circle, lazy, teasing strokes that have me gasping.

"You're already shaking," he growls, voice rough and reverent all at once. "So fucking tight. So wet for me."

My head tips back against the wall, my eyes fluttering shut as pleasure builds deep in my core. It's overwhelming—the thick drag of his fingers, the delicious pressure of his thumb, the relentless heat coiling inside me like a fuse lit too close to the fire.

"Look at me, angel," he demands softly. "I want to see your face when you come."

I force my eyes open, and the second our gazes lock, I nearly unravel. His expression is all heat and hunger and something far more dangerous.

Worship.

"That's it," he murmurs, curling his fingers deeper as he fucks me harder with them. Like the last couple of times, I love that he doesn't treat me delicately. That he gives me exactly what I need. "Fuck yourself on my hand. Show me how bad you need it."

I whimper, my hips grinding into the pressure of his palm as sparks skitter beneath my skin. The friction is perfect, obscene and raw. I can feel the slick mess he's coaxing out of me, soaking through my leggings as his fingers fuck me hard and deep, each thrust sending me closer and closer to the edge. Every time I roll my hips, I bump my clit against his knuckle, and *god* I'm so close already.

"You going to come for me?" he rasps, his voice thick with need as he ruts into me. "Soak my fingers before I even get the chance to stretch you around my cock?"

Fuck, he's good.

"Maddox—" I pant, the tension inside me about to snap.

He leans in, his lips brushing the shell of my ear. "Be a good little cockslut and come. Right here. Let me feel how much you want me."

That's all it takes.

It hits me like a wave—hard, fast, all-consuming. My body arches against him as I cry out his name, clenching around his fingers, pressing my shivering clit against his knuckles. My nails dig into his bare shoulders, and pleasure fractures through me in jagged bursts, white-hot and blinding. I can't think, can't breathe, can only feel—the pulsing throb of release and the delicious stretch of his fingers still deep inside me, his knuckle grinding against my aching bud with merciless precision, guiding me through every last tremor.

He kisses me through it, swallowing my moans like they're the air he breathes, his hand never leaving my body as he murmurs praise against my lips.

"Good girl. That's it. Just like that."

His fingers don't move, still resting deep inside me, like he can't bear to let go yet. Like he's memorizing the way I feel around him. Like he's already imagining how he'll ruin me next.

I just came but I'm already aching for it again.

When I finally sag against him, trembling and breathless, he pulls his hand away and kisses my temple, murmuring against my skin, "There she is."

I nuzzle into him, drunk on the afterglow, on the way he holds me like I'm something precious. Something irreplaceable.

"Your bed?" I murmur, still breathless.

He grins against my neck. "Yeah. But I'm going to make you come again first before I give you my cock."

He carries me the rest of the way through his home, like I weigh nothing, like he's been waiting his entire life to hold me like this. And as he pushes open the door to his room and lays me down like I'm a secret he never intends to share, I realize this is the beginning of something terrifying and beautiful.

And mine.

Not borrowed. Not temporary. Not stolen. *Mine.*

His room is minimal, clean but lived in. A deep navy comforter, dark wood floors, heavy blackout curtains. A space made for privacy. For secrets.

He lays me down like I'm breakable, but the look in his

eyes says otherwise. His gaze flicks over me like he's trying to etch the sight into memory.

"I've wanted you here for so long," he admits quietly, crawling over me, caging me in without touching me. "I didn't think I'd ever get to have you like this. Not really."

His fingers brush down the center of my chest, slow and purposeful.

"You have me," I whisper.

Something flickers behind his eyes—relief, possession, awe. A slow, dark smile curves his lips.

"Not yet," he murmurs. "Not in all the ways I want you, little warrior."

"Oh? And what other ways do you want me?"

He gives me a lopsided smile. "You really want to know?" I nod eagerly. He sighs, looking like he regrets saying anything. "Fine. I want you in my bed every night, with my ring around your finger, and then I want to fuck babies into you. Happy?"

His answer jolts through me. "Really?" I ask, my voice barely a whisper.

"Really. But for tonight, I'll settle for filling up your delicious cunt."

I grin as his eyes linger on me. He crawls on top of me slowly, like he's giving me a chance to bolt, to run from the gravity of this thing between us.

But I don't, because he's already rooted too deep.

I swallow hard, watching him, feeling every beat of my heart hammer behind my ribs.

Marriage? And babies?

Fuck.

His body covers me as he kisses me again, slower now. Not hungry—devoted. His mouth maps every inch of me, like he needs to remember every reaction, every shiver, every gasp.

"You're still trembling," he murmurs, dragging his lips

down my throat, settling between my thighs. His fingers part me again, deliberate and slow, as if he has nowhere else to be.

I can barely breathe. "Maddox…"

"Relax," he says, voice low and reverent. "You'll come for me again, nice and slow this time."

And when he pushes into me and makes me come three more times, when he touches me like I'm the most precious and dangerous thing he's ever held, it's nothing like the desperate nights before.

It's careful. It's consuming.

He kisses me through each one, soft but claiming, swallowing every breathless moan like it's the only thing keeping him alive. He whispers words I'll never fully remember but will always feel—how soft I am, how sweet I taste, how perfect I look spread out beneath him. And when I'm completely spent, his left hand cradles the back of my head, thumb gently stroking behind my ear like he knows I'm hanging by a thread.

"That's it," he murmurs against my lips. "Fuck. You're so goddamn beautiful when you come."

The praise punches through me just as powerfully as the orgasms themselves. I whimper into his mouth, completely at his mercy, shivering in the circle of his arms. His fingers stay unmoving against every inch of me.

When the aftershocks finally ebb, I sag against him, panting, feeling boneless and shattered. He pulls his hand away slowly, carefully, like he's afraid I'll break. And then he presses the gentlest kiss to my temple. I cling to him, shaking with the force of it all. The terrifying, dizzying realization that this man —this obsessive, relentless man—knows me better than anyone ever has.

My head falls against his shoulder, and I let myself be held. For once, I don't resist. He gathers me close, tucking me beneath his chin, one hand tracing lazy circles against the bare skin of my back. His breathing evens out first, then mine, until we're just... quiet.

I tilt my head, looking up at him. "You good?"

He hums. "Perfect." His fingers toy with a strand of my hair, curling it absently. "Stay tonight," he murmurs. "Please."

And I do.

For the first time in my life, I don't hesitate.

A Phantom Obsessed

Maddox

Two Days Later

It's nearly ten a.m., and the sun is already pouring through her gauzy white curtains, bathing her bedroom in gold. A vase of forget-me-nots sits on her bedside table—a reminder of me, from me.

It sits right next to the Polly Pocket I got her, which I find to be the cutest thing ever.

I didn't realize how much it meant to her until she insisted it belonged right next to her bed, and *fuck* if that didn't make me want to buy her a hundred more just to make her happy.

She's curled up on her side, her bare back to me, her hair a soft tangle across my pillow. One of my thighs is slung over her legs, her breathing slow and deep as I keep her close.

I didn't sleep much. I never really do. Not since prison—it was hard to sleep in that place, if I'm being honest. There were a lot of people who wanted to hurt me because of the notoriety of my case, and I had to stay vigilant. And then, once I asserted my dominance, once people realized they couldn't fuck with me, I'd lie awake dreaming about all the things I couldn't have.

And all the things I'd lost.

But now? She's here. Right next to me. Wrapped in her sheets, wearing nothing but the scent of me and the bruises I left behind on her hips over the last two days.

I haven't been able to keep my hands off her when we're together. If I'm not touching her, I'm pretending to work, or read, or cook... but I'm always aware of where she is.

It's like my body is fine-tuned to hers. Even in the next room, I listen, wait, watch. And of course if she catches me looking at her, if she blushes or squirms in the way I know means she's aroused...

It's game over.

Ari hums softly in her sleep, breaking me out of my momentary thoughts, and I stare at her like she might disappear if I blink too long.

My hand slides over her waist, slow, reverent. I press my lips to her shoulder, to that little dip in her spine, and breathe her in. She stirs but doesn't wake—not fully. Her ass shifts back against me, and fuck, I'm already hard.

Of course I am.

She owns me now. Every inch of me belongs to her.

I drag my palm lower, grazing the curve of her stomach, then dipping between her thighs. She parts them instinctively, still half asleep, her breath hitching as my fingers slide through the slick heat waiting for me. God, if I could bottle this feeling of her cunt...

I pull my cock out of my sweatpants and gently maneuver her onto her back. She sighs deeply but doesn't wake up. Slowly climbing over her, I trail a hand up her stomach and lightly brush my knuckles against her nipples. She's completely naked, and I don't think twice about pushing the head of my cock against her slit, working her wetness all around and making sure I have good lubrication.

For whatever reason, despite her giving me blanket consent to do this yesterday morning, it feels wrong to penetrate her without her knowing. Maybe down the road, but not now. Not when she's still so newly *mine.*

I'd never forgive myself if I ruined this before it ever had a chance to begin.

I let out a shaky breath as I thrust my hips up slightly, pressing into her folds but not into her cunt. It must tease her clit, because she moans in her sleep and lifts her hips, writhing her slick channel against my cock, eliciting a watery sound that makes me rumble a groan.

God, she's always wet in the morning.

And she doesn't even know what she does to me like this, how close I am to losing every ounce of control I pretend to have when we're together.

Her hips roll again, slow and instinctive, her soft pussy gliding along the underside of my cock. I hiss through my teeth, fighting the urge to thrust forward and bury myself deep inside her.

"Easy," I whisper against her neck, my voice ragged. "You're going make me come before you even wake up."

She lets out another breathy moan, her brows knitting together, her lips parting like she's chasing the dream she thinks this is. My hand cups her breast, thumb flicking over her nipple, and she arches beneath me, seeking more.

Fuck, she's perfect.

I press a kiss to her jaw, then her throat, working my way down her chest like she's something holy.

"I'm not going to fuck your cunt in your sleep, angel," I murmur, breath shaking as I hold myself steady. "But damn, you're making it hard to stay away."

I keep rutting against her slowly, dragging my cock

through her soaked folds, my tip catching against her clit just enough to make her gasp again, legs twitching.

My whole body is on fire. I begin to shake all over when she lifts her hips, topping me from the bottom and slicking my cock up. It feels *too* good, and she could very easily make me come just like this.

My hips jerk forward of their own accord, grinding against the soft heat of her folds, and fuck, the friction is just enough to make my eyes roll back. I grit my teeth, trying to hold back, but it's useless. The head of my cock catches her clit again and again, and her body reacts like it knows exactly what it's doing to me. Like it wants me to fall apart right here on top of her while she's asleep.

My abs tighten as I bring myself to the edge and pull back as my skin breaks out in goosebumps.

"Fuck, little warrior," I groan, nearly panting now. "You don't even know what you're doing to me." I let my forehead rest against her shoulder as I press against her harder, faster, chasing that brutal edge that's been taunting me since the second I woke up pressed against her skin.

It builds fast—too fast—white heat coiling at the base of my spine, every nerve ending pulled tight, ready to snap. My cock is brutally hard, curved up and close to my stomach as I stop moving, breathing deeply as it pulses with no hard-earned release. *That was close.*

I bite down on the inside of my cheek, trying to wrestle back the wave that's cresting far too fast. My cock throbs—*angry*, insistent—slick with her arousal, twitching with every desperate pulse of need. Every time I brush her clit with the swollen head, I see stars behind my eyes. My vision tunnels. My whole body tenses like a drawn bowstring.

I squeeze the base of my shaft hard, willing myself to hold back, but it just makes it worse. My balls coil, pulling close to my body, and my breath comes out in broken pants, fogging against the curve of her throat. The pressure is molten, blinding, a low burn in my gut that threatens to detonate with even one more stroke. My thighs tremble. I'm drenched in sweat, and I haven't even come yet.

God, when I do, it's going to be *violent*.

My hips jerk again, instinct overriding reason, dragging the slick head of my cock along her folds until I feel the telltale sting at the tip—*that pulse.* The one that says it's happening whether I want it to or not.

I pull back just in time, my fist tightening around myself, squeezing hard to hold it off. "Not yet," I hiss, a snarl of frustration and reverence in my throat. "You're not going to pull it out of me while you're sleeping, angel. You *will* be awake for it. You'll *watch* me come undone and the only place I want my cum is dripping out of your little cunt."

But fuck, I'm close. Closer than I've ever been without finishing.

My whole body's buzzing—an ache in my spine, a throbbing between my legs, an unbearable need. I drop my forehead to her chest, breathing her in, letting the scent of her, the feel of her body against mine, keep me there, *hovering* right on that knife's edge of pleasure and pain.

And still, she sleeps.

And still, I *worship*.

The thought wrecks me. Because even here, half asleep, she's still got more power over me than anyone ever has.

She stirs a little more, lashes fluttering, and I go still.

Not yet.

I kiss her gently, once, then again, lips soft against her temple. "Go back to sleep, baby," I murmur, voice reverent. "I'll be right here when you wake up."

It's going to hurt, but it's going to be worth it when I finally do let myself come undone inside of her.

But I don't stop touching her. I don't stop needing her. I

don't stop rutting against her cunt and bringing myself to the edge, over and over and over.

Even if I have to wait for the payoff.

"Maddox," she whimpers, reaching out for me and shifting just slightly to press her dripping cunt against the overly sensitive head of my cock.

I hiss and pull back, because even one touch will have me throbbing and coming all over her.

Her eyes fly open, and she moans, breathing a little harder as she looks down. "Did you fuck me?"

"Not yet. I wanted—I needed to wait—"

"Then do it."

That's all the fucking permission I need.

I'm just about to slip inside her when there's a knock at her front door.

Ari jerks against me, groggy and confused. "What...?"

I grit my teeth, pressing a kiss to the base of her neck. "Ignore it."

But the knock comes again, harder this time. I stop moving, stop touching her. I'm breathing heavily as she looks over my shoulder with a concerned expression.

"Ari," a voice calls through the front door. "I know you're home. Your car's in the driveway."

"Asher," she says, eyes going wide.

I go still.

The world tilts for a second.

Because of course it's him.

Of course the fucking past has to show up the second I try to give her a future—and the second one small breeze might make me come.

She wraps herself in the sheet and hurries out, and I throw on a t-shirt, my blood already boiling. I hide my raging hard-on under the waistband of my sweatpants, and then I pull a baggy sweatshirt on because I'm too long to hide about half my dick, and I'll be damned if my brother sees it.

I don't follow at first. I let her handle it. But when I hear his voice, sharp and accusing, something inside me snaps.

I push the door open and step outside just as Asher spits it out.

"You lied to me." His eyes snap to mine, and he's not even surprised. How'd he find out? I might never know, but it's apparent by his lack of shock that he knew before coming over here.

And Ari—fuck, she's trying to fix it. Trying to soften it. But I'm already walking closer.

"Asher, I swear, it just... *happened.* I can't explain it, okay? It happened after we—"

"At the house?" he yells, stepping closer.

I'm already standing behind her, then beside her, then *in front of her* like it's instinct. Because it is. Because she doesn't have to be the only one defending herself anymore.

"She doesn't owe you shit," I say, voice calm, even. "You're not together anymore."

Asher's eyes flick to mine, full of disgust. "Fuck you. You think I didn't see the way you looked at her?" His gaze slices into Ari. "I came by the other night. I saw him leaving your house." His eyes shift to me. "What did you do, Maddox? Wait for me to get comfortable, then swoop in?"

"Comfortable? You mean the way you ignored her and still expected her to wait around like a goddamn afterthought?" I grind out, my tone sharp, final. "You don't know a goddamn thing about her. About what she needs. About what she wants." I glance at Ari, and when she doesn't look away, it's all the permission I need. "She chose me. Not because I swooped in, but because you left the door wide open and never even noticed."

And then he hits me with it. "You already fucked her, so I

guess you feel entitled to speak for her too? Guess she didn't waste any time. She always did like to keep her options open when things got hard."

Ari gasps, and my jaw clenches. Red starts to creep into my vision. Maybe it's the fact that I'm so pumped with testosterone, so *fucking* edged, that I feel even more unhinged than normal.

"Say one more thing like that to insult her," I murmur, stepping closer, "and I'll show you exactly how entitled I can be."

"You going to beat me up on her porch, Maddox?" he throws back. "Go ahead. Add a new charge to your record."

I smile. Not a friendly smile. Not the kind you give to someone you once called family.

"You think I give a shit about going back?" My voice drops. "If it means protecting her? I'll go back with a smile on my face and your blood under my fingernails."

Asher's expression tenses. But I'm not done.

"You're not angry because she left you. You're angry because I saw her first. *Truly* saw her. And I didn't hesitate to give her what she needed, unlike you."

He laughs, bitter. "You think you're some kind of fucking savior?"

"No," I say, stepping closer until we're almost nose to nose. "I think I'm the man who'd die for her. I think I'm the man who wouldn't trade her for a promotion or a calendar full of conference calls. I'd never even think of letting let her settle for less than what she fucking deserves. And just so we're clear—neither of us deserve her—but I'm the only one who'd burn this whole fucking world to the ground just to keep her."

Asher blinks. And for the first time, I see it in his eyes—that realization that he never stood a chance.

He looks at Ari one more time. "Is this what you want?"

And she doesn't flinch. She doesn't hide. *My little warrior.*

"Yes," she says, voice steady.

That's it. Game over.

He nods once. No goodbye. Just turns and walks back to his car like a man carrying a loss he saw coming miles away.

I wait until the door closes behind us before I speak. "You okay?" I ask her, even though I already know the answer.

She doesn't speak. Just leans into me, rests her head against my chest.

And I swear to fucking God, I've never wanted to protect someone more than I want to protect this woman. This woman who chose me despite my past, despite everything.

"I'm sorry you had to deal with that," she whispers.

I kiss the top of her head. "I'd do it again. Besides, it's kind of my fault he had to work so much."

She pulls back. "What did you do?"

I shrug, smiling. "I may know a guy who knows a guy who compromised Asher's firm."

Her mouth drops open. "It was you. The reason he had a work crisis."

I shrug. "Whoops."

She gives me a conspiratorial smile. "You really are relentless.

"For you? Always."

THE DOMESTIC
PHANTOM
ARI

TWO WEEKS LATER

The supermarket is the last place I ever expected to see Maddox Cross look out of place.

And yet here he is, standing beside me in the fluorescent-lit cereal aisle, squinting at the shelves like they personally offended him. He's wearing a plain black t-shirt stretched across his broad chest, dark jeans, and a leather jacket like he just stepped off his motorcycle and wandered into the suburbs of Oceanside by accident.

I don't know why I agreed to this.

We were supposed to be laying low. Staying out of sight, keeping things quiet while we figured out what the hell this is —whatever *we* are. But then he suggested it like it was nothing. Like grocery shopping together was just a normal couple thing.

And I was curious to see what that version of us might feel like.

A version where we weren't hiding. Where he could just

be the man who carries my bags and grumbles about over-priced produce.

So I said yes. Even though my heart was racing. Even though I knew better.

Now, here we are.

"Have you been in a grocery store lately?" I tease, nudging him with my shoulder. "Things have changed."

Maddox glances sideways, a smirk tugging at the corner of his mouth.

"Yeah. Commissary didn't exactly offer five brands of almond milk." He picks up a carton, flips it over like it's suspicious. "And oat milk? Still not convinced it's real food. Feels like a scam."

I snort before I can stop myself. I know I shouldn't laugh; his time in prison isn't a joking matter. But he speaks about doing time so casually, I can't help but tease him for it sometimes.

We stock up on my pantry favorites, as well as some chicken breasts and eggs for him. I suppose I didn't realize *how* much protein it takes to keep him looking like he does.

He points at the cereal. "What's your favorite? I should know."

I arch a brow. "You stalked me, Maddox. You should *already* know."

That wicked grin spreads across his face—lazy, smug, devastating. "Fair."

I reach for a box of Cocoa Puffs without thinking. His hand shoots out at the same time, his fingers brushing mine. We both go still.

It's such a silly thing—a box of cereal—but something about the softness of the moment makes my heart trip. His thumb lingers against my knuckles like he's reluctant to let go. His expression shifts, that smirk fading into something softer. Something real.

"Cocoa Puffs?" I ask, my voice quieter now.

His smirk softens even more. "They were Lila's favorite." His voice is quiet, almost fragile.

I don't pull away.

Instead, I nod. "Your little girl had good taste. They're my favorite, too."

And for a beat, we just stand there. In the middle of a busy grocery store, with screaming toddlers and clattering carts and a loudspeaker announcing a sale on canned tuna, I forget the gravity of everything. I forget the weight of what came before. He looks at me like I hung the stars.

Then, without warning, he tosses two boxes into the cart. "One for now, one for later."

I huff a laugh. "You're so dramatic."

He leans in, voice dropping. "You've known that from the start."

And I smile, because it feels good. Real. Like something we're building that might actually last.

We wander through the store like that, bickering about the quality of the produce, sharing guilty-pleasure snack confessions, and somehow, it all feels so... normal. I tell him about how I'm convinced avocados aren't actually seasonal, they just hide them to jack up the price.

Maddox raises a brow, clearly amused. "You think there's an avocado cartel?"

"I think there's a lot we don't know," I say, dead serious.

He chuckles, shaking his head as he kisses the top of my head. "You're adorable."

Meanwhile, Maddox, the man who could snap a neck without breaking a sweat, turns into someone who debates over peanut butter brands because "the organic shit tastes like punishment."

Once we reach the checkout, I realize something strange has happened.

For the first time, it's not the chaos or the obsession between us that's making me feel unsteady. It's the simplicity of it all. The *quiet*. The terrifying, intoxicating idea that maybe, just maybe, this could be my life. Him. Me. Grocery stores. Arguments over peanut butter.

And for once, I don't hate the idea, because it's him.

After we check out and drive back to my house, he helps me unload the food in my kitchen. We've spent the majority of our days and nights here. As nice as his massive penthouse is, I think we both prefer my grandma's small bungalow.

The kitchen is quiet, warm sunlight pouring through the windows as I bend to put the cereal boxes away on the lower shelf.

Behind me, I hear Maddox's low growl, the kind of sound I've learned to recognize immediately. The sound of a man fighting with every inch of restraint he has left.

"You're doing that on purpose," he rasps.

I glance over my shoulder. "Doing what?"

His eyes flick over my black leggings and beige tank top, dark and dangerous. His fists clench at his sides, jaw tight, chest heaving. Slowly, he prowls forward until he's standing behind me, close enough that I feel the heat radiating from him.

"You know exactly what," he says. "Bending over in front of me like that."

My breath catches. His voice, low, reverent, reverberating right into my core.

He presses one palm flat against the small of my back, possessive. His other hand curls loosely around my throat from behind, tilting my head gently back so he can whisper against my ear.

"I need you, Ari. Right now."

The admission nearly buckles my knees.

And God help me, I love it. I love how badly he wants me.

How he doesn't hide it or make me guess. How he's barely holding it together, even now, in my sunlit kitchen on a Tuesday afternoon, surrounded by bags of boring groceries.

He wants me all the time.

And the worst part? I love it. I love being wanted like this.

Like I'm not a burden. Like I'm not too much. Like I'm exactly enough.

———

A few hours later, the kitchen smells like garlic and butter, the faint sizzle of pasta sauce filling the air as Maddox stands at the stove, stirring with surprising ease. I'm perched on the counter, legs dangling, glass of wine forgotten beside me as I watch him move around my small kitchen like he belongs here.

And maybe he does.

I tuck my hair behind my ear, studying him. The black t-shirt stretched across his shoulders, the way his tattoos move with every careful motion, the slight crease between his brows as he tastes the sauce and adjusts the heat.

It shouldn't feel this natural. But it does.

"You're staring," he murmurs without looking up.

I shrug. "You're cooking."

He flashes a rare, soft smile. "I've had twenty years to think about the shit I'd do if I ever got out. Turns out, cooking for someone I give a damn about was high on the list."

The words land heavy. My chest constricts. And yet, it's not fear that rises—it's warmth.

A second later, my phone buzzes with a text from Frankie.

FRANKIE

Dante and I are just parking. See you in a minute. Can't wait to meet your prison yard Prince Charming.

I grin at the nickname she's given him, looking up at Maddox. He's chopping fresh basil, whistling and looking entirely too comfortable in my space.

Something settles deep inside me.

Except for the time Frankie briefly spotted him when she picked me up from the beach house, she hadn't ever officially met him. I held off for two weeks as Maddox and I got used to coexisting—him starting up a new cybersecurity firm with several employees right off the bat... not suspicious *at all*—and me busy with my CPA clients. Truth be told, I was worried about what Frankie and Dante would think... which is silly, considering how they got together.

The sound of the doorbell snaps me out of my thoughts. My heart stutters as I glance at Maddox, but he only quirks a brow and wipes his hands on a kitchen towel, like this is any other day. Like this is normal.

It's not.

Him meeting my best friend and her husband is a *big* deal.

I open the door to find Frankie and Dante on the porch, arms full of wine and a cake box. Frankie immediately smirks when she sees me, but her eyes cut past me to Maddox, who's leaning casually against the kitchen island, knife still in hand.

"Oh my god," she whispers under her breath as we step inside. "He really is Asher's hotter, more dangerous twin." Her eyes sparkle mischievously. "And I do mean dangerous."

Dante grunts behind her, his scowl deepening.

Maddox walks to the front door, extending a hand like a gentleman. "Maddox Cross."

Frankie takes his hand, eyes narrowing slightly, reading him in that way only Frankie can. "Frankie," she says. "This is Dante."

Dante nods stiffly, not offering his hand. "I know who you are."

Maddox's smirk flickers but doesn't fade. "Pleasure's all mine."

The tension is thick, but Maddox? Maddox is smooth. He's charming in that lethal, calculated way of his, but I notice the subtle shift when he glances at me, softening just enough for only me to notice.

Soon, Frankie is laughing softly, helping me chop vegetables while Maddox moves seamlessly around the kitchen, preparing dinner like he's been doing this for years. Dante lingers, arms crossed, tracking Maddox's every move, but Maddox seems unbothered.

"So," Frankie says, leaning close while Dante is distracted watching Maddox. "He cooks, he cleans, and he looks like he'd kill for you. No notes."

I snort, cheeks warming.

Maddox glances over his shoulder, catching me smiling, and I swear he stands just a little taller, like he knows exactly what's being said.

And maybe, just maybe, he does.

Dante leans against the counter, watching Maddox like he's waiting for him to slip up. I don't blame him. He's just as protective of Frankie—and thereby me—as Maddox is.

Frankie nudges me with her hip. "You're glowing."

I huff. "It's just hot in here."

Her eyes flick to Maddox. "Right."

Dante says nothing, but his eyes haven't left Maddox since he walked in. The tension is almost comical if it weren't so nerve-racking.

As dinner comes together, I find myself stealing glances at Maddox, at the way he quietly keeps track of me. He passes me a spoon when I need one without me asking. He pulls my chair out without comment. His fingers skim the small of my back when no one is looking.

I can't get enough of it—of being the center of his universe.

I *needed* this—to be seen without having to say a damn word.

Frankie notices. She always does. "You love him," she says under her breath while we plate the pasta.

"I— Frankie."

"You do. And you're terrified." Her voice softens. "You've never let anyone want you like this, have you?"

My throat tightens. I say nothing, but she knows. She always knows.

At the table, Maddox takes the seat beside me, thigh brushing against mine under the table like he's claiming me. Every brush of contact feels deliberate. Possessive. And maybe I should push him away, but instead? I lean into it.

Dante watches us like a man doing the math and realizing he doesn't like the sum. I have to keep from laughing. He's such an overprotective father figure, and I'm grateful to have him in my life. Plus, perhaps one day the two brooding men will be the best of friends. But for now, they at least seem to tolerate each other.

Halfway through dinner, Frankie steers the conversation into safer waters—talking about work, about how Dante still snores like a chainsaw. Maddox plays along, tossing out dry comments here and there, but every so often, his hand finds mine beneath the table. Stroking. Teasing. Like he can't help himself.

And God help me, I don't want him to stop.

Frankie catches it, of course. Her brows lift like she's about to call me out. "So, Maddox," she says, swirling her wine, eyes sharp with challenge. "What are your intentions with my best friend?" Frankie asks, dead serious. "And please keep in mind that Dante and I watch a lot of true crime, and I'm disturbingly confident I could get away with murder."

I sputter. "Frankie!"

She grins. "Relax, babe. I'm sure he's great. But you know... just in case."

Dante doesn't even flinch, just lifts his glass in agreement. "She's not kidding. We live near a swamp. Bodies disappear there all the time."

"Oh my god," I hiss, covering my face but feeling very well protected nonetheless.

Maddox, to his credit, doesn't blink. His lips twitch like he's trying not to grin. "Noted."

Frankie leans back, eyes narrowed on him. "I'm serious, Maddox. We like you—for now. Screw this up and I'll be the first one making sure you disappear without a trace."

Maddox's smirk only deepens. "Understood. But just so we're clear, I intend to keep her. For good."

Frankie nearly chokes on her wine. She shoots me a look across the table that says *he can't be serious*, and I give her a tight-lipped smile and a barely perceptible nod.

Dante exhales slowly. "Ari is family. Always has been. If you make her cry, we'll be digging a hole in the swamp behind the house."

Then, after a beat, he adds, voice low and deliberate, "Asher knew that, too. That's why he always looked nervous around me."

His tone is so casual it takes a second to register his words as a threat.

Maddox's thumb strokes against my wrist beneath the table, calm, amused even. "I like swamps," he murmurs without missing a beat, but the glint in his eye promises he's not worried.

Frankie's eyes widen like she wasn't expecting Dante to go full mobster, but instead of backing down, Maddox just leans back, looking pleased and like my best friend and her husband didn't just threaten him with murder multiple times.

When dinner is over and we're clearing the table, Maddox washes the pots and pans in the sink, eyes periodically following me like I'm the only thing that matters. Frankie notices too. She pulls me aside as we load the dishwasher.

"You're playing with fire," she whispers.

My stomach flips. "I know."

Her eyes soften. "But I've also never seen you happier."

I pull my lower lip between my teeth so that I don't grin like a fool. "I am."

Pulling me in for a hug, she holds on to me for several seconds. "I bet the sex is incredible."

I cackle and push her away. Dante offers to clean up, but Maddox doesn't budge from his place at the sink. I sip my wine and watch as Frankie and Maddox debate the best way to make garlic bread—apparently she had pointers for him from our meal tonight—and Dante stays close to his wife the whole time, watching Maddox with an unsure look.

They leave around nine to pick Lucia up from Frankie's mom's house, and once they're gone, I saunter over to Maddox to help with cleaning up the cooking mess.

Maddox dries my cast iron pan while I lean over the counter to put the wineglasses away, and then he makes that low, growling sound again.

"You lean over like that one more time," he murmurs darkly, "and I'm going to bend you over this counter."

I swallow hard.

The second I'm not holding glass, Maddox crowds me against the counter, his chest warm against my back. His hand slides around my waist, lips brushing the shell of my ear.

"So, do you think your friends like me?" he asks, a trace of vulnerability tinging his question.

"Frankie does. But I'm not sure about Dante."

"Yeah. I don't say this often, but that guy is intimidating as fuck."

I snort. "He's a big softie at heart. Just protective of me."

"So does this make us official?" he asks, kissing the back of my neck as I let my head fall back against his chest.

"I thought we already were official," I say, my voice a faux whine.

"I want you, Ari. I want everything with you. I want the grocery shopping and waking up with you every morning. I want dinner with your friends and lunch with my parents. I'll even tolerate Asher if he's not a fucking asshole about it."

I laugh. "I want that, too."

We stay like that, pressed together, as his chin rests on my shoulder.

Like we're taking it all in together. And for once, the silence doesn't feel like a weight, it feels like permission.

But... what if it's not enough? What if he gets bored, or at some point realizes his obsession was just because he was lonely in that cell?

"What is it, little warrior?" His voice is quiet, but edged with something sharp, like he already knows the answer.

How does he always know what I'm thinking?

I close my eyes, pressing my back against his chest, letting the steady beat of his heart soothe me. "I'm worried I don't know how to do this," I admit, curling my fingers against his hands resting on my stomach.

Maddox doesn't hesitate. "Yeah, you do."

I turn slightly to glance at him over my shoulder, searching for some sort of reassurance in his eyes. "I don't. I've always just... settled. Done what was expected. Been the good daughter. The easygoing girlfriend. The one who never needed too much. And even with Asher..." I trail off, heat rising in my cheeks. "Even with him, I never felt this close to him. Not even half. It's terrifying, because I've never been able to trust anyone but myself. Yet... three weeks in with you and I feel like I've known you forever."

His jaw tics, but his thumb stays soft as it traces the edge of my jaw. His eyes search mine like he's piecing it together, like he's seeing every part of me that I try so hard to keep hidden.

"That's because you never held back with me." His voice is low, steady, edged with something darker. "Not once." His thumb presses gently against my pulse. "You've given me every version of you—the good, the scared, the stubborn. All of it. You haven't played it safe, not for a second."

The words make me ache. It's true. I've told Maddox more in these past few days than I've told anyone. About my fears, about wanting more, about the exhaustion of always bending myself into what everyone else needed.

"I don't want to be scared of wanting more," I whisper, barely able to admit it out loud.

He exhales through his nose, the sound rough. His hand slides up, curling around the back of my neck. "You think I wasn't scared too? I lost everything, Ari. Lila. Elaine. My whole life. I went from having everything I ever wanted to existing in a small cell. And then I saw that picture of you, and it felt like some kind of impossible second chance, and all I could think was—I'll ruin it. I'll ruin you."

I blink hard, tears threatening. "Maddox…"

"But I don't care about ruining you anymore," he continues, voice thick with something I've never heard from him before. Not anger. Not possession. Something closer to grief. "I want you too much. And I'm selfish enough to take you."

I shiver, the weight of his words crashing into me.

"You don't have to be scared," he rasps. "Not with me. Take it. Take me. No one's stopping you. Least of all me."

My throat burns. The vulnerability of it threatens to unmake me. But I don't pull away. Instead, I lean into him, pressing my lips softly against his.

And it's not desperate this time.

It's not about lust or proving a point.

It's real.

The kiss deepens slowly, like he's letting me set the pace, like he's putting his heart in my hands and daring me to break it.

His fingers tangle gently in my hair, grounding me, anchoring me. When I shift around to face him, he lifts me up as I wrap my legs around his waist before exhaling hard against my mouth.

Before pulling me closer like he'll never let go.

"I've got you now," he murmurs, forehead pressed against mine. "All of you. Don't you dare run."

I take a breath, shaky but certain. "I'm not going anywhere," I whisper.

And somehow, for the first time in my entire life, I mean it.

EPILOGUE: THE PHANTOM FUTURE

ARI

The first time I read the email, I think I imagined it.

The second time, I blink twice at the email, then reread it ten more times.

The third time, I scream loud enough to startle Maddox, who crashes in from the kitchen in nothing but boxers and a "World's Okayest Ex-Con" apron, eyes wild and spatula raised like he's about to fight someone.

"What's wrong?" he asks, scanning the room.

"I got a book deal!" I scream back, holding my phone in the air.

He blinks. "A book deal?"

"I got a book deal on my fan fiction story!"

Maddox lowers the spatula slowly. "The bone collector one?"

I nod, still breathless. "Yes!"

The original dark romantic fantasy, loosely based on *The Nightmare Before Christmas* meets *Beauty and the Beast*, had been blowing up on the fanfic sites, but never in my wildest dreams did I think an actual *publisher* would pick it up.

Maddox's face splits into a grin so wide it knocks the air out of me. "Holy shit, angel." And then he crosses the room in three long strides, drops the spatula, grabs my waist, lifts me into the air, and spins me around until I'm breathless for an entirely different reason.

The email had been clear. A boutique romance imprint attached to a major publisher saw my viral fan fiction, *Monstrously Yours*, and wanted to adapt it into a full-length novel. I'll keep the rights, the IP, and get a sweet little advance that makes quitting my CPA job actually, terrifyingly real. It's been something I've been toying with over the last couple of months, because as much as I love my clients, writing my monster smut makes me so gloriously happy that I've realized over the last year that I would maybe like to do it full-time.

And now... I can.

Plus, Maddox proofreads all of my weekly chapters, and he's been encouraging me to take more time to write.

"Holy shit, Ari," Maddox says, reading the email over my shoulder. "This is a big deal. I'm so proud of you."

"Thank you."

He tucks his face into my neck, arms tightening around me like he might never let go. "You did this. All on your own."

I laugh, blinking back sudden tears. "You helped."

"I just sat next to you while you spiraled about plot holes and questioned if anyone would care about a brooding grave-yard warden who eats bones for power but falls in love with a candlelit librarian. You did everything else."

"You loved it," I whisper, teasing.

He lifts his head, smirking. "I jerked off to it."

"Maddox!"

"What?" he shrugs, completely unrepentant. "Chapter sixteen was filthy, and you know it."

I cover my face with my hands, groaning into my palms. "If I didn't love you so much, I'd smother you with that apron."

"Mm." He leans down, brushing a kiss just beneath my ear. "I'd love for you to smother me with something else."

"I'm sure you would."

I laugh softly, still breathless, still stunned by the email, the spinning warmth of it all. But then his voice drops a little lower.

"So does this mean you're going to say yes today?"

I freeze—not in panic, but in surprise. Not because I don't know what he means. But because I do.

It's not the first time he's asked. Not formally. Not down on one knee. But in passing, in bed, in the small, quiet moments when we're half asleep or watching reruns of crime documentaries while eating cereal straight from the box. He asks me to marry him with that teasing glint in his eye, like it's a joke. Like he's testing the weight of the words.

And I always laugh. I always deflect. I say "Not yet" or "Ask me when I'm wearing real pants," and he always lets it go. Because he knows I needed time.

But now?

Now, everything feels different.

I can *see* our future—me writing in this house where he lives with me now. Him working at the desk next to me, like he does now, and taking lunchtime walks around my neighborhood to get out of the house and enjoy our quiet life. Maybe a cat or a dog, and one day, a baby. Double dates with Frankie and Dante, now that Dante has decided Maddox is worthy of me.

I couldn't see it right away. I needed time.

But now?

He feels like the exact right decision.

I look up at him, his strong arms wrapped around me, his

smile still soft from the excitement of *my* good news. This man—this obsessive, beautiful, dangerous man—loves me better than anyone ever has. Better than I've ever let anyone try.

And maybe I'll never tell him outright that today, *this*, feels like a beginning. Like a shift I didn't see coming.

But I lean in and kiss him once—deep and certain—and when I pull back, I whisper, "Ask me again. *Officially*."

His answering smile? It's slow and devastating and absolutely *knowing*. He sets me down on the couch gently, then backs up. My stomach flips when he disappears around the corner of the kitchen, only to return with something behind his back.

My nerves are shot, and I feel my eyes begin to water before he even gets close to me. And when he does, he holds a tiny, heart-shaped box in front of me, dropping to one knee.

The box is plastic. Glittery pink. With the faintly retro glimmer of something that makes my heart squeeze and a sob escape from my mouth.

"Is that a... Polly Pocket?"

He grins wider. "Custom-made."

"Maddox."

"I wanted something special. Just for you. Frankie told me this was the best idea I'd ever had."

"You asked Frankie?"

He nods. "And Dante. They approve, by the way."

I half laugh, half cry at the audacity of this man.

He pops the box open. Inside, nestled in soft velvet, is a ring. A simple gold band with a dark aquamarine stone in the center, carved into the shape of a flower. A... *forget-me-not*. It's stunning. Bold and uniquely beautiful.

Just like him.

Just like us.

"I wanted to get you something that reminded me of you.

Something unexpected." His voice drops, and I can hear the tremble under the confidence now. "You've changed my entire world, Ari. You made this house my home. You *became* my home. You made me believe I could be more than what I came from, or where I've been. That I could have a future instead of a sentence. That…" I swear I see the hint of tears in his bright blue eyes. "That I could have a second chance at love."

I blink rapidly, trying to hold it together. He swallows, then takes my hand.

"I want to be your biggest fan. Your loudest hype man. Your forever partner. The one who's always watching out for you, and making sure you're happy. And most of all… I want to be your husband." A breath. "Will you marry me?"

I don't even try to stop the tears. I throw my arms around his neck, knocking the Polly Pocket out of his hand in the process.

"Yes," I whisper into his skin. "Yes. You maniac. Yes."

He laughs, that low, delicious sound that always melts something deep inside me, and lifts me off the ground again, spinning us both.

The ring slides perfectly onto my finger.

It's not traditional. It's nothing like I expected.

But I don't think I've ever loved anything more—I don't think I've ever loved *anyone* more.

————

MADDOX

Seven Months Later

My mornings look different now.

No more hustling through federal-grade firewalls, no more burner phones, no more black ops consulting for men who never signed their names. I still take jobs, sure—small ones, clean ones. The kind where I get to work from the office we share while Ari writes her monster fuckery next to me with her little glasses on and my hoodie swallowing her frame.

But the truth is, I'm building an exit plan. A clean one. Because I've had the high-stakes life already, and none of it compares to this.

To *her*.

She's almost six months pregnant now, and the sight of her padded in softness—round belly, glowing skin, that slightly unsteady way she moves through the house—undoes me daily.

I'm going to be a father. Again.

Only this time, I'm not deployed across the world. This time, I get to wake up beside Ari and put my hand on her stomach and feel my son kick. I get to cook breakfast, fold tiny laundry, and kiss her until she moans into my mouth like she used to when all of this was still unspoken.

I'm ready to be a stay-at-home dad. Ready to take care of our son so she can chase down her writing dreams—turn fan fiction into a career, write werewolf kings and tentacle lovers and monster soulmates while I wash bottles and keep them both happy and fed.

Now that I have a glimpse of this life, I'd burn the world down just to keep it—with Ari's swollen belly and our son comfortably existing inside of her.

And today? Today's not special. It's not an anniversary or a big milestone. It's just us. Quiet. Comfortable. *Home.*

But I can't stop looking at her.

She's wearing one of my old t-shirts, threadbare and tight over her growing belly, and humming something under her breath as she wipes down the kitchen counter. Her hair's loose, dark and wavy as it hangs down her back. Her skin glows in the low light. Her ring catches on the edge of the counter, and she turns, smiling at me like it's the easiest thing in the world.

My *wife.*

A shotgun wedding three months ago, before she started showing, and now I get to call her my fucking *wife.*

And just like that, I'm gone.

I cross the room before she even realizes what I'm doing and lift her into my arms.

"Maddox," she breathes, startled but smiling, her hands flying to my shoulders. "What are you doing?"

I don't answer. Just carry her straight to the bedroom and set her down just inside the doorway like she's made of spun glass.

But my eyes?

They're starving.

She sees it immediately. Her smile softens, but her body goes still.

"Maddox…" she murmurs, eyes searching mine.

I drop to my knees.

"I need you to understand," I say roughly, my hands already sliding beneath the hem of her shirt. "I need you to understand what you mean to me."

She swallows. "I do."

"No," I rasp. "I don't think you do."

She starts to speak, but I'm already pushing her shirt up, already kissing my way up the inside of her thighs.

"No one," I say, mouth against her soft skin. "No fucking one—has ever made me feel the way you do."

Her breath hitches.

"You've always been mine," I murmur. "But now?" I place a kiss on her belly as I look up at her. "Now you're both mine. Forever."

She's panting already when my tongue moves down between her legs. One lick, slow and reverent, and she's trembling. She's so sensitive, so swollen, that she comes in mere seconds now.

It's one of my favorite things about her being pregnant.

"I'm going to worship you now. And you're going to let me."

Her knees go soft, and I catch her easily, tossing her leg over my shoulder. My fingers dig into the backs of her thighs as I bury my mouth between them, licking and sucking her engorged nub like a man possessed, letting my tongue pierce into her wet cunt as she cries out.

And she tastes like everything I've ever fucking wanted.

Minutes pass like hours.

Her head lolls back against the wall. Her voice is hoarse from moaning. My scruff and chin are coated with her arousal, and my cock is aching—leaking—but I don't stop. I keep her right on the edge—circling, kissing, murmuring filth into her skin.

"That's it, baby. Let me hear you."

"Good girl. Fuck, you're so perfect like this."

"Open for me. Just like that. Let me taste what's mine."

When she comes for the fifth time, it's with a desperate sob. Her whole body seizes in my hands, and I hold her through it, groaning into her like I might die from the feel of her falling apart again.

But I'm not done.

I lift her—gently, carefully—and carry her to the bed. I lay her down like she's priceless, because she is. I peel off that old t-shirt, trace every curve, every mark our son has left behind on her body, and I strip down beside her.

"I thought I wanted to bend you over and fuck you like a madman," I admit, voice low, peeling off my shirt.

"But now?" she whispers, lips parted, eyes shining.

I crawl up her body like I own it.

"Now, I just want to feel every inch of you. Slow. Deep. If

I could, I'd fuck another baby into you right this very second, letting my cum take root inside of you again." I groan, kissing her. "God, you're so fucking perfect, angel."

I nudge her legs apart and press the tip of my cock against her slick, swollen heat. She's already panting, already ready, already mine.

When I push in, slow and steady, she gasps and arches off the bed.

"Oh my god, yes—Maddox—"

I don't rush.

I don't pound.

I move like I'm etching her into my bones, because I am.

One hand cradles her jaw, the other rests splayed across her belly. Something primal pulses through me, just like it does every time I see her swollen belly.

Me. I did that.

"If you weren't already knocked up," I growl, "I'd be coming inside you so hard you wouldn't stop dripping for days."

She whimpers, and her legs tighten around me.

"Fuck, Ari, come for me. Come with my cock deep inside you."

She cries out, her whole body trembling, and I don't stop. I kiss her through it, hold her close, fuck her through every last quiver, every last tightening around my cock.

And then I come too, deep and hard, spilling inside her with a guttural sound that doesn't even sound human. It's relief and obsession and gratitude all wrapped into one fucking soul-shattering orgasm.

I don't pull out. Don't move. Just hold her.

Our bodies slick with sweat, tangled up, still connected in every way.

"You're still shaking," she whispers, a teasing smile in her voice.

I bury my face in her neck and nod.

"Yeah," I murmur. "But I think it's just because I love you."

She laughs softly, her fingers stroking my hair as she runs them against my scalp. And somewhere in the quiet between heartbeats and steady breathing, I feel it settle.

Peace.

This is what peace feels like, and for the first time in my life, I'm experiencing it for myself.

And I'll do any-*fucking*-thing to keep it.

————

Maddox

Two Months Later

The IKEA crib instructions are in Swedish.

Or maybe it's Finnish. Whatever the hell it is, it isn't English, and even my dad, who was fucking born in Sweden, can't figure them out.

"What the actual fuck is a *fjällsippa*?" I mutter under my breath, holding up a plank of what I assume is crib-side A.

Across the room, Ari's laughter rings out like sunlight, warm and loud. She's sitting cross-legged on the nursery rug, her round belly making her shirt ride up just slightly—just enough to make me want to abandon this entire crib and carry her to bed.

Again.

Frankie lounges beside her, shoving Goldfish crackers into her mouth with the kind of chaotic energy that only comes from being six months postpartum and running on hazelnut lattes and four hours of sleep.

Dante is pacing behind me, reading the directions like he's decoding a bomb. "You're holding it upside down."

"No, I'm holding it like it deserves to be held. With violence," I grumble, turning the piece around.

Ari snorts and leans back on her hands. "Maybe we should've just paid the extra fifty dollars to have them build it."

I glance over my shoulder, and the sight of her—glowing, relaxed, belly full of our kid—makes something tight in my chest loosen all at once.

"Absolutely not," I say. "My son is sleeping in a bed built by my own two hands if it kills me."

Dante grunts. "It might."

Frankie throws a cracker at him. "Let them have this moment. You're just jealous no one ever asked you to build a crib."

He mutters something under his breath and picks up the tiny wrench tool with a scowl, and for the first time, I realize what this moment is.

Full circle.

All the chaos and the dark edges that got us here? They're still part of the story. But right now, we're in the soft part. The golden hour of what comes next.

Ari catches me staring and gives me a small smile, eyes bright, hand resting on her bump.

"Almost done?" she teases.

"If you weren't watching, I'd be done already," I murmur, straightening.

Frankie cackles. "Don't listen to him. He's been glaring at that screw for ten minutes."

"Just making sure it's tight enough," I say dryly.

"That's what he said," Frankie mutters under her breath, and I can't help but laugh.

It definitely breaks the tension, though.

When we finally get the last piece in place, Ari insists on taking a picture. Frankie says it's for Instagram, but I know better. It's for later. For our kid. For when he's old enough to hear about how his ex-con dad got into a swearing match with a box of wooden planks.

As the sun starts to dip below the horizon, Dante and Frankie head out. Frankie calls something over her shoulder about bringing Ari more Medjool dates—*good for softening the cervix,* apparently—while Dante grumbles about traffic all the way down the driveway.

I snap a quick picture to send to Asher and my dad, and the three of us trade a few texts back and forth.

Asher eventually realized that Ari and I were madly, desperately in love, conceding to our relationship. We don't see him much these days—he moved out to the East Coast—but my parents visit often.

Once the last taillight disappears down the street, the house falls quiet.

And then it's just us.

I close the door and turn back toward her, heart aching at the sight of her curled in the rocking chair, one hand cradling her belly, the other flipping through a baby name book we'll never actually use. A couple of months ago, we decided to add an extension off our bedroom to turn her two-bedroom into a three-bedroom for the baby. I wouldn't think of asking her to give up her grandmother's house, and now we don't have to.

"You okay?" I ask softly.

She nods. "Just tired."

I walk over, kneel in front of her, and rest my forehead gently against her stomach.

Her fingers thread through my hair. "I love you," she murmurs.

And then, because I'm me, I glance up with a smirk. "I

love you, too. And I can't wait to fuck more babies into you when you're ready."

She laughs, breathless and fond. "Jesus, Maddox."

I rise, taking her hand, helping her stand with care.

"No," I say quietly, brushing her hair off her cheek. "Not Jesus. Just me. The man who's going to spend the rest of his life making sure you know you were never too much. That you were always worth choosing."

She tears up immediately, like usual lately. I press a kiss to her forehead, then her lips.

"Now come to bed and take a nap," I murmur. "Let me spoil the hell out of you."

Because every piece of this—this family, this love, this second chance—I'm holding it with both hands now.

And I'll never let it go.

———

ARI

One Month Later

It's late.

The kind of late that turns everything blue and soft, with shadows curled around the corners of the room like secrets.

Maddox is asleep in our bed behind me, his hand resting against the curve of my belly, as if he's afraid to lose contact even in sleep. He always ends up there, like it's instinct. Like he's already protecting our son from the world.

I stare at the bassinet across the room. The one he built by hand, despite the trouble he had with the crib... and the dresser... and the rocking chair.

I cried when he finished it. Not because it was perfect—

which, obviously, it wasn't. There's still a tiny scuff on one of the rails from where he threw a wrench and cursed the IKEA gods. But because it was ours. And it'll be the first place our son sleeps before he's big enough to sleep in his bedroom.

Built with care. With love. With purpose.

I still don't know how I got here.

A year and a half ago, I was in a relationship I'd outgrown. I was settling for someone who gave me breadcrumbs and called it a feast. I was exhausted from being good, from being small, from folding myself into the shapes other people needed me to be.

And now... now I'm growing a whole damn person and living the dream as a full-time author of two and a half books.

This tiny boy we haven't met yet? He's already everything. Not because he's perfect, or because I expect him to be. But because I already know what it feels like to be raised by people who believed love was something earned.

I won't do that to him.

Maddox and I talk about it sometimes—what kind of parents we'll be. It usually ends with him tearing up and me pretending not to cry because my hormones are a war crime.

But it always comes back to the same thing.

He'll never have to wonder if he's too much.

He'll never have to tiptoe around his feelings or mold himself into someone else's version of lovable. He'll be wild and soft and loud and angry and beautiful, and we'll love every version of him.

We'll love him when he gets it wrong. When he breaks things. When he forgets to clean his room or fails a test or comes home with a scraped knee and tears in his eyes. We'll love him when he's quiet and unsure, when he's angry at the world, when he's scared.

We'll love him if the only thing that makes him happy is a toy.

We'll love him because he's *ours*.

Because he's made of every brave choice we never thought we'd get to make.

I press my hand to my stomach, feeling the faintest rolling movement against my palm.

And I whisper, "You're already loved more than I ever knew was possible."

Behind me, Maddox shifts in his sleep, and murmurs, "Are you talking to him again?"

I smile, blinking back tears. "Yeah. He's moving."

He makes a sleepy, rumbling sound. Then, still half asleep, he says, "Tell him I said hi. And that if he's anything like you, I'm already fucking terrified."

I laugh softly, my chest warm.

God, we're going to mess up.

But we're going to do it together. Loudly. Softly. Imperfectly.

With our whole hearts.

And for the first time in my life, that feels like enough.

———

Thank you so much for reading Play with the Phantom!

I have another release later this year, so if you'd like to get notified about what's next, sales, giveaways, and just generally support me, the best thing to do is subscribe to my newsletter:

http://www.authoramandarichardson.com/newsletter
(Psst... you also get a free student/teacher novella as a thank you for joining!)

If you enjoyed this book, you might enjoy my Ravaged Castle

series. Five billionaire brothers? More rich, possessive heroes? Yes, please:

Prey Tell
(Brother's best friend, primal play, angst and steam)

Marry Lies
(Marriage of convenience, plus-size heroine, voyeurism)

Ward Willing
(Age gap, father's best friend, student/teacher, pleasure Dom)

Masked Sins
(Stepbrother, hidden identity, masked man, sadistic Dom)

Holy Hearts
(MMF, bi-awakening, poly rep, religion kink)

Acknowledgments

Thank you to everyone who loved Frankie and Dante, because without them, Ari and Maddox would've never happened. Ari was just supposed to be a fun side character in *Dance with the Devil,* but sooo many people asked me for her book! Before I knew it, the idea of Asher/Maddox came about, and then there was no stopping me.

Thank you to Erica, Macie, and Bryanna for alpha reading! This book started a lot differently and about halfway through, I realized I needed some more forced proximity, so the vacation house idea was born. Thanks to them, I ironed it all out in record time without having to push the release date back! I have the best team. Truly.

Thank you to my husband for once again being my rock, my source of sustenance (I mean food/caffeine... get your heads out of the gutter) and overall my biggest support system. Love you!

To my *Heated Glance* and *Surrender* Patreon members... Lori, Tabitha, Drea, Devon, Jaime, Kristen, Kay, Ashlee, Jenna, Tina, Hannah, Pam, Rhiannon, Shannai, Megan, Mary, Stephanie S., Markayle, Aimee, Shayla, Calleigh, Nita, Gabriella, Shannon, Vivi, Candace, Sarena, Carla, Heidi, Allie, Suzi, Deani, Nicole, Katherine, Darcy, Stephanie K., Elizabeth, Jess, Hayley, and Delanie... you guys are the true MVPs. THANK YOU for the support, comments, love, and all-around amazing-ness! ILY.

To everyone who's lost someone they love... I hope this

book gives you some hope that love and light can be found even after our darkest moments.

Thank you to Rumi for the fantastic edits. I'm sorry for all of the *wrecked* and *tightens* and *furrows*. I promise to try and be better next time, haha!

Thank you to Kirsty for bringing to Maddox to life... three times! THANK YOU for being amazing and quick.

And to my readers, thank you for trusting me. I wrote *Dance with the Devil* as a way to sort of fight back against tropes that get a lot of hate (pregnancy), and with *Play with the Phantom*, the cheating trope. I know a lot of people don't like those tropes, but I do hope I've done them justice for people who do enjoy them (like me!) I hope you've enjoyed these palate cleaner books. They were so fun to write.

Love to all of you!! Thank you for making my dreams come true!

ABOUT THE AUTHOR

Amanda Richardson writes from her chaotic dining room table in Yorkshire, England, often distracted by her husband and two adorable sons. When she's not writing contemporary and dark, twisted romance, she enjoys coffee (a little too much) and collecting house plants like they're going out of style.

You can visit my website here:
www.authoramandarichardson.com

9 798281 249546